TAKEDOWN THE TAKE

By W. Hock Hochheim

Paperback ISBN: 978-1-932113-98-3
Digital ISBN: 978-1-932113-99-0
Copyright 2023 Published by
High Home Endeavors: Books
All rights reserved.

Other Titles by W. Hock Hochheim
Fightin' Words
Knife Combatives
Impact Weapon
Combatives Footwork and Maneuvering
My Gun is My Passport
Last of the Gunmen
Rio Grande Black Magic
American Medieval
Blood Rust
The China Alamo
Be Bad Now
Swellen's Reckoning
The Great Escapes of Pancho Villa
Training Mission Series 1-5

Table of Contents

Chapter 1: The Certain "Call" to Duty

Huntsville Penitentiary, January, 1998...

"I want a conjugal visit," Inmate Number 474898, Shelly Mongrieves said.

"I think that you can do that," State special agent, Jumpin Jack Kellog said, "they have those visitation rooms here. All you have to do is ask one of the guards and they can set that up for you. There's some paper-work to do, and..."

"I want one with you," she said.

"Me?"

"You."

"Surely, you have some guy that you know that..."

"No. And only after our conjugal one-on-one visit, I will tell you all you need, and all you want to know."

Jack looked at the orange-suited Shelly, leaning on her elbows on the interview table. Shelly was a white female in her early 60s, about the same age as Jack. She barely knew him once from some 30 years ago, just as a victim (her), police (him) acquaintance. Was this conjugal visit request why she asked to speak with him in the first place?

Just three days earlier back in the Houston Department of Public Safety Intelligence Office, Jack's sergeant Peter Dull sauntered up to Jack's desk, and he said,

"Jack, there's an inmate in Huntsville, a Shelly Mongrieves, that claims she knows about the most corrupt cop and biggest crime operation in the State of Texas. She wants to talk about it."

Jack leaned back in his desk chair and looked up at him.

"She asked for you, Jumpin'."

Dull laid the penitentiary written request form on Jack's desk.

"Me?" Jack said.

"You. Don't know why. Maybe she read your *Be Bad Now* book?"

"That ain't all true," Jack reminded in a sigh.

Jack always grimaced at the term his "book," as he did to everyone, every time that true crime book subject came up. The late 1980s crime book Be Bad Now was three-quarters-true and about one-quarter fiction. It was not written by him, but instead by a pretty famous crime writer. It was all about him fighting the New York Mafia in Texas in the 1980s. Yet, some of it was truer than Jack would ever admit.

"Maybe she read your name in the newspapers after the Muzak deal?" Dull said.

Jack snatched up the request form and looked it over. He had to think a moment, then it came to him. He did meet a Shelly Mongrieves from West Forge years ago. She owned a small interior design shop on a main street back in the 1980s. Running a business, she inevitably fell victim to some small crimes like property theft and bad checks. As a result, she first met Jack when he was a West Forge P.D. patrolman.

To Jack's memory, she was a cute, young thing then, and somewhat successful. Then it all went south for her about three years later when she picked up with a pair of cocaine and drug dealing, flashy cowboys. They were high-rolling, ambitious cocaine dealers. They flashed a lot of cash around, wined and dined her and she melted into their world. The sex. The drugs. The country rock and roll. Within a few months she was a coke addict and tottered on the verge of losing everything.

He did find her vivacious at best he recalled. But that changed when she later met the "detective" version of Jack Kellog. Her mother ran to the police, sat down and cried to detective Jack with the sad tale of her tail-spinning daughter. She hoped for an intervention on his part, of some sort, any sort. The mother had met the two con men drug dealers in the beginning of their seduction, so she supplied whatever background she knew on them.   Jack promised to talk to her if he found her somewhere, but reminded the mom that might not change anything.

"Try," momma Mongrieves begged.

Jack drove by the empty, closed shop on his rounds about town and finally one night he saw a few lights on inside. He finally caught her there. He knocked on the front glass door and walked into her degraded, barren store. He was shocked when he saw her. Shelly was a gray pale, a skinny shadow of her former self. Teeth looked bad. Jittery nervous. Left eye twitched. She had the appearance of what is called a "speed whore." She tried to act nice at first, but she just couldn't behave when she heard that her mother had talked with him. She ordered Jack to "buzz-off" and stay out of her life and business. Jack buzzed off.

Shelly soon left West Forge with these two wheeler-dealers. A bank foreclosed and seized the shop and her home. Then about six or so years later, Jack saw her mother in an HEB supermarket, and the mom reported that Shelly was arrested in Dallas as an accomplice to murder!

"That Shelly Mongrieves," Jack whispered.

Dull handed him a mugshot.

"Know her?"

"Hmmm. Yup. Yup I do," Jack said, studying the almost unrecognizable prison picture. She appeared healthy again, thanks to prison life.

So, three days later, there Jack sat with an 18-year sentenced Shelly Mongrieves in a penitentiary interview room. Dried out, blood clean, psycho-analyzed, teeth fixed, normal and fit-looking once again. She'd asked to see only him. And now, she asked for a conjugal sex visit with him.

"Shelly, you know I can't do that, it would look strange for a state police investigator to have a conjugal visit with an inmate," Jack said, with about a half a chuckle. "It won't look right. Why don't you just tell me about this corrupt cop?"

"I will tell you right after our little visit. That's the deal. And why not Jack. We knew each other once."

"Barely."

"But you knew me before I lost my mind. There was a twinkle in your eye and a little hungry smile when you first met me. You remember?"

"A…twinkle," Jack repeated. "Was I, was I that obvious?"

"I sized you up too. You were hot."

"Were."

"Oh, come on, take a day off and come back to see me. I am not the bad girl you last saw or heard about. I am in here for 9 years now. I work out in the gym. I go to college classes here…"

"In what?"

"Architecture. I already have a BA in interior design."

Jack nodded.

"And I'm working on a degree in Philosophy too."

"That'll learn ya."

"I read in the newspapers and in the Texican Monthly in the library about your big hunt for that crazy Muzak and I…I remembered you. You once tried to talk me out of my addictions and stop me from hanging out with those two con men dope dealers. I should have listened to you. You are memorable, Mister Jack Kellog."

"Memorable enough for aaaaa…conjugal visit, huh?"

"Oh yes, and then, then, only then, I will tell you all about the worst criminal in Texas, a cop who runs the biggest criminal organization in Texas."

"A cop."

"A cop," she said.

"So, what else you want? Some kind of deal? Shortened sentence?" Jack asked.

"That would be nice, but right now? I am just looking for a booty call."

"A…booty…call," Jack repeated with regret.

She smiled big. Her teeth were indeed fixed up. Jack realized this conversation would not advance without a "call to booty." He pulled a business card from his leather jacket, wrote his home phone number on the back and he slid the card across the table to her.

"You ahhh…you set the visit up and you call me at that number on the back. I will take the day off and it will be mostly…largely unofficially, official. Huh? Better be big news."

"Oh, it's big. Big. It's so big. And it will be worth it. I'll make it worth it. Oh, they only allow wine with a visit. Merlot for me. So, Jack, so is it me, or is it the information? What will bring you back?" she asked with a new wry smile connected to an eyebrow raise.

Jack stood and looked her over.

He said, "A…little of both."

He drove back to Houston, thinking this whole messy thing over. He sipped his bottle of Dr. Pepper,

catching some of the salty peanuts in his mouth that
he'd poured inside. Who or what cop and crime organization could she be talking about? How big? How bad?
How would he officially justify a sex-act, conjugal
visit with an informant-inmate if such was discovered?
Usually, such things would be scandalous.

He would be fully id-ed to enter those pseudo "jail-
hotel" rooms. He'd be listed on official records. Would
they know, could they tell he was a state cop? He
would drive there in his Caddy and produce a driver's
license, not a badge and state ID. Would he or would
he not do this for such a possible big criminal intelligence coup? And…well…he had not had any sex in a
while. And…well…she was kind of cute for her age.

Chapter 2: A Murder in Screed

Christ's Church, Screed...

Paul Massaport stepped out of his detective car at 5 a.m., and onto the dark, empty, church, back parking lot. He was already dressed in his gym clothes. His two kids and wife were still sound asleep at home. He pulled a big bag out of the back seat with some gear and his suit and tie, dress clothes folded within, to change into for his workday.

It was "workout Wednesday" for Paul and he always hit the church gym Monday, Wednesday and Friday for weightlifting and cardio before showering, changing into a suit and tie, and reporting to work at the detective division at Screed Police Department by 8 a.m. Screed was a smaller, somewhat rural city about a two-hour drive south of Houston.

Paul was a church deacon with keys to the building and enjoyed working out alone and watching the morning news on the big screen TV in the gym. He blasted the sound, while pumping iron and running on the treadmill.

He walked across the lot to a back metal door, keys in hand and unlocked the lock. He walked inside to the long hall and motion detector lights popped on as stepped along the way. His destination was at the far end of the hall, past the church office lobby.

Then…a man in a black police-like uniform appeared in the hall by the lobby, hat and all. He looked like a security guard, and this surprised Paul as he'd never heard any word about the church hiring guards.

Why would they? Wouldn't they consult him first, as a deacon and a cop? The guard was average height, but with a slight limp in his right step. Paul noted the man was armed, a gun in a police belt rig.

"Well ahhh, hi!" Paul called out.

The man said nothing and continued to approach him. As the lights paved his approach to Paul, Paul saw the man had a black, cloth mask of some sort on his face. What the…?

"I didn't know there was..." Paul started to ask, feeling the situation was getting stranger by the second.

The man's silence? The mask? What…? Closer. The uniform man pulled his pistol and shot Paul in the face. Paul went down fast, like he was hit in the nose by a high-speed brick. The uniform man limped up to him, looked him over, then shot Paul in the head again.

At 6:50 a.m. church office manager Patricia Loudin entered the building through the front lobby doors. She tossed her purse on a desk and flipped on some lobby lights to help the rising sun's illumination. She walked to the hallway and turned on the hall lights.

"What the…" she said, looking at the big lump halfway down by the exterior door. With a curious expression she marched down the hall. But as she got close, she wanted to stop but knew she couldn't. She stepped further still. It was a man's body in a pool of blood. She gasped, turned and ran back to the lobby. She called 9-1-1.

Another employee walked in the front door as she hung up.

"What, Pat?" she asked her despondent boss standing and writhing her hands."

"Renee, there's a dead body down the hall. I…his face is…is gone…destroyed," she said.

"Oh dear, God, dear…Paul's car is parked on the side lot. Is It him?"

"I don't know," Pat whined.

"Let's get outside and wait for the police. It's not safe in here."

The two ran out for Pat's Chevy. They locked the church doors behind them. Pat started her pickup truck and she drove across the two-lane street to park, a spot where they could see the front and right side of the church. Pat had a small .32 revolver in the glove box.

She got it out and laid the pistol on her lap. They waited, shaking at times, for the Screed police and ambulance. They heard sirens in the distance.

"Oh my God if it's Paul," Pat said.

"Oh my God if it's anybody!" Renee said.

Chapter 3: Cinnamon Dunker

Conjugal Visit Room, Huntsville Penitentiary, January, 1998...

Jack Kellog, naked but for a white robe once hanging in the bedroom closet, stretched out on the couch of Conjugal Visitation Cabin #11, a 3-room cabin-pre-fab construction building that resembled a trailer but wasn't really an official trailer. It was more like an old motel in many ways.

Rushed into the bedroom by Shelley upon his arrival, he hadn't had time to look around. But now, 90 minutes later, after what one might call "desperate sex," he was free to scope the place out. It was stocked with things like condoms, linens, soap, towels and snacks. You could cook in a small kitchenette beside a small dining room table, if one packed in the food. He didn't know about the food, otherwise he might have.

The structures were made to perpetuate overnight inmate, family unison-life, so they had up to two bedrooms, some even three rooms, so kids could also visit their incarcerated mommas and/or poppas. Jack noted that it was also furnished with board games, cards, dominoes and a color TV with basic cable in what could be called a "living room" area.

Jack turned on the TV as a smiling Shelley walked in, wearing the bedroom's second white robe, fresh from the shower, brushing her hair. She walked to the kitchen and poured two glasses of wine and grabbed a small bag of supplied pretzels from a cheap, fake wooden bowl. Then she handed one wine to Jack and sat down next to him, just as a segment of disturbing news reporting a murder came on the tube...

"A Screed Police Detective, Paul Massaport was murdered in his church, the Christ's Church here in Screed, Wednesday morning while on his usual, routine morning workout trip to the church gym. Massaport was married, father of two and a 14-year veteran of the Screed Police Department. Our on-scene reporter Alicia Gonzalez reports…

"Thanks Jim. The detective was shot in his gym clothes walking down the hall to the church gym, presumably about 5 a.m. He was then discovered by church employees beginning their day at about 7 a.m. The detective was also a deacon at the church. Jim, the Screed Police Chief Calvin Methods told us that parts of the church, not all, parts inside and out, and parts like the lobby and the main parking lot have some surveillance cameras. Chief Methods said the footage contains the probable suspect. Jim, here's the lobby film of this mysterious, uniformed person wandering the lobby and turning away from the lobby camera into the hallway, all about 4:40 a.m. to 5 a.m.

Chief Methods has asked that we show this video clip of the suspect on television. Anyone with any information should call the Screed Police Department."

Jack leaned forward on the couch to study the sketchy black and white footage. There on screen was a stocky man in a police uniform, complete with a police hat AND a face mask. Black shoes. No patches. A police belt with a gun. He walked around as if he was killing time, like he was a bored security guard. He had a slight limp, an odd gait, and his right foot was turned out slightly.

"As you can see…" and Gonzalez repeated the suspect description as Jack and Shelley saw it.

"Who in the hell is that guy?" Jack said.

"That's pretty bad," Shelley said. "Will you be

working on that?"

"Nooo. No. Screed's far off. Couple of hours. And probably the Texas Rangers will get involved. I just work intelligence, not…not homicide cases anymore."

"You miss it?"

"Yes and no," Jack said.

Jack turned on the couch so as to lean on the side arm rest and threw a left leg up over and atop Shelly's legs.

"And so," he said," speaking of intelligence information, what's this big story you promised to tell me?"

"Okay, you deserve it," she said as she shifted over to her side of the couch to face him, their legs now entangled.

"Jack, you ever heard of Captain Sam Dunker? They call him 'Cinnamon.' From the Harris County Sheriff's Office?"

"Ah, yeah. I think so. Years ago. He was a sergeant in the detective division for years. Then he bounced all over the S.O. Promoted. Been all over. Narcotics. Internal affairs. I've never met him in person. Just seen him in meetings and on the news when big cases broke. What about him?"

"Internal affairs? That's a comical waste," she said.

"He's retired from the Sheriff's Office now. He's now the commander of the Gulf Coast Drug Task Force."

"I didn't know that. I don't know much about these state-run, drug task forces, but I do know they are like their own little super, police force, beholding to almost no one. The state gives them huge grant money and great power. They work in secret. I hear that some of them get in trouble once in a while. How do you know about that?"

"He, Dunker is your biggest crook in Texas. And his

task force is the worst criminal operation ever."

"You think? And how's that? How do you know this?"

"When Dunker was a detective in Harris County, he created his own little crime ring of detectives. Seduced or even blackmailed other detectives to work for him. You remember those two slick Dallas cowboys I picked up with years ago? Got me hooked on crack and coke?"

"Yeah."

"Billy Delarosa and Mike Ackens. They blew into Houston and West Forge in their new Mercedes selling coke and heroin. I stayed off the 'H.' I met them in a happy hour at the Little Ferry Ramada Inn bar on all-you-can-eat shrimp night."

Jack chuckled and said, "ohhh, I remember those nights. Biiiig shrimp. Don't know how the Ramada could afford that week after week?"

"Those boys charmed the…well, they charmed the pants right off me. They got me toasted and that very night the both of them did me. In a room with a heart shaped, spa tub."

"Now there's a picture. You get in the tub?" Jack asked.

"I did. To cool down. Are you talking about them both doing me, in the tub?"

"No, I…"

"They were trying to connect with everyone, promising everyone everything. They had a connection with people as far away as Italy and France. They were working on Thailand. They promised to fly me over with them, but they never did. All they ever did, you know, was ruin my life. They met a lot of people, so many, well, one-too-many people in East Texas and cut a dope deal with a dangerous guy, 'Triangle Al.'

Al was really working for Cinnamon Dunker."

"Undercover cop?"

"Nope! Oh no. Not like that. Al was forced to work for Dunker to sell Dunker's drugs and make deals. Failure to work for Dunker? Death. Al's job was to make more versions of himself to work for Dunker. Dunker makes dealers his slaves. Dunker and his corrupt cop boys just oversee, enforce and ramrod the slaves. So, Triangle tells Dunker about them. Dunker and his boys jumped Billy and Mike one night, set up by Al. Beat them almost to death, took their drugs and money and commanded them to work for Dunker, or else."

"Or else."

"Do or die. Dunker wanted all their dealer and customer names, and a big percentage of their money."

"And this was when? What time? When he worked for the Sheriff's Office?"

"Yes. He wanted names and numbers of dopers. Not to arrest them, no. To replace them. And Jack, all the time Dunker kept getting promoted, getting more and more power in the Sheriff's Office. Then he spread out and started a ring that stole cars."

"Chop shops."

"Yes. They killed people, Jack."

"And you know this…how?" Jack noticed that Shelly's tone and pitch had changed a little. She suddenly sounded just a bit like a hood.

"I was told every bit by Billy and Mike, and they were scared shitless. I don't know, I…I was too wasted to really understand exactly what was going on. I mean, I wasn't scared, and I never knew fully what all they did. And now I am in jail now because of Billy and Mike. They killed Triangle Al. I was there."

"You where there?"

"Yeees. Al was shot in the back seat of a limo. He

got into an argument with Billy. We were all in the back seat, drinking, doing drugs. Snorting coke. They were supposed to work under Al, Al under Dunker. But this idea aggravated Billy. Billy suddenly had a look come over his face, like a gray wave, like a monster.

He just pulled out a big pistol and shot Al. The driver of the limo pulled right over, jumped right out of the car and ran away. I shoulda ran right out with him, but I was too close to Billy and Mike, and they would just find me. I had no place to go anyway. I lost my house and was living with them in a big hotel suite. So, Mike told me to get behind the wheel of the limo and drive. Drive to the coast, he said. I got behind the wheel of the limo and…and started to drive east."

"What happened next?"

"Next…I just drove. Got south of Galveston. Mike and Billy ditched the body in a sand dune on a beach. Back in Beaumont, the police met the limo driver – who should have known better – who should have just said his limo was stolen. But no. He told them about the murder too. Ooohh, I should have known better too, Jack. The police found me next, and here I am, doing time, an accomplice to murder. The DA said since I drove the car, I was an accomplice. But, I was scared to death and just did what Mike told me."

"Where's Billy and Mike? Did they go to jail too?"

"They're dead. I mean they are gone, but I just know they're dead. Billy's mom wrote me a letter here years ago – I met her once. She asked if I knew where Billy was. I wrote her back and said I didn't. I don't. But he's gone. He hasn't called his mother in years? He's dead. Even the witness, limo driver is dead. I saw that on the TV news. He was shot, they say 'random' in a so-called 'drive-by' shooting."

"What about Triangle Al?" Jack asked.

"The cops found the body. I confessed. I told them where he was dropped," she said and shook her head in disgust. "I thought they would treat me better but no."

"And so, Dunker was in charge. And now he's running a task force. For the state. You are only assuming that..." Jack said.

"Oh, I am not assuming, Jack, she interrupted. "I know women in here. Women in trouble. Wives and girlfriends of dealers and dopers. Sam Dunker is doing the same thing but on a grander scale. He's hidden away in a task force with a great alibi. He's locating and making new slaves. When the task force arrests somebody, they decide what to do with him or her. Book them or they turn them into an employee."

"Will any of these women turn state's evidence? Talk?"

"No, I don't think so. Dunker will torture and kill us, and we know it. These gals were just unlucky like me, caught up on the outsides of things and arrested. I guess Dunker doesn't think we know enough to bother him? And he would easily just deny it, anyway, saying the task force was...you know, working on them or something."

"Yeah, working the leads with informants. Yeah. Easy lie."

"That's why you cannot use them and...or use me. You have to solve this problem independent of us."

"Yeah," Jack sounded disillusioned.

"You've done this before. You took on the Cowboy Mafia and the New York Mafia years ago. You put them in jail."

"No, actually not, Shelly. I killed most of them. Legit! Justified. Legit shootings though but making cases on these guys is almost a waste of time. They have the greatest lawyers and behind the lawyers stalling and playing court games, these guys…these guys don't play by any rules at all. They just…kill the witnesses. Scare or bribe the jurors. Even the judges."

"Even the judges. It's so one-sided. Rules versus no rules, huh? It's impossible," she said.

"It's…not…impossible," Jack said.

"I know I cannot cut a deal for a shorter sentence over this. Somewhere would be the – like– secret paperwork at the state police or the DA's office, or Pardons and Paroles…somewhere…and Dunker would have access to all that with his task force. He could say he wanted to use me as an informant and look me up. Get me out, or find me and then do me in."

"He might well," Jack said, "these task forces are very powerful."

"I am safer here in the pen."

Jack nodded and stroked her calf.

"You never used any heroin?" he asked.

"No. Just coke. I never did. Well, some speed. Mostly coke. I'm afraid of needles."

"Good thing to be afraid of," Jack said.

She sipped her wine and ate another pretzel.

"Sound worth it? Was I worth it?" she asked.

"Ah yeah, you were, and it does. I have to look into it."

"Will you come back to see me even if I have no crimes to trade?"

Jack smiled and looked at her for a few seconds.

"You know, probably."

"The doctors here say I am obsessive-compulsive," she said.

"Eh," Jack grunted, thinking about taking down this Cinnamon Dunker, "aren't…we all?"

Chapter 4: The Gestapo of Texas

Next Morning, Department of Public Safety (DPS) Headquarters, Houston, TX…

"Cinnamon? Dunker? Yeah, I know him," Texas Ranger Weaver Wisdom said, seated behind his office desk in the Houston Department of Public Safety headquarters. It was a room that looked like a mix between a cowboy museum and a church.

Weaver was Jack's first stop with all this new info, and the Ranger offices were just down the hall from the state intelligence bay. Weaver was the state's first black Texas Ranger, a powerful man of 6'5", and Jack's best friend. Their life and times went back two decades, starting with Jack as a detective in West Forge. He and Weaver had been through several "big-case-police-hells" together. Shot at and shot up, their crime fighting actions were both reviled and revered by their admins and the public, depending upon the political times. But they persevered.

Jack revealed all the intel on Cinnamon.

"Who told you this?"

"Ain't saying just yet." Jack said. "I will have to confirm it all independently."

"Hmmm, one of *those* informants. Hold on," Weaver said and reached for his phone.

"Nip, you in?" Weaver asked.

"I'm answering the phone, ain't I?" DPS Narcotics Sgt. Daniel "Nip" Budsten replied.

They say in the police and military business, one never gets to choose their own nicknames. Nip hadn't either. Thanks to the old deputy Barney Fife character on the 1960s Andy Griffith Show, and the deputy's famous line, *"Nip it, nip it, nip it in the bud,"* his last name of BUD-ston with a "bud." somehow connected him with the nickname of "Nip." Budston took to it and thought it better than just being called "Bud." Younger troopers unfamiliar with the classic show never know why he was called Nip.

"I mean in-in," Weaver said, "had coffee, been to the shitter, all calmed down. Can you come down to my office?"

"There in a minute," Nip said.

Nip showed up with a cup of coffee in hand, in a minute. He was a rangy, lanky thing, with long grey hair and beard, about 60 years old, from Abilene, TX. Dressed in a plain shirt, jeans and boots, with a nickel-plated .357 Colt Python strapped to his tooled belt, he took a seat in the second empty leather guest chair next to Jack. Always on the "get-things-done" level, Nip in Narcotics was a straight-up, must go-to-guy.

"Weave. Jack," he said.

Jack repeated the same story to Nip. Nip never took a single sip of his coffee. He was that hypnotized by the frightening tale.

"Could that be true?" Weaver asked.

"Could be," Nip said. "Firstly, I know this guy. Use to be a linebacker for Texas A&M. Almost made pro. Power broker in the Harris County S.O. for years. He worked narcotics when I met him. He was in everybody's office over there, politicin, a wheelin and a dealin. Then, got himself appointed, or he himself wrote the grant for this Gulf Coast Drug Task Force. He retired from the S.O."

"That's their official name?" Jack said. "The Gulf Coast Drug Task Force?"

"Yes sir. Official so named within the State Congress drug crime bill. His task force pretty much runs up the Gulf Coast from Louisiana to past Galveston.

There's another task force that runs south from there to the border. They are busy bastards what with the border and all. There are…I don't know…15, 20 of these task forces working in Texas these days. Made by the Texas State legislature."

He finally took his first sip. It was a little cold.

"These drug task forces…they are made from the ground up to be secret," Nip said. "Root out corruption high and low. Protect informants. They are officially called 'DTFs' Multijurisdictional Drug Task Forces. They are all nicknamed "jump-out boys," because of their black tactical uniforms and the masks they sometimes wear during raids. Most work in rural and suburban areas, but these boys you are talkin about operate on almost the whole coast. Big cities too. They get money from the Feds, from the Byrne Grant."

"What's the Byrne Grand?" Jack asked.

"Grant. With a T," Nip corrected. "The Byrne Grant Program. It was created by the Anti-Drug Abuse Act of 1988. For controlling violent and drug-related crime and serious offenders.

They also subsidize their own selves with seized money. Which is the loosey-goosey part. Who knows how much they really take in and how they spend it. What do they do with it? DPD Narcotics don't even get any Byrne money. Right now, I hear, because we don't know for sure, but I hear that all the task force members outnumber our DPS narcs by 3 to 1. I mean, we state folks are out in the cold. They get money from the states, money from the Feds and generate their own money."

"I did not know any of the details on this," Weaver said.

"Your snitch is probably right, Jack, this would be the worst. They keep the seized money for their budgets and that's where the real money is. Unaccounted for money. Seizures. They could easily lie about what they got. The task forces run informants, their own highway interdictions with official squad cars. They run raids. They are like independent little police departments. Little gestapos are what they are. The commanders get to recruit the members, and some ain't even PO-lice. Just whoever they want as officers with no police academy training. As the saying goes, 'they have no ruling authority.'"

"This sounds a lot like what my snitch said," Jack added.

Nip said. "ACLU and some Texas congressmen think they've become problematic and have investigated some horror stories about them already.'"

"They can't be too secret. They still have to file cases with the local DAs," Weaver said.

"They do," Nip said. "And I bet they do some. They have to look good to somebody. Somebody somewhere in Austin is watching the numbers. It ain't us! It ain't D.P.S. Narcotics. You think we'd be a good choice for that. But no."

"Asking for performance records at the DA Offices would surely tip them off," Weaver said.

"Yup," Nip said.

"Asking for records at the state grant office would surely tip them off too," Weaver said.

"Yup," Nip said. "And some laws protect that information. Can't get it. They surely have to report annual stats somewhere, in some office of the legislature. Finding that office, showing up and asking for their task force numbers alone, would, could get back to them. Tipping them off."

"I might be able to get some access to that information if a certain someone I know were to ask for all the statistics, and not just from one task force. Someone they would suspect would be nosing around," Jack said.

"Gail?" Weaver asked.

Jack nodded. Weaver nodded back.

"Where might their headquarters be?" Jack asked.

"Don't know, bubba. Nobody knows. That's the beauty of it all. It's all secret-squirrel shit."

"Huh!" Jack said.

"Whatcha gonna do Jack? Whatcha want us to do?" Weaver asked.

"Okay, well, right now, nothing. I got two-three ideas I am going to work on."

"Keep your Sgt. Dull happy and don't tell em. This will flat freak him out," Weaver said with a smile.

"Yeah," Nip said. "Keep Dull, dull."

"I just wanted y'all to know about this," Jack said, "what I heard."

"In case you get kilt tomorrow or something," Weaver said.

"Something like that," Jack said.

"Consider yourself heard," Nip said.

Jack winked, stood and left the office.

Nip and Weaver looked at each other.

"Think he'll find something?" Nip asked.

"Ohhh, probably," Weaver said. "I've seen him like this many times. When he gets like this, onto something like this? Praise the Lord, nothing but a long, string line of horrible things happen."

Chapter 5: Free Lance Expressions

League City, Harris County, Texas...

Samuel "Cinnamon" Dunker finished shaving his face in the personal wing of his big house which contained a private bathroom and closet. He was 6' 6" and at age 55 in terrific shape, as he was able to work out and run in his task Force headquarters almost daily. Not quite as tough a routine as his college football days. But close. On weekends he and wife went to a local gym.

He needed a special wing in his home, with a safe and secure, locked-away closet for all his guns and gear. He had but a few minutes before his wife would be rounding up their two kids, packing them in an SUV and carting them off to elementary school, so he quickly slipped into a pull-over polo shirt and 9-11 pants and jogged barefoot to the main part of their enormous house.

"Kiddos!" he yelled.

"Bye daddy!" they yelled back, in a smiling melody that always warmed his heart.

"Are you going to speak to your father?" his wife Katie asked as she gathered up two large purses full of her daily real estate paperwork and brochures.

"Yes, yes I will."

"Now?"

"Yes."

She kissed him on the cheek and bounded off into the garage. Dunker went back to his wing and put on socks and black sneakers, stalling for a time before the dreaded father-son meeting. What would he say this time to his cantankerous old man anyway?

He took a deep breath and walked through the

house, bound for in what would be called in real estate terms, the "mother-in-law" wing. In this case, this wing was where his 83-year old father lived.

"Pops?" he said, entering the rooms.

"What?" the pops said in a grunt, seated in a plush lounge chair eating a dish of ice cream, some of it had already having landed on his t-shirt, according to the fresh stains. The TV was on, blasting the Today Show.

"Ice cream again for breakfast, huh?" he said.

Another grunt.

"Ice cream..." Dunker started.

"It's close to cereal,"

"Pops, I got to go work but I have to tell you something."

"Uh-oh," Pops said never looking away from the TV.

"Katie and I were thinking and, you know, after that car accident last week..."

"That small accident..."

"We think you need to stop driving, Pops."

"The shit you say."

"This is the fourth one, small or not, in three months."

"You can't stop me from driving. How am I gonna get around to my club meetings? My shopping? The podiatrist?"

"Taxis. Taxis, Pops, or we'll drive you. Anyway, you haven't shopped for anything in a store by yourself in years."

"I haven't? Huh? How do you know? You're gone most of the time. Well, what if I have to? What if I need something? You can't keep me in adult diapers forever."

"You don't have to shop."

Pops successfully spooned a lump of ice cream into

his mouth.

"Most people don't eat ice cream for breakfast," Dunker added, "It's not healthy."

Pops finally looked at Dunker and sneered. The look that tore through Dunker's childish core.

"Okay Pops, think about it? Huh? Will ya?"

"Goodbye," Pops said in a growl.

"We are going to take your keys away at some point!" Dunker said over his shoulder as he walked away.

"It's my car!"

"No," Dunker stopped and turned at the doorway. "It's my car."

Then he left, sighing, "Jeee-suuus." It wasn't meant as a curse to Jesus Christ, just a free-lance expression.

With too many other things on his mind, Dunker backed out of the four-car garage in his new, red Mustang. He drove the few plush, hilly, treed blocks out to the neighborhood's main exit street and onto Windswept Ave.

At the intersection, Dunker didn't notice the Cadillac sedan parked in the shopping center across the street. Jack Kellog had been studying each face in each car as it left the elite housing edition until he spied Dunker's mug behind the wheel of one.

"There…he…is, and he is linebacker big, the son of a bitch," Jack mumbled as he turned on the ignition. Jack didn't know Dunker's mother. It was not a curse meant for her directly, just another free-lance expression. One of his two plans were now in serious play.

Jack Kellog's Idea #1: The Klatch Girls
Just the day before, right after leaving the Texas Rangers office bay, Jack sat with the six senior women secretaries in the intelligence office. They were nick-

named the "Klatch Girls," many years earlier. Lydia, Jocelyn, Wynona, Reba, Stella and Christina. None under 50 years of age, all divorced, overweight, smokers, drinkers, sewers, knitters and occasional swearers.

No one knew where the nickname "Klatch" originally came from. Coffee Klatch perhaps? Sewing Klatch? They did have a sewing club. These women not only did a ton of office chores, but also were veteran experts in information collection, scouring the libraries, phone books and new, expanding internet and microfiche, all items unofficially and officially attached to all government agencies and files. They were always toiling away in the background, responsible for cracking, tracking and capturing some of the baddest, bad guys, gals and gangs in Texas history, and never getting a lick of credit for it.

Right after Jack's massive heart attack, nervous breakdown, brutality charges, and firing from West Forge two years ago, Jack was hired on full time by the state police DPS (by Governor George Bush's decree), he was introduced to the Klatch by Ranger Wisdom.

"Ladies, this is Jumpin' Jack Kellog, my best friend and the best detective you'll ever met," Weaver said.
Weaver Wisdom then slowly introduced each woman to him, their faces expressionless, as much as to say, "here's another one," despite the Ranger's enthusiasm.

Then came the publicized successful manhunt for the killer John Phillip Muzak. Then came Kellog's visits to their office, not just to ask for their work, but just to stop and say hi. Chat briefly. They all started "chatting" back.

So that day, Jack stopped by and dropped a newspaper photo of Samuel "Cinnamon" Dunker on the big table in the middle of the room and asked for help.

"Ladies," he said, "I need to know everything we can find on this guy. In particular, one thing for sure, for starters, where he lives."

Taking turns, he sat near each one, searching for what they could, and they realized by mid-day, that much information required a trip to the library and a deep dive into newspapers and their related micro-fiche. Such a trip would have to be approved by Sgt. Dull though, and Jack wasn't ready to tell him about this yet.

Plus, the ladies had no access to any secret, state task force information. None. But, by the end of the day, they at least found his house. It was not in Cinna-mon's name. Dunker was 55 years old, born in El Paso, Texas. County and city marriage records found his wife's name. She was a real estate agent still using her maiden name and their near-mansion-sized house was in her name alone. The home was in League City, known to be one of the richest cities in Harris County.

"What's the scoop, Kellog," Christina finally asked, knocking the ash off the end of her Marlborough ciga-rette. "He's a cop. Why?"

"I don't want everyone to get excited…but this Gulf Coast Task Force. Dunker is in charge of it..."

"Ya ain't telling Dull about this, are ya?" Reba asked.

"Ahhh, not yet," Jack said.

"Oops! Say no more handsome," Lydia said, "we get it."

Plan underway...
Armed with this new info, the grateful Jack Kellog left for his own house, switched vehicles from his state

Ford Crown Vic to his 1994 El Dorado Cadillac. In his trunk he had several rubber, magnetic signs. He pulled out two that read "Wilson's Reality" and stuck one on each side. This and a big clipboard of papers on the dashboard was "cover" to slowly prowl any neighborhood several times and have an immediate eye-witness excuse for doing so when spotted by curious residents. He drove to League City for some drive-bys of the Dunker house.

It was never wise for corrupt cops to have big houses, newer cars and boats – Jack himself had two of those three – a big house in West Forge and a nice car. But Jack lived like a monk and was single. The Dunker house was indeed massive, surrounded by other massive houses. All things considered, no one knew what a commander of a big task force made, and Dunker also had the excuse of being married to a deal-finding, real estate agent, all great cover for a cop to have a really big, big house, and a new Mustang.

An Atlas map revealed that there were two big entry-exits to the housing edition, one street led onto a bigger avenue than the other street, which was more of a back road. Jack went with the odds the next morning and sans those car door signs, he parked on a high-dollar, small mall, parking lot by the main avenue exit. And there appeared Cinnamon Dunker in a new Red Mustang waiting at the red light to turn right. It was 7:40 a.m.

Jack followed the Mustang for about 5 miles, then at a major intersection he pulled off into a Skaggs-Albersons parking lot. Dunker drove on. Jack noted it was 8:10 am. Tomorrow he would wait in this supermarket lot in his old pick up truck, waiting for Dunker to pass. Jack worried that if Dunker was worth his salt as a veteran, and a corrupt cop, he might be on the lookout to be followed once in a while. So just in case Jack pulled off. He learned this "segmented surveillance" method from old Houston PD detectives when he was a young Houston PD patrol officer.

The next morning, Jack waited on the Skaggs-Albertson lot in his "war wagon" 1990 Ford pickup. He got lucky, because Dunker was on time and following a normal schedule like the day before. Jack pulled his truck out on the street several cars behind him and followed. How far would he go today?

They drove on and on until Dunker eventually turned left into a small commercial airport called Beachem Air, far enough away from Bush and Hobby airports to operate. Jack was somewhat familiar with the place. It was not too small of an airport because they flew private jets city-to-city, state-to-state via the small airline headquartered there called "Cloud Air." And there were also numerous private hangars for rent. Jack did not turn into the complex but rather drove right by the entrance so as not to be spotted.

About 200 feet farther on, he turned onto a factory parking lot across the street and parked facing the airport. He snatched up a pair of binoculars from the passenger seat and watched the red Mustang travel past the small jet service terminal and on down to the line of rented hangars. There were eight horseshoe-shaped hangars. Dunker turned left into one section and out of Jack's sight. Was this the task force headquarters? A rented plane hangar in an eight-hangar airport? Why not? Isolated. Big. Rather brilliant.

He scanned the landscape. The whole airport was surrounded by an 8-foot chain link fence with three strands of barbwire across the top. He noted that there was a single lane asphalt service road outside the fence. He decided to chance a closer look. He drove across the street and onto the narrow, border, service road outside the fence to take a look at the hangar complexes. He passed the jet airline operation and continued on to spy on the hangars.

There were four large horseshoe-shaped two-story, square hangars all in row following close to and along the airstrip and another four behind them a ways back. The center space of each horseshoe shape was quite large allowing for parked cars. The third one down, Jack spotted the red Mustang among other parked cars.

There was an office door to the right side of it and above the door was a giant sign on the metal wall which read, "The High-Flying Aces" in a hand-painted red font that resembled all the other signs on all the hangars, obviously a rental requirement.

He continued around the circumference and eventually examined the other side, the back side of the hangars. The outside rear of the horseshoes had the standard, tall, large hangar doors. These were all high-dollar operations for big businesses. Some doors were open and he easily saw several planes, some boats, some factory machinery and people milling about in all of them.

As he completed the circle, he spotted behind the *Cloud Air* terminal, an overweight, uniformed guy in a golf cart. The airport had its own security, worth noting.

Jack got back on the street and said aloud, "And there you have it, the secret headquarters of the Gulf Coast Drug Task Force. And I will be paying y'all a surprise visit tomorrow."

Jack Kellog's Idea #2:
Jack called an old friend.
"Gail? This is Jack."

"Jack? How are youuuu? Are you calling to see if I am still married? I am."

Gail Conchas was the lead, popular, award-winning crime writer of the famous Texican Monthly magazine, and long-time "close friend" of Jack's for many a year. Close also included "using" each other for investigations, stories and even some sex. Their paths seem to mysteriously cross with some frequency since his 1980's "war on the New York Mafia" days.

"No, I know you are still married. I spy on you. I just have your next big scoop, honey."

"Oh, that's nice," she said skeptically, "and what might that be, mister?"

"It involves going to the capital and conducting an investigation into all the state-funded, drug task forces, like an audit for a magazine article. Task forces are always a hot topic."

"They are. And growing," she said.
"Now I say all…because we really want information on just one of them, secretly, under the guise to study them all for Texican Monthly."

"I am interested," she said. Can we meet tomorrow or maybe the better, the day after? Your place?" she said.

"Gaiiiillll, this is strictly business now," he said. "My place has always meant a lot of drinking and sex."

"Darn, Then, well, meet you halfway at our usual barbeque place. Lunch. Noon. Thursday? Prairie Station Barbecue?"

"Wonderful. You won't regret it." Jack said.
"I never regret it."
They hung up. He wouldn't tell her the whole story, just enough to stir the pot, and…keep her alive.

Chapter 6: Jack the Giant Killer

DPS Headquarters Houston, TX...

Since Weaver Wisdom had a private office and Jack just had a desk in an open bay with partitions, he, Weaver and Nip met privately in the Ranger's office.

"An airline hangar," Nip said, "that's a pretty nice little airport. Expensive. Private. Smart."

"I think I am going to pay them a social visit," Jack said. "Just ahhh, - hi, my name is Jack, new in DPS Intelligence and I wanted to stop by and say hi and offer my services in the war against drugs."

"Whatcha gonna tell them when they ask how you knew where they were?" Weaver asked.

"Probably say someone told me where they were, like from the DA's office."

"That'll raise a red flag," Weaver said.

"That'll damn sure shake the tree," Nip said.

"If I walk in, I'll see what they have. Reckon they have a plane or two in there? If so, reckon what they are flying around in it?"

"We need some more scoop on them from the state records," Nip said. "Somewhere in the Austin capital."

"I'm working on it," Jack said.

"Gail?" Weaver asked.

"Gail."

Weaver looked over the top of his reading glasses at Jack for a few seconds after the mention of Gail's name. Jack had never married, never settled down because of long trysts with married women through time, one being Gail Canchas.

"Okay," Nip said, "go visit em, get a look inside and see if there's anything suspicious. And get some intel from Austin. I think if we get some meat on this, we can get budget money authorized for a surveillance on the place. I've been out there. Eight years ago we worked on a dope ring out there, flying dope in there. There are fields and some trees three quarters around the airport, and we might set up a 'deer stand' surveillance from afar."

"When ya goin?" Weaver asked.

"Now. How's about the two of you go have coffee in the terminal cafeteria while I do. Be nearby. I'll have my portable radio with me and yell for help if I need it.

"Yell for help. HEEELLLP! Sounds like a simple plan," Nip said, as he, Jack and Weaver stood up to leave.

Weaver and Nip had the lead in the drive over to Beachem Airport so that they could park and get set up at a table in the small cafeteria first. Jack Kellog stalled for a few minutes and drove his black state car, Crown Vic onto the airport grounds. He knew right where to go - that third hangar. And the red Mustang and other cars and trucks were there outside of the High-Flying Aces sign. Upon this closer inspection, Jack noted Dunker's operation took up two-thirds of the U-shaped hangar, a whole back and right side.

He parked and with portable radio shoved in his back pocket, walked up to the metal door under the sign. He opened it...

Five men were seated in a well-furnished lobby of chairs and couches, all dressed in subdued colors. All were really shocked to see him. All stood up and pulled pistols! Aimed right at him.

"Hey, hey guys!" Jack yelled with his hands up, palms out, "I'm with you!"

He pulled open his sport jacket and displayed the

state badge on his belt.

They still had their guns on him, but their facial expressions changed somewhat. Then two or three lowered their guns, then all five did.

"Well saints be praised," came a voice behind him. Sam Cinnamon Dunker himself emerged from a side office door. "If it ain't the infamous Jumpin' Jack Kellog."

Dunker walked toward him with a big smile and open hand. They shook hands.

"This is Jack Kellog, boys. The man who brought down the cowboy mafia and the New York mafia around here in the 1980s. And a few months ago, hunted down the most wanted criminal family in Texas."

Jack smiled and shook his hand. Dunker looked the same as his older press conference and newspaper pictures.

"What brings you around here?" Dunker asked.

"West Forge P.D. fired me. The State hired me thanks to the Governor. I am OO-ficially, full-time, with DPS Intelligence now, and I am just making the rounds to introduce myself and offer my services to every agency in the region. Just say hi. Leave a card."

"Great. How'd you find us?" Dunker asked very nonchalantly.

"Somebody at the DA's office," Jack said.

"Oh, somebody," Dunker said.

"This is Larry Drumwald, from the Panhandle S.O. up there."

They shook hands.

"Greg Williams once from Harris County."

They shook hands.

"Lassiter Gaston from El Paso P.D."

They shook hands.

"Collier Jones. Once Houston P.D."

"Me too, once," Jack said, and shook his hand.

"And that is Tyrone Tyson."

And they shook hands.

"Let's ahhh…well…let's show you are around," Dunker said.

They walked through double doors on the back wall of the lobby and into the hangar. The hangar was huge, crowded with various cars, and a newer style plane. The hangar had its two giant back doors open. The inside of the hangar revealed an array of old and new cars, some expensive sports cars, two SWAT vans, a business meeting area of tables and chairs before a rolling chalkboard, a battery of desks, all not unlike a common police detective bay.

"Wow," Jack said.

"We got it all," Dunker said, "from grant money or seized money from dopers. The whole area over there are all seized cars from dopers."

"Wow," Jack said again.

"We have four highway interdiction squad cars too. The four officers use them as take-home cars, so they are not here, coming and going from their homes. They run the roads, make traffic stops. Two of them have dope dogs. They have brought in a lot of our business running up and down the highways. Come here, look over here," and Dunker guided him to a set of rooms along a wall.

"Holding cells," Dunker said. "They catch em and we talk to them in here. Wheels and deals are made as we try to shoot up their distro ladder."

"Great," Jack said, eyeing the four cells up, all replete with big center drains for…cleaning with hoses.

"Amazing," Jack said.

"Amazing what seized dope money will do,"

Dunker said, "When used properly. Here's our walk-in armory."

Dunker motioned again for Jack over to a two-door, walk-in, metal, stand-alone gun safe, the double doors open, offering a view of weapons hung and stacked inside to rival a war movie. Pistols. Rifles. Machine guns.

Jack looked the whole place over. To the left aways off, he saw a man in a dark green, mechanic's outfit walked around some unmarked cars. Normal height. Stocky build, black wavy hair which was almost wig-like-looking. The man had a Central American, or maybe Aztec-looking features. But, what Jack noticed very quickly, the man, once in motion between cars, had a limp, an odd gait, and his right foot angled outward, like the man in the church, detective murder caught on film.

Jack quickly looked away, as though his study was one big, sweeping scan of the interior, but he felt a chill.

"Well gentlemen, I know now that if I get anything worth your time, I will send the info or the snitch your way," Jack said as they all turned to walk back to the front office. "Do you have a phone number I can reach you?

"Yup. I even have a card, but with the 'Aces-High' name. That sounds mighty fine, Jumpin," Dunker said.

"And you know not to send them here, we'll meet him somewhere else."

"Oh yeah. Sure."

"This here's the Batcave. And no one knows where Batman goes."

"Yup."

"In fact, don't tell anyone where we are, okay?"

"Okay," Jack lied.

Once back in the front lobby, Dunker walked through a side door into what must have been his office and emerged with a card. Jack traded him his DPS business card.

With a big, social grin, Jack said goodbye to them all and left. The men could not help but watch him walk out the door and across the parking lot through the windows.

"What the…" Collier Jones said.

"DA's office my ass," Greg Williams said, "they don't know where we are. No one does."

"It's not impossible to find us here," Dunker said, also watching Jack leave. "But something ain't right. And it's especially ain't right that it's him," Dunker said with a sigh. "Him. Him nosing around. He's a buzz-killer. He's no normal cop. He's a giant killer. He's got the jazz. But we did good. We acted normal like we would for any such legal visitor."

Jack Kellog returned to his car and sat inside. He tried to jot down, as many license plates of the cars around him as he could. He knew it was standard practice for all city, county, state narcotics people to have false names attached to license plate names and origins. But many of the cars there were not at all official looking. And what of that man with the odd limp? What?

"Meet cha back at the ranch," Jack told the waiting, nearby Weaver and Nip over the handheld radio, holding the radio low on his lap and de[depressing the mike switch.

Back in Weaver's office, Jack, Weaver and Nip sat. This time they finally invited in Jack's supervisor, the Intelligence Division Sgt. Dull, for the pow-wow. They briefed Dull. Dull seemed mildly impressed and somewhat interested.

"This guy walking around, like a janitor, or a mechanic, with the…that…that strange limp," Jack said, "just like the shooter of that Screed city detective in the church they caught on film. Ahhh… could be nothing. But I got a chill when I saw him. I got a chill."

"Respect the chill," Weaver said, knowing his old buddy.

"Otherwise, it all looks like a top-notch, task force operation," Jack said. "Lots of money involved. Almost, almost too much money. Lots of unsupervised chances to hide lots more."

"What do you want to do, Jack?" Dull asked.

"In a perfect world, I'd like to set up a surveillance on that task force."

"That's a lot of money," Dull said. "We're not there yet."

Jack nodded, then said, "I'd like to go down to Screed and look into their shooting. Look to see if there are any drug angles to it. See if they know yet why that detective was killed."

"All this just on a guy with a limp?" Dull said.

"And a hunch. Yeah. It's an odd limp," Jack said.

"I don't think they have any leads down there yet," Nip said, "they're scrambling for anything right now I heard tell."

"Any Rangers in on it yet?" Dull asked Weaver.

"No, not yet," Weaver said. "We usually get asked in. Invited in, especially from a small or mid-sized city like Screed. I suspect they haven't gotten around to it yet. It's in our region, though. And surely, they need some big-league help."

"Can you get approval to go?" Dull asked.

"I can," Weaver said. "I can by just going. I am my own approval."

Jack smiled.

"Can you take Jack?" Dull asked.

"I can."

"Okay then," Dull said, "take a couple of days on this, Jack. See what you can find out. This could be big, or it could be nothing."

"Thanks, Sarge," Jack said.

Dull left the office.

"We go tomorrow?" Weaver asked.

"We go. Yup. I'm gonna see if the Klach girls have anything," Kellog said.

Jack walked into the Klatch Girls' rows of desks holding a thin stack of copies.

"Ladies!" he declared.

"Jack," and the ladies replied with variations of his first and last name, and nickname.

"Any news?" he asked.

"Sure. The bad news is the task forces are about as protected as the CIA. They have legislative, built-in walls covering all their activities. Only a few appointed Texas congressmen, the Lt. Governor and Governor Bush can look into their activities," Lydia said.

"That bad, huh?"

"That bad," Joselyn said, "we're still working on it."

"Mr. Dunker has quite the public record. Sterling super cop so far," Wynona said. "He should have his own TV show."

Okay…I have this," Jack said, handing out the sheets of paper to all six of the ladies. "These guys, part of this task force, introduced themselves to me when I made a surprise visit this morning."

Jack read the names out loud, and the girls scanned

the papers with him.

"Larry Drumwald, from the Panhandle area Sheriff's Office. Greg Williams once from Harris County. Lassiter Gaston from El Paso P.D. Collier Jones, once Houston P.D. Tyrone Tyson, origin unknown. I can only assume surely, they should all be police elsewhere, detectives, narcotics, somewhere to be hired on a task force. Can you check? And…at the bottom are some license plates I copied down. Can we see where that might go? I know that narcs can have phony license plates, and a task force must do this too."

"If they're legit police people, they'll be on the police rolls of each state. We'll find em," Christina said.

Jack winked at them, but they didn't see his eyelid move as they quickly burrowed down onto the computers.

Chapter 7: The World Series of Policing

Since Weaver was still recovering from his wounds and the last of his surgeries from the Muzak shooting in El Paso, Jack drove them to Screed, Texas. Weaver co-piloted by scanning the Atlas map-book and guided them to the city police department. Like so many mid-to-small sized police departments, the agency was connected with the complex of city offices.

Unannounced and uninvited, Jack and Weaver strolled into the lobby and asked if the Chief of Police was in. The civilian stationed at the front city desk, went eyes wide at the sight of the 6' 5", black, Texas Ranger in his white Stetson, white, long sleeved, starched shirt, tan vest replete with thee legendary "cinco peso," Mexican coin, badge, tan polyester pants, boots and leather tooled gun belt, holding an engraved .45 semi-auto pistol. He quickly took off for the police wing.

"Where would we be without Walker, Texas Ranger?" Weaver said of this instant, front desk awe and respect from the front desk civilian.

"I really don't think you need Walker, Texas Ranger," Jack muttered, not bothering to look at him. "You kinda got something going on alllll by your own lonesome."

Within a few minutes, a bald, elderly man, pot-bellied in a blue uniform entered the lobby. They introduced themselves to each other. The chief's name was Method, and the chief stammered, with an added left eye twitch and slight sneer, when he learned he was in the presence of one Jack Kellog.

He led the way back to his office. He sat at his desk and the visitors sat in the quest chairs.

Weaver began, "We were wondering if your department needed any state help with the murder of your detective?"

"We are still gathering information. He was one of our finest, and other than his many arrests and cases, we have so far found no strong motive for such an ambush at this time. Even amongst those he's arrested."

"Any idea how this killer got into the locked church?" Jack asked.

The chief looked at Jack for several seconds, and said, "Now, you're that detective…that detective that last year or two, what beat that child killer almost to death up in West Forge. All on the TV news. Filmed the beating from a traffic chopper."

"I am," Jack said.

"And how is it you are still wearing a badge? Any badge? Sitting in my office asking me questions?" Weaver knew to sit this one out.

"Because I'm very good at this. At that moment I had a heart attack and a nervous breakdown. I lost my mind. And otherwise, I may have some important information that might help in your case."

The chief made a distasteful expression and said, "I find that unlikely. I find you unlikely. If it weren't for the Ranger here…"

"You liking it, ain't got nothing to do with it," Jack interrupted, "who you got working on the case?"

The chief stared at him for another ten distasteful seconds, then reached for his phone.

"Patty, is Linda here? Send Linda in here," he said, then hung up.

After a moment of uncomfortable quiet, a woman, thin, pale in her late 20s, with brown straight hair parted down the middle and a bare trace of make-up, stepped in the doorway.

"This is Detective Linda Pathways," the chief said.

"Linda, these two men are from DPS. They think they have some information on Paul's murder. You want to show them what we have?"

"Ah, yes sir, sure," she said, and she waved her hand for them to follow.

Weaver stood and winked at the chief. Jack ignored him, and they left the office.

Pathways' so-called "office" was an open, three-sided cubicle. She dragged up two chairs and all three sat as best they could at her desk. Pathways crossed her legs lightly, tightly and efficiently as only a skinny person can.

They introduced themselves.

"You've seen the video on the news?" she asked.

"Yes," Jack said.

"We have a little more. We have just have the lobby and part of the hallway on film. And we have the busy part of the church outside, the side parking lot records 24-7 too. No cars that night. They run the camera 24-7, but really to record Wednesday and night and Sunday morning."

"No cars that night. What about the other nights?" Jack asked.

"I…we…ah…"

"This church was cased, had to be," Jack said. "And probably a suspect drove around it at least one time, days before the murder. At night. Before. Days before."

She just looked at Jack with a blank expression.

"Detective Pathways, I…" Jack said.

"You can call me 'Path.' Everybody does."

Jack smiled and said, "Path, does the church still have the parking lot videos from the nights before the shooting? Like a week or so?" Jack asked.

"I would think so, yes," she said.

"Good. We need to see them. How did this killer get into the church?"

"We don't know."

"Was the church all for sure all locked up?"

"Yes, they say. They think it was locked," she said, "it seemed all locked up. No forced entries."

"Did Paul work any drug cases?" Weaver asked.

"Once in a while. We all do, once in a while. We have two narcs here. They do most of it. But if something falls into our lap? We work narcotics. Why you ask."

"We need to talk with your narcs. Is there any connection, any chance of any of Paul's cases involving any drugs that you know of?" Weaver said.

"No. I have all his open and recently assigned cases right there," she pointed to a pile on her desk. "I've looked them all over. I can't find anything that would make someone mad enough to kill Paul like this. This odd, organized, planned way. Please, y'all look them over too. Are you here…do you think he was killed by a drug ring or something?"

"Or something. Just an idea, right now. Now you say assigned cases," Jack said, "how about self-initiated cases, cases not assigned. Ones with no formal crime report yet. No formal file. Working leads and hunches? They'd be in notes maybe? Or known in conversations," and he moved his hand around in the air, "with y'all?"

She shook her head with an expression of ignorance.

"Who knew him best? Who'd he hang out with here?" Weaver said.

"Ramsey…" she stood and looked over the cubicle wall, "he's not in right now, but they deer hunt together. Play softball. They are…were…in the VFW together. He says he is clueless about who would do this. Hey…there's Gallanty, narcotics."

She shouted out to Gallanty to come see her. When he got there, introductions followed. Gallanty remained standing and rested an arm on the cubicle wall.

"We are wondering if there are any recent narcotics cases that Paul might have been working on?" Jack asked.

"Drugs?" Gallanty said, scrunching up his face, "no, nothing official. Nothing to get himself killed! I think. He did say to me last month, that an old high school and Army buddy of his – he asked me about this – drowned in a lake near here. He was in the Army with Paul and Paul said the guy came home from Iraq and became a dope addict. A dealer. Cocaine. Smack. After the drowning, the guy's mother called Paul and she was crying…begging for his help. She said that there was something odd about the Paul's death. She begged Paul to look into it because nobody else would. You know…the 'mom thing.' Paul mentioned it to me when we were fishing, because the guy was a drugee. PTSD maybe? Too? They were in Iraq together. Enduring Freedom."

"Yeah, what they do in the Army?" Weaver asked.

"Helicopters. They flew choppers. You know, but the guy probably drown out there on the lake because he was too high? Not too many suicides by drowning."

"Not too many. Remember the guy's name?" Weaver asked.

"Naaah, I don't. There's no report here on it here because it happened outside the city."

"I can dig it up, look it up if they were school and Army buddies," Pathways said. "And the nearest lake is Trail Downs in Pleasant Prairie. It'll be big news there."

"Can the dispatchers here compile a record of criminal histories and license plates Paul has asked them to run…in, oh, maybe a month? Two months? That might cover anything he was working on off the record," Jack asked.

"I think so," she said, "I haven't…thought of that."

"Well, so that's not a problem," Jack said with a big smile. "I can't think of everything either, which is why I hang out with this big somabitch right here. We each think of things."

Weaver remained stone-faced.

"Path, you ahhh, you ever work any homicides before?" Jack asked.

"Well, no, sir," she said.

"Just call me Jack."

"Okay. We only have about one or two a year here and Paul worked all of them."

"And now, you are 'homicide.' Welcome to homicide," Jack said.

It was her turn to grimace. She shook her head.

"Homicide is the World Series of police work," Jack added, "and you can't lose even one game. And you play on a team."

"Can we go take a look at the church? Now?" Weaver asked.

"Sure," Path said, let me stop at the dispatcher office and ask about those NCIC requests. That's a good idea."

They all stood, and Jack wandered over to Paul's cubicle.

"It's still same as the day before he was murdered," Path said, heading to the dispatcher section.

On one wall, hung several color photos in frames. Some were military photos and Jack leaned in for a look. He saw several photos of Paul in and around helicopters in the desert.

"Pilot," Jack mentioned to Weaver.

Weaver was also surveying the desk and the photos.

"An office empty of a soul what flew away." Weaver said.

"Upwards I hope," Jack said. "Haunting in a way," Jack whispered.

"Yup," Weaver said. "Always is. The shallow, empty belongings of the dead. Leftovers. The righteous man perishes, and no one lays it to heart. Devout men are taken away, while no one understands. For the righteous man is taken away from calamity, he enters into peace."

Jack took that speech in, all the while looking at his friend's profile.

Weaver looked back at him and said softly, "Isaiah 57:1-2."

"Gotcha. No peace for we the survivors. Let's go."

Chapter 8: Texas Roulette

Late night, Beachum Airport...

"What we got?" Dunker asked his task force, highway, drug interdiction patrol officer Reynolds Rebadoux as they hustled toward the holding cells. Rebadoux had just made an interesting traffic stop and arrest.

"Boss, this guy had 2 pounds of coke and 5 pounds of Maryjane in two suitcases in his trunk. He just looked funny to me in traffic on 45 and I thought I'd pull him over. Instinct. The guy went freaked-out, shaky-nuts when he saw the K-9. Then Buster went nuts when he got near the trunk."

"Anything special, Reb?"

"Passport trip. Mexico. Just earlier today," Rebadoux said.

"Ohhh, okay. Sounds good."

"And he also had two empty suitcases."

"Ho! So he had some drop-offs already. He got business. He got game." Dunker said.

"He got, we got, about $14,000 cash too."

"Brazen roadster."

"Yes, sir."

Rebadoux stopped outside the cells' hallway door. Dunker entered the hall and walked to the first cell. The suspect was seated at a bolted-down, metal table on a bolted down metal chair with the two front legs cut off by about 2 inches each, an interrogation trick, leaving the suspect leaning, tipping uncomfortably forward. He was handcuffed to a metal loop in the center of the table. Task Forcer Collier Jones stood in the corner of the metal room.

"Thomas Jessica," Collier advised Dunker, "lives in

Austin."

"Keep Austin weird," Dunker declared the old motto as he sat across the table from the arrested driver and smiled at him.

"I believe I have a right to a lawyer," Jessica said

"Ordinarily," Dunker said, "but this? You and me? This ain't ordinary."

"I want a lawyer."

"I want…everything you know," Dunker replied.

"Your people in Mexico, your customers between here and Mexico. And Austin."

"What is this?"

"This is the PO-lice Twilight Zone. Twilight Zone P.D. and I am Rod Fucking Sterling." Dunker said, "you think you are where you are, but you ain't."

"It's Serling. Rod SERLING," the man corrected, "and I know where I am, and you are not going to trick me. I want a lawyer. I want a phone call. I want…" Thomas Jessica said.

Dunker stood up, leaned over and hook punch-belted Jessica right in the mouth. It was a wallop! And Jessica would have fallen right out of along with the chair, had it not been bolted down.

"I got all night, dipshit," Dunker said. "You are under MY arrest. And it's your nightmare, Auschwitz arrest. You dig that hippy boy? You don't have enough individual teeth in your mouth to say no to all my questions."

This was a shocker to Thomas Jessica, and he sat back up, with a long, red stained drool hanging from his lips.

"I am not going to arrest anyone that you know. Mexico or round here. Or Austin. No sir. I am only going to replace you. I am just going to rework your place. Or! Or you will work for me. Continue to work for me and do exactly what you are doing now. Except, I am your new boss. That dope in your car? It's still yours. Your car? It's still yours. You will be making less money for a while, but you will still be alive."

"A while?"

"Yeah, you will be making less money, but for a little while as we grow. You see bubba, I am into 'profit sharing' and this will pay off in the end."

"I was stopped by a real cop!"

"Yes, you wuz."

"In a cop car!"

"Yes, you wuz."

"I was cuffed and taken to this jail cell!"

"Yes, you is."

"And you aren't the cops?"

"Yes, we are, and no we're not. That is your problem. Your dilemma. We are as powerful as the cops, but, we'll also do anything we want to make money too. So, with us, you won't go to jail, won't pay thousands of dollars to lawyers. You'll just pay us. And eventually if you are good boy, you will be protected and rich."

"I don't believe it. Where am I?

"Secret. That's why our officer bagged your head on the way here. Now, let's get started with Mexico. Start at the top. Where do you get your product?"

"This is a trick. A scam. You're not fooling me. And, I want my lawyer."

"Okay…get the pistol," Dunker said.

Collier Jones nodded, left the cell and the jail section. In a moment, he returned with a nickel-plated magnum revolver in his right hand.

"Ready? One bullet?" Dunker said to Collier.

"Ready. One bullet," Collier said as he spun the cylinder down his left arm.

"We don't waste time here at Nightmare P.D."
Dunker said. "We start playing Texas Roulette right
away. It would be nice to have you as an employee,
buuuut…we already got $14,000, lots of dope and
your car. We'll change the VIN numbers and sell your
car in Mexico. It's a nice little sideline for us. Cars.
U.S. of A. Cars sell well in Mexico. If I could sell
your bones for soup, I would too. So, no matter what
shithead, it's a win-win for us. It's a lose-lose or…or a
half-lose, maybe a quarter lose only for you. Stick
with us, and you will make even more money."

Thomas Jessica looked up at Collier as Collier
pointed the handgun right at his head. Then he looked
back at Dunker.

"Now," Dunker said, "Who do you work with in
Me-heeco?"

"This…this ain't right. Ain't real. No. No, I don't
trust this. It's a trick to get me to talk."

Dunker lifted a pointy finger as a signal for Collier
and Collier pulled the trigger.

The unexpected magnum blast next to him about
blew Dunker out of his chair and Collier almost
dropped the pistol! Thomas Jessica was smacked with
a .357 round in the left forehead that seemed like it
would tear his head right off at the neck, what with his
being so secure in that chair and table.

"WHAT THE..?" Dunker yelled, his ears scream-
ing like two jet engines.

"Shit!" Collier yelled.

He looked at the pistol and popped out the cylinder.
The gun had been fully loaded, instead of empty. He'd
grabbed the wrong pistol! They'd never had anyone
last past two empty clicks without giving up information and would never load the roulette pistol anyway, not even with even one round. They wanted a

deal not death. If they needed to kill someone? They'd always do it elsewhere. Smarter.

"I grabbed the wrong gun!" he yelled over his own screeching ear drums.

Rebadoux and a few of the task force members still there in the hangar charged into the hall and cell.

"What?" they all seemed to say.

Dunker broke out into a fit of laughter and shouted, "Well, this goofy mother-fucker brought a fully loaded gun in, to play Russian Roulette!"

This did amuse most of them, but they were still amazed-shocked. Then, that man with limp, still in a mechanic's jumpsuit, ambled in among them.

"Bluto!" Dunker said to him, "can you imagine this? Russian roulette with a loaded gun!

Bluto limped over to the corpse with a wry smile. He looked back at Collier and grinned.

"Don't feel too bad, amigo" he told Collier with his deep, Hispanic accent, "I have seen this happen before. Still…100% fuck up. Ha-haaa."

"Okay, you get to clean this room up, Collier," Dunker said as he stood, shaking his head and popping at his ears lightly with his palms. "I will probably need hearing aids after this. Jeez! And still good work, Reb. You did good. We got drugs, money and a car. Keep em coming."

"I guess I will be working on his car for Mexico auctions. It's a nice car," Bluto said, "you got his tele-phono, Reb?"

"I do. I do," Rebadou said.

"Give it to me. I will break into it. See who he's called in Mexico and then around here. His life, his business…is in that phone."

"Yeah, good work Reb," Dunker said again. "Keep em coming. We get that Mexican contact phone number, we'll just try and replace Jessica here. Fact a business, Collier, take a Polaroid of his dead self and we'll show it for proof he's gone if need it."

Collier stood there, hands on hips, looking at the mess. There were white bits of skull bone blown all over the cell back wall, stuck there in the blood and flesh and brains.

Chapter 9: Unlocking the Unlocked Lock

Christ's Church, Screed, Texas...

The two police cars pulled onto the church front lot, Pathways in hers and Weaver Wisdom and Jack Kellog in his. They all got out and met.

"I wonder why they didn't just shoot the detective out here in the parking lot. Maybe the gunshot noise would travel. Maybe some random witness…?" Jack wondered aloud, sizing up the building and the area. "Easy drive-by. Boom and leave. Why create the mystery of the inside, armed security guard and all it took to pull that off?"

Path raised an eyebrow and curled her lips to that.

"That back door over there is where Paul entered in," she said. "No lights. No cameras. Just that street light way over there," she pointed, "very dark at night. He got inside about 20 feet and was shot dead in the hallway.

They walked through the church front doors and into the lobby. Pat Loudin stood from her welcome desk.

"Hello Detective," she said, "any news?"

"No Pat, fraid not. Is the pastor in? These boys are from the state police and want to help."

"Oh, sure, come on back. Follow me."

Within a few minutes of introductions and catch-up, Jack started in…

"I hear that the main parking lot, the west side, is filmed 24-7."

"Yes, it is," Paster Adding said.

"I hope you still have recent tapes on the days before the shooting?"

"We do. The murder was on the 17th. We have 16

days of films and then we cycle them through for another month. But with what happened? I went to K-Mart and bought a new box of tapes. In case we needed to save the old ones."

"Oh, that's smart thinking, Padre," Jack said.

"I'll get them," Pat said and left the pastor's office.

"It is frightening," Adding said, "that man with the limp, just floating around in here in the middle of the night, like a…like a ghost. It's just haunting. We are getting an alarm system installed."

"You need one. Y'all are kinda isolated out here." Jack said. "How many side and back doors do you have?"

"One. The back one. The building is old. It was constructed before Screed had any fire codes. We should have at least two more doors, on either side, but we grandfathered in and the city did not mandate more doors."

Can we look at the door Paul walked in through? From the outside?"

"Well, yes, sure," the pastor said. "Come on."

In a few moments," the pastor, Path, Weaver and Jack stood on the back parking lot outside the door. There were three steps and a cement pad-landing, wider than the metal door, with some bushes and dirt on the grounds either side of the door and pad.

"We fingerprinted the door," Path said, "the whole door. Nothing."

Jack nodded and stepped forward and looked down on the cement. However minute, the cement, like all cement had an irregular texture to it. The irregularities collected "things."

Jack ran his fingers across the far right corner to corner's edge to confirm the roughness.

"Can we get a lab tech out here?" Jack asked

Weaver.

"I can get NASA out here," Weaver said, then seriously added, "I'd rather call in Austin, they have more gear and a better lab than we have in Houston."

"What for?" Path asked.

"Once in a while Path," Jack said, "we run across professional burglary rings that use half criminal locksmiths to make keys to businesses they want to burglarize. This requires a locksmith trained...a criminal locksmith to do some drive-bys, and then in the middle of the night, sneak back out to the business, to doors and make a key. They have to sit out, like here in the dark and do it."

Apparently, Pathways did not know this as she listened intently.

"The key process starts with a...a...raw shaft. A key blank, they call it. They file on it, insert it in the lock as far as it will go, and they have to start filing on it to go deeper and deeper into the key form, the shape. Those filings," Jack waved his hands out, palm down and pushed them downward, "fall down like...like a fine dust. If this was done here, the locksmith probably sat down or kneeled down here, and filed away right over this cement pad. I'd like to confirm if a locksmith snuck out here and made a key. There might be dust unique to black keys on this."

"I...we...did not do that...did not know..." Pathways started to say.

"That's okay," Jack said with a wink, "lots of people...police...don't know this. I had to work a few pro burglary teams – safe crackers - working all of Harris County years ago and up until then, I didn't know about this either. In those cases, a locksmith was part of the burglar crew. He confessed. This slab here has a texture to it and if there are any filings, we might at least prove a theory. We also need to disassemble the doorknob. Take the whole doorknob. The lab will look to see if there might be some dust inside the lock too."

"Has it rained since the murder?" Weaver asked.

"No sir," Pastor Adding said. "No sir, we were praying that it would, but maybe the good Lord kept us dry for this."

"I hear ya," Weaver said.

"We'll have some crime scene people high-tech vacuum that landing and take the lock. I'll radio DPS," Weaver said.

The Ranger started back for the sedan with a big open hand, palm up. Jack tossed him the car keys, and of course he caught them.

"It might not seem like much," Jack told Path and the pastor, "but we'll know one more thing than we didn't before. And that one thing might lead to something else. And we might see a locksmith or suspect vehicle make a pass, a drive-by or two on those tapes from the first of the month. They knew where the cameras were, and they knew this door was not covered by cameras. But they also knew Paul's routine, to catch him here at the right time. They had to follow him for at least two weeks I would think."

Weaver walked back to them.

"Team in route," Weaver said.

Paster, you have a custodian handy?" Jack asked.

"Yes, sir,"

"Can you get him and tell him if he has any plastic or a big canvas," Jack said, "we need to cover this whole area outside the door. Cover it carefully, so as not blow anything off the pad. In terms of crime scenes, it's very legally, crime-scene-late, maybe too late, but better late than never for the sake of information. And the janitor needs to get a new doorknob, we'll be taking this one."

"We can't…we shouldn't leave this after we have officially…this late, rebooted it as a crime scene," Pathways said.

Jack nodded in agreement, then said, "Can you stay?"

"Yes," she said.

"Pastor, the crime scene team will need all those surveillance tapes. Not us. Them. They can enhance them and protect them."

"We'll have them ready," the pastor said.

"They organize fast in Austin. They'll be here in… oh, in three-four hours." Weaver said, half smiling at Pathways.

"I'll just…I'll just get a chair from inside, sit here and watch the door."

"Weave and I got stuff to do. We gotta go. But one more thing."

"What?" she said.

Jack pointed a finger all around them and said, "Cameras. You know Paul had to be followed to get his routine down. I wonder how many of these businesses out here have cameras outside. View the street?"

Path and pastor looked around. Their expressions said they did not know.

"These cameras are becoming popular. They may have had someone parked near here, following and… and watching Paul. From a distance."

Pathways nodded.

"Yeah. Parked on their lots. Away and watching. And…it's becoming so popular to have these red-light traffic cameras and traffic cameras these days. In some cities intersections are recorded, 24-7."

"We have some here and there, but I don't know where they all are," Pathways said.

"See if there are any critical intersection, lights right around here, streets everyone must or are most likely to pass through," Jack finished up his advice as Weaver walked to their car.

"I'll get you a comfy, padded folding chair," Pastor Adding told Pathways, patting the padded shoulder of her jacket.

"Thanks Jack. Ranger," Pathways said, now armed with a few ideas no one at their agency had even dreamed of yet.

Chapter 10: Justify the Existence

Gulf of Mexico, Texas coast...

"If you throw anything overboard, we will shoot and kill you!" Gulf Coast Drug Task Force Officer Greg Williams announced through his bullhorn. "Si tiras por la borda, te idparamos y te matamos!"

The three Hispanic men on their fishing boat some 40 yards away raised their hands.

"How many? Three?" Williams asked Collier Jones.

"Three so far. That's a pretty nice Viking 53 boat they got there," Collier Jones said, studying the men in the open rear of the vessel with his binoculars.

The eight task force officers were aboard their Swedish, CB-90, Fast Assault police boat, a real military-looking craft, painted pale blue and flying US, Texas and police flags. Removable banners on each side hull of the CB-90 also read, "POLICE." The very shape of the ship was frightening to all enemies, lest of all from the two Browning, .50 caliber machine guns mounted in front of the helmsman position.

Even the US Coast Guard was envious of the macho ship design when talking with them by radio, or in passing and/or waving at each other. Given the official police appearance alone, the Coast Guard never questioned the authority of the Task Force and also never knew what they were up to when trolling by each other in the few miles off the Texas coast – both hunting drug smugglers.

The CB-90 boat was purchased by Cinnamon Dunker in an international, military weapons convention, the annual LAAD Security Arms market in São Paulo Brazil. Dunker bought it with a combination of

Texas grants, legally seized drug money and their own illegal drug sales.

Dunker next had his eyes on acquiring a military helicopter of some sort, and any of these little high-seas episodes would help finance that cause. Under the same style banners and signage of a police helicopter, Dunker knew they could fly, pick up and land anywhere, delivering just about anything, a drug dealer's dream. No airstrip needed. No helicopter landing permits needed like those by civilian choppers in various cities, counties and states.

The task force boatmen were adorned in coast guard-like uniforms, with body armor vests and ballcaps that read "police."

"We are coming aboard!" Greg Williams said, "Estamos subiendo a bordo!"

One of the three men on the Viking did something stupid. First, he started shaking from fear. Then he looked at the other two, before suddenly dashing to the far side of the advancing CB 90. He dove over the side into the Gulf! This was an insane act because they were about three or more miles from the shoreline.

The quartermaster-pilot of the CB 90, Lassiter Gaston laughed when saw this vain escape attempt and immediately veered away from the Viking and steered around her front-bow. Rocky Snelling ran forward on the CB 90 with his Remington sniper rifle in hand. The assault boat slowed, slowed…and all the task force men watched and waited.

Finally, the swimmer surfaced, unable to hold his breath any longer. Lassiter Gaston raised his rifle, took his own deep breath and shot the man in the head, like shooting a floating, bobbing basketball.

The remaining two on the Viking quaked at the gunshot as a shock wave of sound and reality ripped through them. A few of the task force members laughed. One clapped. Rocky Snelling turned the Remington on the two men. The men raised their hands even higher, babbling words of surrender in Spanish.

The CB 90 pulled up beside the Viking. Two task forcers leapt aboard and chunked the two men face down to the deck. Other officers followed. Greg Williams joined them and stood on Viking platform while Collier Jones went down below through a narrow, short staircase to search. In a moment Jones emerged with a smile on his face.

"My estimate? About 50 pounds of coke. About 50 pounds of Mary Jane."

Greg Williams nodded. Though the deck was getting crowded he shouted for Arturo Benavidez to come aboard. Arturo was a former Mexican Federale, fired down there for corruption and as a result, recruited by Cinnamon Dunker as one of their "intelligence" officers and translators. Once aboard, Greg Williams jutted his jaw toward the two men down on the deck.

Arturo began his interrogation. He flipped them face up, pulled his Glock and pointed it at their heads, waving the barrel back and forth. He kicked them several times. The duo started talking in amongst pleading. Then he walked over to Greg Williams.

"Our snitch was right. They are taking the shipment to a dock in an inlet of Holiday Beach. Meeting the Cornwall gang at their dock."

"Okay," Greg Williams said, "You know…" and flicked his fingers toward the captured men.

Arturo knew what the finger flick meant and what to do next.

"Get up!" Arturo said, "Ponerse de pie!"

They did. They were shoved to the side. Arturo shot them in their faces, and the bodies tumbled over the side.

"Unload the booty, maties," Greg Williams told Collier Jones.

Greg Williams jumped back over to the CB 90 and told Lassiter Gaston to run the Viking's registration numbers. Then he got on their military secure line phone they nicknamed the "Bat-phone."

Dunker, in his backyard pool with his kids, heard the phone's annoying, unique alert on the patio table. He was well aware of the mission underway and wanted any immediate news, so he'd carried the little phone in a suitcase out in the yard with him, antenna fully extended. He climbed out of the pool and answered.

"Our guy was right," Greg Williams told Dunker, "The shipment was going to Holiday Beach. We're running their boat registration now. Coke? About 50 pounds. Mara-hootch? About 50."

"Okay," Dunker said.

"Wait…okay…the number on the boat is coming back," and Greg Willams leaned into the police computer screen on the bridge to read it. "Yeah, the Viking belongs to a guy in Brownsville. Nobody we know. They probably just stole the boat from a dock and owner doesn't know it yet."

"Yeah," Dunker said, knowing that these boat docks were often surveilled, and unused boats stolen by drug mules. When the mules identify boats in docks that show some signs of neglect and, or are hardly used, they often steal or borrow them. These crafts are rarely, quickly missed and therefore unreported stolen for weeks. At times, the smugglers might even return the boat, as is-was, after a short run.

"We'll contact the owner and hell, give him his boat back on this one," Dunker said. "Looks good on paper. Makes us look good. We'll keep us 25 pounds of each, then log in the other 25s on the state report."

"Yes sir," Greg Williams said.

"We have to…justify our existence," Dunker said.

"What about the mules?"

"Three. Davy Jones' locker."

"Another gun battle at sea with evil doers!" Dunker said.

"We'll tow the Viking into the Port Aransas Coast Guard. Check out and contact the owner. "

"Excellent work, Greg. See y'all when you get back."

Dunker switched off the phone, and to the giggling delight of the kids, let out a holler and cannon-balled into the big pool.

Chapter 11: Team Extra

With a magnetic, rotating police light he stuck on the roof of his car and with some needed "blurps" of a siren in tight traffic, DPS Intelligence Special Agent Jack Kellog sped through the City of Houston streets. His mission? Retrieve a Mrs. Calista Lamont from her apartment and rush her back to the hostage scene at the Walmart as soon as possible. The SWAT team negotiator needed her to talk with her son Reggie inside the store.

Reggie was holding four employees and two customers under his pistol inside there. SWAT did not know how many other customers were cowering inside the store. Some were collected up after crawling through some back doors, loading ramps and the automotive garage section.

The armed robbery went bad about three hours earlier in Peak, Texas, a suburb within Harris County, covered by a small police agency without a SWAT team. The State SWAT was called in. Call sign "Team Extra." The SWAT team tossed a negotiation phone into the store and started a conversation with the suspect, a Larry Lamont. The SWAT Commander, LT. Worth asked Jack to run Lamont's background via the police computer systems – NCIC.

Part of the DPS Intelligence Division's job was to support the state SWAT teams with intel before, during or after incidents, and Jack was called to perform such duties this night, which usually meant waiting for hours at some hostage scene on the chance they needed someone to run somewhere, find out something, or as in this case, go get someone.

In the van, Jack suggested the mother angle, since the negotiation was going nowhere. The commander liked the idea. Jack called Mrs. Lamont and she was awaiting Jack's arrival to get her to the scene and try to talk her son down and out.

On the way, Jack's car phone rang.

"Kellog."

"Jack, Lydia."

"Hi Lyd." It was a woman from the Klatch, and she wasn't calling him to help with the Walmart standoff.

"Jack, we ran all those officers' names you gave us through 49 states. Hawaii is a hand-search of index cards, and they are slow. There were a few Greg Williams, but all are working active duty in their faraway states. None of the others you gave us were officers anywhere."

"Thaaaat fits. Fake names," Jack said. "No wonder they were so quick to introduce themselves. Then you know these task forces…these task forces will change the names of their agents for security reasons too. Fake IDS. Many do that. It's legit."

"Like our narc guys. Yup," Lydia said.

"Yeah, like our guys," Jack said.

"Okay, tell everyone mucho thanks. If you can think of anything else? Please do …think of anything else."

"Good luck out there!" as she knew what he and SWAT were trying to do in Peak.

They hung up.

"Huh!" Jack said to himself out loud, drumming his right thumb on the steering wheel.

The phone rang again.

"Kellog."

"Jack," he recognized Weaver's voice, "we got some word back from the Austin lab. There were key filings inside the doorknob and on the cement slab. Somebody shaped and made a door key right there like we thought."

"Okay."

"And, get this. The lab boys sat and watched all those church tapes back to the first of the month. A small pickup truck with tool chests in the bed made a few passes over a few weeknights. Old Datsun truck. There were no signs on it. But they got half the license plate enhanced."

"Some sombitch locksmith, huh?" Jack said.

"Yup. Probably."

"We'll get Auto Theft to run the partial with Datsuns registered in Harris County, and I guess…I guess…I will have to hunt every one of them down in the county and see who has a tool chest in the back… who is a locksmith."

"I'll hep ya. Pathways will help. But, that's some good news huh?"

"THAT is something."

"Yeah. Anyway, I know what you are doing out there now," Weaver said, "so I'll let you go. I'll get with Auto Theft on the plate search tomorrow morning. Good luck, bubba."

"Adios, bubba, see ya tomorrow."

When Jack pulled up to the apartment complex, he saw a black lady, must have been Mrs. Lamont, in a house dress and big purse, hair up in a bun, shuffling her feet side-to-side, standing outside. She ran up to the car.

"Hello, ma'am and thanks for coming.

"Of course, I will come. My boy has never done anything like this before."

Jack u-turned and the two talked a bit about the overall situation…

"We have to give him a reason to live, some hope," Jack advised, "an out, rather than you know…hell, dying in there. Or hurting one of the hostages. They are, you know, just regular people."

"I know, sir. Thank you for thinking of me. Has he hurt anyone yet?"

"Not yet. That's important. Be thinking about that. Think of any happy memories. Reasons to live," Jack said, "reasons not to spend a lifetime in prison."

Then the phone rang yet again.

"Kellog."

"Jack?"

"Gail?" he said, recognizing that voice. It was Gail Canchas from Texican Monthly.

"Jack, I wanted to call you on my progress, well, my lack of progress. Darlin, the congressional office will not let me see any information on task forces except for the most very superficial. The task forces in total, cost a lot and take in a lot of drugs and seized cars, money, houses, planes, boats. But which one did what is…like is top secret, and they say I will put police lives and investigations in danger by seeing the individual reports and by reporting on them…"

He and Gail spoke for several minutes about this, then the police radio announced,

"Team Extra calling State 101."

Jack recognized his newly requested call sign of "101" part of his old West Forge number badge number and call sign. Team extra was the on-scene SWAT commander back at the Walmart.

"Go ahead, Team Extra."

"Jack, been trying to call you on the phone but It's been busy. You can cancel the pick-up of the mother, the suspect just shot himself inside the store. No hostages hurt."

Mrs. Lamont turned in the passenger to Jack, her jaw and eyes wide open.

"Is the guy dead?" Jack asked.

"Ten-four," Team Extra said.

The mother let loose a baleful, wild animal scream. It was pitiful. Jack pulled over. He grabbed her left arm with his right hand.

"Gail, I got to go," he said into the phone.

"Sounds like it," she said.

Chapter 12: Mission Impossible

"You're here to drown, Skelton," Dunker said, opening up an aluminum folding chair at the water's edge.

Skelton Rhoades was already neck deep in the Gulf's rising inlet waters. His left ankle was shackled and chained to a metal pier's post about 6 feet down. His left hand reached up and gripped the floor of the dock. Skelton looked over the shoulder of a seated, re-laxed, resting Dunker. Behind Dunker some 50 yards was the task force's current, secret, party house, up on quite higher ground than the water level. Everyone in-side was probably even higher than that. He'd been to several of these Friday night hullabaloos, and he knew their task force confiscated drugs were abused by the task force, accomplices and trusted girlfriends.

Some of the very men on the task force were down there at the dock, all holding Lone Star, Coors and Mexican beers. They looked at Skelton Rhoades and laughed a bit. Even the madman Bluto limped up and stood behind Dunker with his arms folded.

"Shouldna done it. Skel!" Greg Williams sang out.

The Gulf water touched Skelton's Adam's apple. There was no question high tide was rolling across the Gulf shores and into its inlets. Inlets like this one.

"I can fix it!" Skelton yelled out.

"You know we rent a half a mile north, south and west of here," Dunker said. "Yellin out so loud will get you nowhere."

"I can get those cars back," Skelton said. "Or the money!"

"But cha can't get our trust back," Dunker said. "And that is the problem."

Adams apple deep, Skelton Rhoades was an ex-con,

a professional car thief, wheeler and dealer of swiped autos and parts, with connections all over Texas and Mexico. He was recruited by Dunker and the Task Force to manage, chop shop, fix up, alter VIN numbers and get rid of all the cars they legally and il-legally seized in dope raids and traffic stops.

By law, legally seized property like cars could be sold and the monies put right back into the operational budgets. The illegally seized ones were sold also, and the bounty split up by Dunker for himself and the task-force members.

They gave Skelton 3 acres and a mobile home just north a bit toward the Piney Woods of East Texas for the steady chop shop job. His salary, his take, was a hefty one. The place looked like a backwoods, auto wreck yard out front, but deeper inside, Skelton and a few of his able buddies would-could dismantle and re-mantle just about any car, alter VINs, mileage, paint them, and you name it. Then at one point there were so many cars, Skelton thought he could sneak-sell some of them off and keep all that money, but Dunker's fas-tidious, record-keeping and evil, paranoid eye caught him.

Some women holding drinks, stepped out on the back balcony of the party house and started begging the boys to come back.

"Y'all come on! Pizza is here!" one shouted.

With that announcement, Dunker stood, stumbled a bit from too much whiskey, and folded up his chair. "Pizza calls!' Dunker declared, "got to go. And they say, you know, we all die alone. So…die mother-fucker."

Dunker and all his cohorts started up the hill. No more good-byes. No last meal. Die alone. And now chin deep, Skelton knew he was bound to drown when the high tide rolled on it, when? Within an hour? A few hours?

Then, he knew what they would do to him next, in the morning, just as they'd done with other "problem-children." They'd cart his corpse off and drop him in some canal or waterway somewhere. Cause of death when found, if found? Drowning. Accidental drowning. Just like he'd heard the whispers about that helicopter war vet they recruited to fly a new chopper they wanted to buy. The new pilot was in prison. They got him out of prison. When he learned their real plans, he suddenly freaked out, and wanted out. But there was no way out with this task force. Like the Mafia. He had to turn up…drowned in some lake in central Texas. Just like he will be, if he doesn't figure out a way to escape.

Skelton cursed. He's been through numerous hells in the Texas pen, in car chases and drug crew threats and beatings. And he was hell-bent not to die in this one like a drown dog. If he'd had a knife? He swore he would cut his foot off rather than die like this! He'd already tugged on the chain and leg iron shackle enough to know that pulling his foot out was a lost cause. The shackle covered his whole ankle. It wasn't super tight, but tight enough.

He still had his black, lace ankle boots on both feet and the round 4 inch, shackle was half on the boot, half on his skinny calf. He took a deep breath, ducked down and unlaced the left boot. Up again for air and down again to unlace. Unlace by touch only in the murky water. He finally pulled the boot off his foot.

There! Some ankle space! There was some more space inside the shackle, but not enough to get his foot out. That damn heel of his. He wrangled and twisted and turned his foot, but he still couldn't get his foot free. His heel stopped him.

"OH, GOT-DAMN IT!" he yelled out to no one.

He kicked his left foot in anger with his right foot. It hurt but the water was getting colder. Then the solution struck him. If he would dare cut his foot off, if he would go to that extreme…so…but…what if he could mash the bones in left foot, flatten that heel, squash the bones enough to slip free instead. Yeah! Break his ankle and foot! Smash them into mush!

Skelton Rhoades began this horrible, nightmare task of slowly destroying his foot! He placed his left foot up against the hard pier leg. With his left hand he grabbed more of the floor of the pier deck above for some stability. With his hard-booted, right foot he began mercilessly kicking and beating his bare left foot. He couldn't see it from the brown waters, but he tried to aim at the bare heel with the boot's hard heel.

He didn't hurt too badly at first, then…it did. But it was do or die. Every few minutes he glanced back up at the party house. Music. Lights. Laughing. No one cared to spy on him. It was Friday night!

He re-positioned the bare boot and beat it again. He started to cry, not just from the pain but the pitiful, fool's position he'd put himself into. He started groaning with each kick as the pace slowed down. The foot was now numb. He pulled on it. He put the right foot boot on the shackle top pushed down and pulled up. The mashed foot finally, tightly slipped through!

He was free. Okay, what now? He swam out to the small pier's end where there were support beams like a ladder he could climb up on. He still had the strength from adrenaline to haul himself up and out of the tide waters. He laid for a few seconds, chest down on the deck and headfirst to the house to study the two-story vacation home and the some 14 vehicles parked to the south of it. There were more cars and trucks around the front. All were from task force members, their girlfriends and maybe some other invited criminals, such as he himself was once a guest.

Those cars. His only hope. There was nowhere to limp off to. If he was lucky, they wouldn't think to fish him out till mid or late morning. That's what usually happens. Those sleepovers would sleep late, get up, eat breakfast, then wander down and pull out the bodies. If they looked out the windows and could not see him, they would think he was dead, drown and down. He got up on all fours. His mashed, broken foot was somewhat numb, somewhat sore and he looked down at it for the first time. It was bleeding but not too badly, not too much. It was black and blue and malformed. It made him nauseous to look at this mushy, lumpy "thing" attached to his leg. He stood with the help of the railing and limped to the grassy, sandy land, swinging wide, south of the cars and the house.

He stopped at the farthest vehicle. It was locked, but the next one over, a Ford truck was unlocked. Inside. No keys, but so what! Skelton was a master at stealing cars. There was a folding knife in the console, and he went to work, with eyes darting back and forth. Steering column. House. Dashboard. House. He saw a gun belt and a police raid jacket in the back seat. He reached for the 9mm in the holster. If they saw him and ran to him? He would shoot it out. Better to die like that in a gunfight than drown like a rat.

Wires connected. The Ford started up. He got behind the wheel, and slowly steered the truck to the left side, dirt driveway, watching the house. The driveway. The house. He kept the headlights off. The driveway was long, but he made his way out to the two-lane asphalt road! Looking back, no one was charging out of the house to chase him. He did it! He did not speed away until he lost sight of the party house.

His foot. It was bleeding more. He saw his ankle was severely cut open from the shackle. What? Where next? His old rental house in Houston was still his, from before his temporary move to the Piney Woods car lot. It was about an hour away and he had no choice but to go there. That would be one of the first places they'd go looking for him in the morning, or whenever they noticed the Ford was gone, but he had to go there. He had to wrap up and treat his foot, get clothes, food and he had an old Corvette in the garage. He had to get there, get fixed up fast and...flee.

There was one Twinkie left in a torn, open package on the passenger seat. He ate it in a gulp. His foot started to really ache, in a funny way that he had never felt pain before. It seemed now to be oozing blood. He was dizzy. Dizzy but still alive.

What would he do tomorrow? He couldn't trust the police. He couldn't go to any hospital. The Task Force would use its police authority to contact all the hospitals, claiming he was an escaped fugitive or some such scam. Dunker would have every one of his friends quickly contacted. And the task force guys would probably beat every one of them nearly to death to ensure they knew nothing.

Then he realized - there was one law enforcement person he could possibly trust, someone honest but hundreds of miles away in El Paso, untouched by these Gulf Coast people. That Texas Ranger. The Apache one, Wilderaydo Acorn. Skelton was once a snitch for Acorn, 3 years back, working off an auto theft rap. He fed Acorn information on two Mexican American car theft rings. Acorn, yeah! Acorn treated him fair and square, and always kept to his promises. The Ranger got the charges dropped. He'd call Acorn. Yup. Acorn. He would get him some help. He still had Acorn's private phone number on one of his cell phones at the house.

Skelton drove to his old house. All his keys, even his wallet, were still in his wet pants pockets. Just like they would be if people found him drown in some lake somewhere. He parked the Ford out on the street and limped to the front door, dragging his foot like a small suitcase with bad wheels. He unlocked it and he was… inside. Home. He turned on the living room light and looked at his ankle and foot. They were almost unrecognizable, like a…like a giant mushroom and leaving a trail of blood. Now malformed, it was even more shocking to look at.

With pitiful gasps he went to the bedroom and wrapped the ankle and foot with a white t-shirt, got some duct tape in the kitchen and wrapped it further, tightly. At least now he didn't have to look at it. And maybe the bleeding would slow down. He only had stale pretzels and potato chips to eat from the kitchen cabinets, since he was barely home of late and out at the country car lot.

In his bedroom, he lifted his mattress and snatched all the loose cash he tucked away there. He got one of his many "business" phones off a charger and headed for the back door and for his pristine, 1994 Chevy Corvette in the garage. But he stopped at the door, backed up to a kitchen drawer and snatched a bag of marijuana, papers and a lighter.

In the garage, he started the Corvette and left. Bewildered and still dizzy, he drove toward the center of Houston, parked on a Holiday Inn parking lot, and called Texas Ranger Wilderado Acorn from memory, not needing any notes. In answer to an agnostic's prayer, Acorn answered the phone in three rings.

Two hours later…

In bed, Jack Kellog groaned when his bedside phone rang.

"Jack. Weaver."

"What's up, Weave?"

"Jack, I got Wilderaydo Acorn on the other line."

"Ray…Acorn? What…what for?" Jack knew Acorn well from their manhunt of John Phillip Muzak.

"Acorn was on the phone with one of his old snitches, talking to a car thief here in Houston he turned years ago. Proven snitch. He said the guy was working for the Gulf Coast Task Force and they tried to kill him earlier tonight. Drown him. And he escaped."

"What the…" Jack said, sitting up.

"The snitch is sitting in a red Corvette on a Holiday Inn parking lot, bleeding to death. I sent a trooper nearby to check. He said he can't trust anyone here, especially the police, so he called Acorn in El Paso."

"Yeah, the guy can't trust anybody," Jack said, "he's right."

"The guy says can't go to any hospital. The Task Force will track him down."

"That they will, yeah. I…ahhh…well, take him to the West Forge Heights Hospital. Yeah. It's Saturday a.m… yeah. I know the midnight shift doc and nurses working there for years. I can talk to them, and we can hide the records. Yeah."

"That's a plan. I am gonna head out to the Holiday Inn too."

"Okay, I'll beat feet to the hospital," Jack said and started to get dressed.

"Betty! It's Jack Kellog!" Nurse Nancy Seaton yelled out to her co-worker at the sight of the former city detective walking in through the emergency room doors. Jack was not formally dressed, but in jeans, boots and an Astro's t-shirt, but they had seen him dressed this casual before, many a night through the years, when he'd been called out to investigate violent crimes back when Jack was a West Forge city police detective.

He shook their hands, and the evening shift doctor appeared in the lobby, as did a few more nurses. They too all shook hands, but the catch-up talk had to be brief.

"Can I...can I talk with y'all in one of the rooms?" Jack asked.

"Sure," Dr. Beekeridge said, and he led the crew into one of the ER rooms, away from the patients waiting in the ER lobby.

"DPS is about to show up with an organized crime informant of ours. He's...they tried to kill him, and we don't know all the details yet, but he's in some really rough shape. This involves some bad cops, and we have to keep this a secret as best we can."

"Okay, we'll see what we can do," Beekeridge said, and the nurses nodded.

"They should be showing up with him any minute," Jack said.

And they all returned to their normal duties and stations. Jack walked into their break room and poured a Styrofoam cup of coffee. Then he nervously paced between the desk and the outside doors. He did get to speak with some of the nurses. They asked about his health, his massive heart attack, and what he'd been doing since he was fired by the West Forge Police Department. He explained he was now working only

Intelligence for the state.

Then Jack saw through the glass doors out into the parking lot, Weaver's unmarked sedan pull up, followed by a marked trooper vehicle. As Jack approached the doors, Weaver was already coming in, holding an unconscious man in his arms. Weaver's face was grim.

"This way," Jack said, and they turned into a treatment room, followed by Beekeridge and some nurses. Weaver laid the man on the bed, then backed away as the night shift initiated trauma team work.

"Injuries?" Beekeridge asked while checking his pulse.

"His ankle Doc," Weaver said, we know that he escaped a shackle that was going to hold him underwater until he drowned. He...told another Ranger that he kicked that left foot with his right foot until it got mashed enough for him to pull his foot through the leg iron."

"Whoa," the doctor mumbled.

A nurse unwrapped the duct tape and removed the once white t-shirt, now brown and red, to expose the foot. The crew never missed a beat, but Jack and Weaver were taken aback at the sight of the appendage.

"He did all that to himself?" Jack asked Weaver.

"Apparently so," Weaver said.

"Betty, get..." and the staff went to work.

Jack and Weaver stepped out into the lobby and then back out on the parking lot where they could talk freely. The uniform trooper who first found the wounded man walked up to them.

"He say anything?" Jack asked.

"He was out cold when I got there. When I got him in my car, he came to and mumbled some stuff to me.

He said he ran stolen cars for the 'task force.' Changed them and resold them. Then he stole some cars, and some money and some guy named Dunker was going to kill him. I asked him where this happened, and he said an inlet off the coast, their party house, and then, and then he passed out. I thought he died right then, Jack, but he mumbled and groaned a few more times. I got blood on my passenger seat floorboard maybe an inch thick. Lots of blood loss."

"Inlet off the coast," Jack repeated in a whisper.

"He had a longer conversation with Acorn on the phone."

"Recorded?"

"No. The call went to Acorn's personal cellphone. And he was home in bed."

"Damn," Jack uttered.

"The El Paso Ranger Company is sending Acorn up here to hep us. He was Acorn's snitch on some auto theft rings years ago which was why he called him. Captain said they would fly him up here in the morning."

"Good. He's a solid dude. What's this guy's name?" Jack asked.

"Skelton Rhoades," Weaver said. "Wallet in his pocket. Ex-con. A wiz-kid, car theft and chop-shop gang leader." He turned to the state trooper, "Wilson, thanks for your hep, we got this from here."

"Goodnight, gentlemen and good luck," the trooper said and left.

"Acorn told me that Rhoades told him, that to escape from the house, he stole a task force member, truck and drove it to his house," Weaver said.

"Truck's still there? Where's his house?"

"When I got Rhoades sopping, wet-ass wallet off of him, I sent Chilton over to take a look at the house."

"We need to search that truck and print it before the task force gets out there," Jack said.

"Yup."

"Right now, my gut reaction is to search and print the truck then leave it there to be found," Jack said.

"Yup. I don't know about a warrant," Weaver said.

"Yeah. Not much time. Callin it close. We can get a warrant started at least to show good faith in trying, but I don't think we have much time," Jack said. "We can explain the time crunch later. Expediency."

Weaver's cellphone rang.

"Wisdom. Yeah. Yeah. Hold on." And Weaver turned to Jack and said, "It's Chilton. The Ford truck, it's still there. Hot-wired. Gun belt in back. Police jacket. Rhoades took the gun. Gun was in the Corvette. I got it in my car."

"Prints. Can you get a crime scene guy out there for a clandestine search? Just one guy. No big production. Mission Impossible style. Plain cars. With a backup in an unmarked car up the street in case someone shows up looking for Rhoades?"

"Yup," Weaver said, "Tony will do it. And we'll get Chilton to watch up the street. The captain knew I was responding to all this, and he told me to order up whatever it takes."
Weaver made the arrangements on the phone, then shut the phone.

"I guess I'll wake up Rygh Eadleston at the D.A.s office and get a warrant going," Jack said, "car and house. Course…if this guy lives he can sign a waiver for his house. If the truck was stolen, we believe it to be stolen, we can seize it and routine inventory it. But then we lose the intelligence of watching to see if someone recovers it."

"Call Rygh. I'll sign the warrant. Since I spoke with Rhoades and Acorn, I'll be the best affiant right now," Weaver said.

"Yeah, you're right."

"What's another all-nighter," Weaver said.

Jack grunted, pulled out and opened his flip-phone to call Rygh at home, when…

"Guys! Guys!" Dr Beekeridge said walking outside the doors, "sorry guys, but this man's dead. You might say he bled to death. I'm sorry."

"Sweet Jesus may he rest in peace," Weaver said quietly, somberly. "Death-bed statement? Like a death-bed confession?" Weaver said to Jack.

"Kinda, maybe. Might work. We'll see what Rygh says. The death shouldn't interfere with the search warrant for the truck."

Jack dialed Rygh's home phone, waking him up. It took 10 full minutes to explain to him the events of the night.

Jack hung up and told Weaver, "Okay, Rygh said head to the DA's Office. He'll meet you downstairs at the front doors to let you in. Call him on the way, he'll get started on the warrant."

"I got his number," Weaver said and took off.

Jack walked inside the ER and the doctor was at the desk.

"Jack, when someone dies in a hospital, it's a big deal," he said.

"I know, Doc."

"I have to fill out a ton of hospital and insurance paperwork. And… basic details will become public information. The corrupt cops you're worried about could dig it up if they start calling around looking for him. Eventually."

"I know, Doc. Maybe we can do something to slow

it down? Maybe call him a John Doe? Say the standard 'heart attack' thing?"

"Hmmmm," the doctor smirked in a grunt, "yeah, everybody dies of a heart attack."

Ranger Chilton and Tony Menting decided to wait a while for the search warrant. Chilton ran the plate and the truck returned to an Alicia Ledbetter, with a Houston address. The related driver license came back to Ledbetter, a 27 year-old, white female with no criminal history. Chilton informed Weaver of all this to add to the vehicle search warrant.

At the dark and empty DA's office, Rygh Eadleson and Ranger Weaver Wisdom whipped up two, fast probable cause search warrants, one for the truck, one for the house. Rygh had been conversing with the Ranger on the way as they both drove in.

With most of the warrant prep set in Rygh's mind, he pounded the warrants out. Rygh called and woke up a district judge in Houston to sign the documents. Weaver drove out to the judge's house at 3 a.m., and Judge Savi Reddy, in her robe and pajamas sat with

Weaver at her kitchen table and read and signed the warrant. No specific details of the Task Force itself were included in the legal document, should it fall into the wrong hands, as it surely eventually would. Now, any evidence garnered from the search of the stolen car and house would soon be admissible in court and open to the public, and the Task Force.

Weaver sat back in his car, called up Ranger Chilton on the DPS radio and said "Got it. Go."

Weaver knew Jack went home and decided to let Jack sleep and not notify him of the warrant's progress. He drove back to DPS headquarters to lock up the 9mm found in Rhoades' car, originally from the

Task Force truck, into evidence. Fingerprinting the pistol was a priority. Unlike Ranger Chilton, Weaver was in his assigned, recognizable, fleet, unmarked police car. Hanging around the Rhoades house in such a vehicle might scare off any people hunting for the victim and the Ford truck.

With this search warrant, go-ahead, crime scene investigator Tony Menting stepped out of the unmarked, older car and approached the Ford pickup with a small tool bag and small flashlight. Chilton sat back, watching and waiting. After about 15 minutes, Tony walked back to Ranger Chilton's car.

"Prints. I got a lot of prints and photos. There is a Police style gun belt in the truck, but no pistol. A raid jacket. Blood. Lots. Otherwise, nothing else in the truck. It must really belong to a woman, there's a lot of female stuff in there." Tony said. "I'll take a quick look around the house, but we should get out of here ASAP."

Tony jogged over Skelton's house and saw the thick blood trail down the sidewalk to the front door. The door was unlocked, and he entered for a fast look around. More blood trails. He took pictures, then left.

They drove off to Tony's nearby parked car. Next, Tony would head off to DPS headquarters.

Ranger Chilton eased back to a spot not too near the Rhoades' house for a hunkered-down vigil of the house and truck. Who would come hunting for the Ford truck and the freshly deceased Skelton Rhoades.

Chapter 13: Tender Young Alice's Wheels

Tender Young Alice was up at 8 a.m. The Task Force nicknamed her "Tender Young Alice" after the famous Elton John song and because of her youthful, seducible persona. She was the main squeeze of married task force member Josh Elliot, in and out of the beach inlet party house. She was available whenever Josh beckoned, but she was also "available" for some of the other members in Josh's absence.

She left Josh's bed, grabbed up her clothes and high heels and stepped outside the bedroom into the hall where she got dressed, balancing herself on the wooden railing. She walked barefoot down the steps, shoes in hand. She found her jacket and purse in the front room and left the house, bound for her Ford pickup. But…within a few minutes…

"MY DAMN TRUCK IS GONE!" she yelled out, running back inside the house. "It's gone!"

All the task force members and their girlfriends, still in the house from the prior night's festivities, scrambled out of their upstairs bedrooms, in various levels of dress and undress and out to the second story open hall.

"What?" Josh said.

"My truck is gone. Stolen, Josh!"

All the members and girlfriends exchanged glances.

"My… gun!" Josh said, "shit, my gun belt was in there. My raid jacket."

"Skelton!" Greg Williams declared in a growl, "That…could…?"

The men ran back into their rooms and got quickly dressed, but Josh emerged in a scuba wet suit for it was to be his job to unlock and recover the dead Skelton anyway. The members dashed out the back door to see the calm waves by the dock. Was Skelton down under and drown? Or did he somehow escape in Alice's Ford?

Josh dashed down the water's edge and dove right in by the dock. The men waited. Then Josh's head bobbed up.

"He's gone," Josh said.

"Gone like dead-gone?" Lyle said.

"No, gone like gone. He's not here gone," Josh said.

"The leg iron is fine. Still locked."

"What the…"

"He's a magician!"

"Dunker will kill us."

"He must have gotten hissef out and swiped Alice's truck."

"I put him in the shackle," Josh said. "And he could not slip through it. No way."

Greg had his cellphone with him and walked off, calling Dunker.

Dunker was at home, watching Saturday morning cartoons with his kids, eating cereal. He answered.

"Boss, Skelton is gone. He stole Alice's truck and he's gone."

"He…well what, how?"

He got up and walked into the kitchen where his wife was making breakfast, so he passed through the kitchen and out the back door.

"How the hell did he do that? Did he cut his foot off or something?" Dunker asked.

Despite his departure, his wife still heard the tail end of that, shook her head in disgust and refused to dissect that conversation.

"We don't know, sir."

Silence.

"He had to do something…to…to get his foot out of the leg iron. He had no knife." Dunker said.

"Josh said the leg iron is still intact, boss," Greg said.

"If he did cut his foot off, or forced it through the shackle, he'll bleed to death fast. Well, okay. Look, you know what to do. Send the boys out looking for him. Just down all the roads…if he bled out while driving away. And the car lot up in the woods. His house. He's probably too smart to call the police or an ambulance knowing we'll track him down and find him."

"Will do," Greg said.

"I'll be at the airport hangar in an hour." Dunker said.

"Ten-four," Greg said.

"Tell Josh to saw off that hook on the pier. If that skinny bastard survives, he may still call the police."

"Yes, sir."

"You know, if we can't find him? We'll have to barbecue the house," Dunker said.

"Yes, sir. I know."

At 9:30 a.m., a new, black SUV drove by the hunkered down Ranger Chilton in his old sedan. Chilton spied and wrote down the plate number, even though at this point, the Ranger knew the plates would probably be false. Two white males dropped out of the vehicle and approached the Ford truck. It was unlocked and they examined the insides. Then they pulled pistols and slipped into the unlocked doors of Skeleton's house, they just barged right in, to emerge moments later. One man reentered the truck and pulled an empty gun belt and raid jacket from it.

Chilton knew they would drive by him again when leaving, and with such a "face to face" he could easily be spotted slumped down in his car, so he waited for a moment when they were preoccupied by the Ford and drove right on by them, never giving them a glance.

Given the damage to the truck from the hot wiring, the two men left in their SUV, driving off the same way they came in and they would have passed Chilton just as the Ranger thought, possibly spotting him. Chilton also guessed a tow truck would be in route with an unsuspecting, less-suspicious, tow truck driver. But still, he would re-position himself, wait for the tow and follow the truck.

Sure enough, a tow truck appeared within the hour, but when he saw the odd gait of a limp of the Hispanic, tow truck driver, he recalled his briefing on this and was glad he'd parked way up the street. The man hooked up the truck, pulled it aboard the flat bed and drove off.

At 10:37 am, Weaver Wisdom called Chilton. Chilton gave him a rundown of the evening, to include the arrival of the limping man, and that he was tailing the tow truck.

"Where are you now?" Weaver asked.

"Right now, I am turning down Buster Blvd. and… and just ahead is the Bleacher Airport."

"Makes sense. That's their headquarters. I think when they enter Beachum, confirm they took it to the Flying Aces hangar. We need that confirmation for a warrant. Then you can break off, we know where he's going."

Next, Weaver called Jack Kellog, again awakening him, the second time in 12 hours. Jack had not even undressed, he'd just dove into the bed. The Ranger filled Jack in on the night's events. He quietly listened to the developments.

"I've been thinking, Weave," Jack said, "Do you remember who else drowned lately?"

Chapter 14: It's a Thin Line

"Boss, we can't find him," Greg reluctantly told Dunker over the protected line, cellphone. Greg was still at the inlet house, reporting on the 5-hour, failed search.

"I got three men here calling all the hospitals," Dunker said. "We got Alice's truck here at the hangar. We found it right where we thought, at Skelton's old house. And Bluto is going to fix it up for her. We'll get it back to her. Skelton must have abandoned it at his house and took off in one of his other cars."

"Skelton took Jason's pistol with him from her car," Greg said. "We sent Jason, Lyle and Steller out to the chop shop, car lot. The crew up there all acted stone dumb shocked about Skelton. Jason said he was convinced they were telling the truth," Greg said."

"Then we can't trust Skelton's demise," Dunker said. "He could have gone anywhere. Still alive. Escaping a murder, he's plenty mad at us. He'll go to the Feds? State police? Greg…barbecue the house. We can't have it searched. It is loaded with fingerprints. You know the routine."

"Yes, sir."

And they hung up.

Greg, the last man standing at the party house, was already prepping for the infamous…house barbecue. If Skelton got to anyone, talked to anyone, and the location of their party house was revealed, and some evidence found of his attempted murder? This was probable cause to bring the whole task force down. The house had to be destroyed, burned down to the last possible fingerprint and pubic hair. It had been about 18 hours since they walked away from the captured, water-logged, neck-deep, Skelton. Somewhere in that time period, Skelton either died alone, bled to death, or went to the police and told them everything. Or did both and died before talking. Every hour that passed without action could mean the police are ignorant of the full events. But still, just in case, the house. It had to go!

This was another lesson Greg learned from his boss-man, "Cinnamon" Dunker. Dunker never ceased to amaze him. Two years ago, when he and Dunker bought this house and property pretending to be a gay couple with false names and finances, they looked for home advantages that other shoppers ignore or even fear. How easily, how thoroughly could a two-story house…burn. A lesson in criminality that Greg could only learn from someone like Dunker, a legal-beagle and master-criminal, tightrope walker. So, when party-house shopping, they noted the propensity for quick-burning, "crispy wood." This entire house was essentially an older wooden structure.

Dunker, acting with an effeminate lisp, also told the real estate saleswoman that they were buying the house for rental property and a rare, occasional stay for them, the "couple." Not a fulltime residence. That was about half true as it was an occasional weekend, party house, stuffed with cheap furniture for the task force and friends to crash all over.

He'd already attached a big, heavy metal plate hooked by chains to the back of his pickup. He began riding over the dirt parking lot and dirt road on the property to destroy all tire tracks. The scene of an attempted murder meant the authorities would collect tire tracks for future comparison. With those tracks flattened, he parked the truck on the shoulder of the asphalt road, loaded the big plate in the bed and walked the grass lawn back to the backyard of the house.

Greg lit the charcoal in the rolling grill on first floor patio and put two of those long burning fireplace starter logs in the grill. The two logs burned bright. He let that cook for a few minutes.

Then he tipped it over onto the wooden wall and struts of the balcony. With a stick he rolled one of the fully engaged fireplace logs over to another nearby strut. As hoped, as planned, the fire took off. Greg stepped back and watched it grow. Fast. It was catching on nicely.

He jogged off to the main road, got in his truck, now sans that metal plate and drove off. The only clue left was the colored smoke that increased in the sky. It would grow much greater as the house engulfed.

Maybe then someone would see the dark clouds and call the volunteer fire department in the area, normally a group of citizens at their real jobs with a terrible response time, especially in the daytime when the volunteers would be busy at their fulltime day jobs. They would have to go through many machinations to finally arrive at a scene and fight a fire.

Greg knew not to use any suspicious arson accelerants that investigators might find. This fire started by a clumsy, abandoned barbecue. Plus, there would be no insurance claim filed anyway which would prompt an even closer examination.

Driving away, Greg reminisced about the good times there. Drugs, booze, sex, rock and roll…lots of sex.

"Lyle's albums!" Greg blurted out.

Task Force member Lyle Emerson had a terrific collection of vinyl record albums in the living room. Now doomed for a total meltdown. What a tragedy.

"Ooohhh no! Lyle!"

David snapped his fingers overhead. Dunker pacing the hangar, finally saw and heard David's alert. The two other task force members left their telephoning chores, and with Dunker, closed in and crowded around David's desk.

David hit the speaker button on the phone…

"My commander is here now, and could you repeat that?"

"Of course, officer…last night we had a DOA in our lobby."

"And the details?"

"The night shift paperwork says he was a white male in his 40s. Name – John Doe so far. He died of… it says here…a heart attack."

"About what time?" David asked.

"2:48 a.m. There will have to be more investigation, police or insurance, to discover his name and more details. We have nothing more as yet, which is unusual because we usually can glean more than this right at the visit. So, officer, this might could be your suspect you're hunting for."

"Thank you, sir!" Dunker said loud enough to be heard, "and this hospital is…?"

"Yes, of course, West Forge Heights Hospital, sir. Anything else we can do, sir, call us. In a few days we should know more."

They hung up. David's eyebrows popped up. Dunker nodded.

"West Forge," Dunker growled. "Kellog. Fucking, Jack Kellog. His old stomping grounds. In all of Harris County, about 100 hospitals, this guy drops dead in West Forge."

Special Agent Jack Kellog and Detective Linda Pathways accepted the invitation from Mrs. Ginger Newlan to sit down at her old, ornate kitchen table and chairs. She folded her trembling hands atop the vinyl, orange tablecloth that still had the fold lines in 8-inch squares visible from recent storage.

"Can you tell us about your son?" Pathways asked, "Paul's friend?"

"It's hard to picture both of them dying in a way, you know? First Randy and then Paul. Within 3 months of each other. When Randy died, I called and asked Paul if he could look into Randy's drowning. It wasn't in his city, but he said he would. My Randy was never near water. To be found in a lake? Drowned? He'd never went fishing or boating or jet skiing..."

"He was found in a lake?" Jack asked.

"Yes, sir. Postican Lake."

"Was there an autopsy?" Jack asked.

"Yes. By the county. They declared it was an accidental drowning," the mother said. "I still couldn't believe it. I had to ask Paul to do something about this. You know, Randy and Paul...when they were young-uns they ate many a meal right here at this table when they were growing up. They both joined the Army when they growd up more."

With a little pain and a grunt, she stood, walked into the living room and returned with two 8x10 photos in worn, chipped picture frames. She sat again and laid the frames before them.

Each frame contained a collage of photos, one where the two were young teens on up to high school age. The other one full of Army photos.

"They both became heelio-copter pilots in Iraq. Kuwait. The wars. They had meeedals galore! Then, they came back. Paul become a police officer, but my Randy…he became an addict. A drug addict. The counselors at the vet hospital said he had this P-Dest S-m T? He still flew helicopters for a whilst, at Dranston Commercial. But he slowly fell deeper and deeper into…this crack stuff everybody was using. Crack cocaine. Maybe it was the wars that made him do it? My God, I don't know. That's when Randy and Paul broke it off…their friendship."

"And Randy went to jail?" Pathways asked.

"He did. He did. He sold crack. He lost weight. Skinny. All gray, the grayest of skin. Lost hair even. Teeth yellered like corn on the cob lookin. The laws caught up with him. A couple of times, and he was sentenced to 5 years for dealin and possession."

"And he got out early?" Pathways asked.

"He did, Miss. He told me that some lawsmens came to see him in Huntsville, and they wanted him to do some flying bidness and thanks to them, they got him out of the pen early."

"Flying business," Jack repeated.

"Yes, sir. Heelio-copters. Doing something. He wouldn't say, but I was grateful he got out and came home. I know he told Paul he was out – proud – doing something like Paul does with the po-lice. Randy and Paul met again, Paul said, one more time. Then, shortly after that, Randy done drownded. I think it's murder, detectives. Something he was doing for those lawsmens that got him out of the hoosegow and got him murdered. Randy said they weren't state police, they weren't federals or city. Who were they?"

"Do you have any copies of the autopsy? Here at home?" Jack asked.

"No sir. That don't mean nothing to me, sir. They's

liars all."

"Okay."

"Will you hep me? Will you look into this mess?" she asked.

"I think we will, Mrs. Newlan," Pathways said, "do you have any pictures of Randy? Recent ones? And what has he been driving since he got out?"

"I'll get you some pictures we took at the picnic when he got out. And they, the lawsmens, gave him a used Chevy Caprice. It was fixed up real nice though."

"What color was it? Where is it now?" Jack asked.

"Don't know where," she said. "You see maybe somebody kilt him and stole the car? And they dropped him off in a lake. I don't know what happened. It was a dark green. Four door."

"Ever get the license plate? Write it down anywhere?" Pathways asked.

"No, Miss."

After some more discussion, the two investigators left with some photos of Randy Newlan in hand. They climbed into Jack's Cadillac.

"Where would the autopsy report be?" Jack asked.

"Our county contracts a pathology company that does them for us and the three adjoining counties…" Pathways said.

"Let's go."

Since Pathways was local law enforcement, Jack let her take the lead at the office front desk and the conversation at the medical examiner's office. Soon they sat at a Dr. William Burst's desk, someone she knew well. An aide handed Burst a large, thick envelope. He pulled out from within a folder and an inch thick pile of photos. It was obvious there was a video tape of the autopsy still in the bottom of the envelope.

"Here is the report. Some photos," he said. There was no sign of foul play from any struggle. His face. Neck. His hands and arms. No gunshot wounds or knife wounds. And as I recall…yes…look, there were drugs found in his system. You folks call it Black Tar Heroin. Some LSD. Not enough for an overdose, I don't think."

He handed Pathways the report. It was the classic, primitive human body drawing on the front page, as old as Da Vinci's, with handwritten notes and several typewritten pages for a follow-up.

"These photos…" Jack said and reached for them. He looked at the prelim, the before-cutting-open ones taken of the naked body.

"These photos, black and white…"

"We have the color negatives. We just process them first in black and white to save money. We can always process them in color later, if need be," Burst said.

"Look at this," Jack said.

He laid a few photos of Randy Newlan's legs out on the desk.

Pathways and Burst leaned in closer.

"Look at the left ankle. Bruised? About 4-5 inches long? This side shot looks like the bruise goes all the way around the ankle."

"Yesss," Burst said. "It could be from…we don't know? Water skiing, or some odd, accident-injury unrelated to the drowning. It didn't cause the death. We don't know about that."

"We do," Jack said. "That video tape. Stationery, overhead? Ever zoom in on anything? Zoom in on the ankle bruise?"

"No, the ankle bruise was very incidental to me."

"Uh-huh, okay," Jack said. "The drowning. It happened in a freshwater lake. Was there ever a sample and test taken of the water in his lungs? Testing to see for salt water or fresh water?"

"No sir. There was no evidence overall, ya know, in toto, that this was a murder investigation. It presented as a drowning, so no, we didn't."

"Toto," Jack whispered, still scanning the photos, "if we exhume the body, could such a sample still be collected and tested, Salt water versus freshwater? Not sure yet if we need to know, just yet, but maybe."

"It is possible, Mr. Kellog. But the bruise? Postmortem, skin discoloration. The funeral home prep. Might be a problem. Probably gone, but we have color negatives of it from the night he was brought in."

"Can you order us up some? And let me know when they are ready?" Pathways asked.

"Sure, Lin. Can I ask what is going on?"

Pathways explained aspects and parts of the investigation. She suggested the killers were a drug ring, which was half-true, and how they drown their enemies.

They left the office with copy machine copies of the leg bruise. Once in the Caddy...

"You have spoken with Paul's wife..." Jack started.

"Oh yes, but not about this angle. Let's see...it's 3:30, she's a teacher and will be home from school by 5. Let's run by the P.D."

At the station, Pathways wanted to keep Chief Methods abreast. Seeing him in his office, she knocked on the open-door, frame and they walked in. By his expression, he was still not too happy to see Jack Kellog again.

But, after the dissertation of their progress from the church and the corpse in West Forge, Methods began to become excited. Path's explanation held a lot of

"Kellog did this, Kellog did that, Kellog saw this or that, and Kellog thought of…"

"That is certainly good news," the Chief said, "good progress. Y'all are bustin something open."

The two started to leave and Methods said,

"And thanks for…for your help, Detective Kellog."

Jack usually reminded people that he was no longer an official, "detective," anymore, just in intelligence, but he winked at the Chief and followed Pathways to her desk.

The Massaport Residence, Shreed, Texas…

"Linda!" Candy Massaport said, answering the front door, "come in. Any news?"

"Some, Candy. This is Jack Kellog from DPS Intelligence. You know, the state police."

Mrs. Massaport shooed her two children off to their rooms and they all sat in the living room. Pathways briefed her on the developments. She pulled a photo of Randy Newlan from her purse.

"Randy. Oh yes. He was once one of Paul's best friends. He was the best man at our wedding. Then…" she shook her head side to side in a manner of shame, "drugs. Then no more, a few months back Paul told me that Randy was out of jail early and going to work for some police department."

"Police department?' Jack said.

"Well, a special police team, a…"

"Task force?" Pathways suggested.

"Ahhh yes. Yes, that's it."

"Anything else? Did Paul say anything else about all that?" Jack asked.

"No. Then we heard Randy drowned! Paul said he had not seen Randy but that one time they talked after he got out of jail. Then we heard from Randy's mom. She asked Paul to…you know…look into Randy's drowning. She refused to believe it was an accident. But the drowning…it wasn't even in the city. He had no…"

"…jurisdiction. Did he? Look into it?" Jack asked.

"I think so. So, you think Randy's drowning has something to do with Paul being shot?"

"Could be, Candy," Pathways said.

"How?"

"The lines are not all neatly drawn yet." Pathways said, folding her hands on her lap, "but we are working on it."

On the drive back to Screed P.D. they were quiet, until Jack spoke up.

"I think we will have to make this a formal state investigation now, ask for our own special, state task force because we need steady workers, surveillance, crime scene, intel, a drug unit. Probably they'll put Weaver Wisdom in charge of it. You should be on it, Path. Can you? We need someone like you that knows Screed. And we need to run down all the Harris County locksmiths, figure out just why Dunker needed Randy out of the pen. We need Randy's visitation list …Man! There's a whole lot to do."

"I can be on a few things to do. This is all I have been doing now since the murder, and now we have specific leads to follow. I am sure the chief will let me."

"It's going to take some convincing at DPS to pull all the folks together. I'll call you very soon about it all. And you know, I know, that Dunker and them, tracked down Paul, followed him, trying to find the best place to slaughter him. So, if this gets out, if you

seem to be asking around with the same right questions, you too are in danger."

"So are you," Pathways said.

"Tell me about it."

"The Chief was not…you know…not fond of you
being involved in this, until this afternoon," Pathways
said. "He said last week you were a dinosaur, like a…
a…'Dirty Harry' crazy cop. A lawsuit waiting to
happen."

"Do you even know who Dirty Harry is?" Jack
asked.

"Not…really."

"It's a movie way before your time really. 1970,
1971 I think. When cops did a lot of things differ-
ently."

"Okay," she said.

"I do have a, kind of a…Dirty Harry background,
Path. A reputation. A past," Jack said. "Some cops
kinda love me. Some kinda hate me."

"Well, I'm starting to love ya, and so is Candy
Massaport and Ginger Newlan."

"It's a thin line between…"

Chapter 15: The Tale of Two Meetings

Meeting 1: Beacher Airport, Task Force Hangar

Cinnamon Dunker clapped his hands several times to shush the 18 members of the Gulf Coast Drug Task force. He looked them over as he took "center stage" in front of them. In the last 3 years he'd judiciously handpicked each member before him. Each one was once in some form of law enforcement, then resigned or were fired for three main reasons, drug abuse, violence or corruption. Some did time for their violations and crimes, most not.

He looked them over. This was the worst crucial moment in those 3 years. Knowing each were law-and-rule breaking rebels in some way, he recreated a kind of mafia-like world of respect, comradery…and fear. Every suspect, every traitor, co-worker he'd tortured or killed was an abject lesson in personnel management. The men took seats before him in a variety of folding chairs and rolling desk chairs. The 19th member was Bluto, who stood in the back leaning against the parked SWAT van. He did not handpick Bluto. Bluto was forcibly suggested by his overseers. Bluto had a different acquisition story…

"This monthly meeting is more than just a monthly meeting due to what has happened," Dunker started.

"You all know by now what has happened with our car thief dude Skelton Rhoades. He stole from us. He needed eradication. He escaped the "drowning pool." He must have destroyed his shackled foot somehow.

Squashed it with his other foot. We can imagine how. We think he showed up, we'll they say 'DOA,' at the West Forge Heights Hospital and under the "John Doe" name. The hospital first told us this, then they shut up about it, claiming medical privacy rules. They stopped talking with us without a search warrant. No ambulance delivered him there that we can find out about. Somebody brought him in. That hospital is on the northwest side of Harris County. A long way from the beach house and the house Rhoades owned, where we found Alice's stolen truck."

Dunker sipped his Whataburger iced tea through a red straw and continued, "A week or two ago, a Jack Kellog from DPS intelligence walked right in here. Right in that lobby. He found us. Some of you dudes met him. He claimed that someone from the DA's officer told him where we are."

"Impossible," Lassiter Gaston said.

"Right. Well, we're not impossible to find, but very hard to find. A pro could follow one of us and find us. But he somehow found us. Don't know how. Kellog came in and said howdy and wanted to offer 'help.' Would, could the DPS help us when needed. We gave him a friendly hello, like you'd treat any police visit, showed him all the legit gear and place, suggesting we are legit. You know, the congressman tour. Then we said goodbye. But the more I thought about it, the more I worried about it. I thought about it afterwards…he's…it's not too, too suspicious…but… anyone here recognize that name?"

"He just caught and killed John Phillip Muzak," Larry Drumwald said, "the escaped convict on the big Texas crime wave months ago."

"He did," Dunker said. "And in the 1980s, he killed about half the mafia that came down here from New York. Killed them. Shot them. Beat them up. He was a West Forge city detective for many years. Solid as a rock. He's not Sherlock Holmes, he's not that bright. He's just…tenacious. Really tenacious. And much worse guys…he's lucky. The visit here, plus this West Forge, John Doe hospital thing, I am not jumping to conclusions when I say that one plus one equals ten with Jack Kellog. Rhoades may have been working with him, or conning him for something, I don't know."

"We have Rhoades' phone?" Lassiter Gaston asked.

"No. And he had several phones like we all do. We don't just have one of them.

"What we gonna do?" Tyrone Tyson asked.

"We already barbecued our beach house. Into cinders," Dunker said. "It would have made for quite the crime scene if Rhoades talked. But there was no move to search there, 18-20 hours after the hospital DOA, which is…good news. I mean, the state would have jumped on that search the minute Rhoades would have talked and they learned the location. But, I learned the state arson investigators were there at the house after the fire department called them. But without investigating an insurance claim, there won't be much follow-up to a backyard, cooking fire accident. They are probably trying to find the buyers, but we covered our tracks on that."

"Maybe Rhoades was talking to Kellog, but never got around to mentioning the house? And he died before he could?" Tyrone Tyson said.

"Maybe. My plan for now?" Dunker said, "business as usual, boys. I think we're going to start following Kellog around, like we did that Paul Massaport guy. See where he goes. Who he talks to. His habits. In case we need to take some 'action' on him, we need to get Kellog's routine down."

They all nodded in agreement.

"Last on the agenda, Bluto and I are going to Washington, D.C. to an international, military arms sales.

We are still going to buy us a freakin helicopter. This Randy Newlan thing ain't stopping us. We'll get a great pilot we can trust this time. We already have a fantastic boat. A SWAT van that's a tank. And a plane, but a long-distance chopper? One marked 'police' on the sides? Our plane needs a landing strip, but a chopper lands up and down and anywhere, and a PO-lice chopper needs no local pre-approval to land any-where. Like a medivac. We can pick up and deliver drugs and contraband in a traveling range from Mex-ico to South Carolina. We still don't have a pilot we can trust yet, we tried, but we'll get us one. We'll find one. We're looking. We cherry picked y'all carefully and we'll pick a pilot the same way."
Silence for a few seconds.

"Okay then, that's all. Keep doing what you do. Josh and Larry, hang back with me."

The others left, and the designated remained and sat at an empty desk in the hangar.

"Josh, this Tender Alice? Your squeeze?" Dunker asked.

"Yeah," Josh said.

"You ran out to Skelton's house and saw her truck there. Your gun was missing. Surely Skelton took it for protection. And it is probably in police custody recov-ered from wherever he drove his Corvette," Dunker said, "or still sitting in that car somewhere? Aban-doned? We don't know."

"Yeah…they probably got at least a partial on the gun if they have it. If they got the gun, I mean. We don't know. But it's a print of an ex-Omaha cop no-body up there knows where he…I…am. He's a long-gone daddy from up there. I mean, I am Josh Elliot now."

"Yeah, yeah. Right. And you found the truck. Bluto

towed it in and is fixing it up. Looked untouched?"

"Yes sir. No signs of fingerprint dust anywhere. I don't think the police found it."

"Should we give it back to her. Do you think there's any way the police got that license place and will start fucking with her?" Dunker said.

"Can't see how, boss. They woulda seized it when they saw it. Right?"

"Yeah, probably, I think so. I do," Dunker said, "but this Kellog? He's a smooth operator. Well, okay, we'll give it back to her then. But I want you to keep eyes on her and her surroundings for a while just in case."

"Okay."

"Collier,"

"Yeah?"

"Collier, I want you to get eyes on Jumpin' Jack Kellog. You met him here, few weeks back. Pick up on him at oh, probably DPS Houston. Find a hidey-hole and watch the place till you see him. See where he goes, eats, sleeps, shits, screws. We may have to put him down."

"I will, boss," Larry said.

"Okay! To work then!"

Meeting 2: DPS Headquarters, Houston, TX.

9:40 a.m. Time to gather in the break room for the 10 a.m. meeting with DPS Lt. Colonel Daniel Murth. Murth was very much an influential second or third in command of Texas DPS, being the Deputy Director of Criminal Law Enforcement Division. By the book, Murth ran its investigative, analytical, and regulatory functions that were split between three major services - Narcotics, Criminal Intelligence and Motor Vehicle

Theft. And, also inside all of these with its own unique brand, the Texas Rangers.

Drinking coffee in the break room, were Jack, Ranger Weaver Wisdom, Narcotics Nip Budsten, Surveillance Sgt. Manny Vasquez and Screed detective Linda Pathways.

In walked Texas Ranger Wilderardo Acorn, just there in time, all the way from El Paso.

"Ohhhh, kid," Weaver said shaking Acorn's hand. Weaver introduced the young Ranger to the others in room, 'this is Acorn, the kid who replaced me when I was shot to bits in El Paso with him," said Weaver as he threw a thumb toward Jack.

Jack winced.

"Chief," Jack said with a smile, shaking his hand. Acorn was a full-blooded, Comanche and Acorn and Jack had hunted down the Muzak gang, after Weaver was shot and replaced by him. The death-defying bond between Acorn and Kellog will never be forgotten.

"Kemosabe," Acorn replied.

"Well, it's time. Let's head that way," Weaver said.

Jack was about to pour the rest of his coffee in the sink, but Weaver stopped him.

"He won't care," Weaver said, "take it in."

Murth's secretary guided them into the enormous office with many chairs. This would be the first time Jack met the Lt. Colonel in person. Jack was appointed by Governor George Bush over a year ago into his intelligence position just to hunt down John Phillip Muzak. After catching and killing Muzak, Governor Bush then ordered Jack's appointment permanent.

This order ran against the wishes of most of the DPS administration to include Murth. Jack was not a graduate of the DPS Academy and did no time on the Texas highways as a patrolman-trooper, which was ordinarily a pre-requisite to any state, plain-clothes duty. Jack was a Texas police academy grad and a Houston PD and West Forge PD veteran, but not a DPS Texas Police Academy grad. All were aware of Kellog's nervous breakdown and public firing at West Forge P.D. All of DPS admin thought that Jack was a "loose cannon." Despite DPS "tribal demands," what the Governor says, goes in the end. Bush demanded that DPS leadership keep Jack Kellog after he killed Muzak.

"You can't let him go. Are you nuts?" Bush reportedly said, "You keep that crazy son of a bitch. We need the likes of him in our bullpen!"

Murth was in his Texas Highway patrol uniform and waved a hand for all to take a seat, then he did, behind his desk. And the whole group sat in gathered chairs.

"Well, Ranger Wisdom what do you have?"

"Colonel, this is all Special Agent Kellog's doings from start to now, and I think it best he do the telling." Murth grunted a bit, then looked over at Jack.
And Jack started off with the summary details on the Detective Paul Massaport murder.

"Yeah, I remember that. Saw the footage on TV," Murth said.

Step by step, Jack reported the Massaport-Newlan connection and what they knew about Dunker and the task force.

"Huh," Murth said, and leaned in.

Jack turned to Ranger Acorn for him to describe Acorn's prior informant relationship with the deceased Skelton Rhoades and the surprise phone call.

Acorn described the cryptic, "wounded" phone call he received a few nights earlier from Rhoades about how the Dunker Task Force tried to chain, shackle and drown him and his gruesome escape.

Then Jack continued reporting about the escaped Rhoades bleed-out, and his left ankle injury causing his death. Detective Pathways stepped up to the desk and displayed the color photos of Detective Massaport's friend, Randy Newlan's "drowning," autopsy photos of his shackle-like, left ankle.

"Newlan had the same shackled-like ankle injury. The fingerprints we found on the pistol, Jack continued, "once in Rhoades' escape vehicle beside the raid jacket came back to a fired narcotic's officer from Omaha, Nebraska by the name of John Springer. As far as Omaha is concerned, Springer moved off. Gone. In fact, none of the names I was given on my first visit to the hangar were real names, either. Our girls have not found any prior police employment under those names."

Murth looked again at the autopsy photos, then back up at Jack.

"Detective Pathways contacted the Department of Corrections for visitation records on Randy Newlan. Newlan was visited four times by Samuel Dunker and a Greg Williams. They, the Task Force, organized his early release from prison, but then, he was found drown about four months later."

"Why get him released?" Murth asked.

"Don't know," Jack said. "Contacts I have and people in our intelligence branch tried to glean anything about the Task Forces stats from Austin, but they and all drug task forces' info are well protected and locked up tight by law."

"This is true. I know they are insulated, fearing corruption," Murph said.

"Colonel, they are the corruption," Jack said. "We need our own task force on this. We need to run down

the locksmith that supplied the key to the church. We
need to follow the girl who owns the Rhoades' escape
vehicle. We need to set up surveillance on their airport
hangar. We need to drill down on the Dunker, Newlan,
Massaport connection. We need to solve this murder
of a Texas peace officer."

Murth leaned back in his big chair.

"A drug task force like this is a perfect storm for
massive corruption with built-in cover," Jack concluded.

"And this Rhoades snitch, did he name names?"
Murth asked Ranger Acorn.

"Yes sir, he did, "Acorn said. "He named Cinnamon Dunker and he named the Gulf Coast Task
Force."

"And they tried to kill him? Drown him?"

"Yes, sir. By chaining his ankle to a pier."

"Was this phone call to you recorded?" Murth
asked.

"No sir, he had my private cellphone. I was in bed
asleep when he called. And he passed out while talking to me. I was lucky to first find out where he was
when he told me was bleeding badly. Then he started
telling me what happened."

"Hummm," Murth growled.

"I know Dunker and the Task Force will just shake
that off as a disgruntled doper snitch," Jack said. "We
need more. We can't make a move until we have
more."

"Okay," Murth said. "Okay, this does need to be
our own task force. A DPS one. This is serious and it
involves the murder of one of ours in the State of
Texas," he nodded toward Pathways. "Weaver, I know
you are busy with your own cases, and you can help
out, and I want you to help out, but you can't run this

thing. Neither can you Wilderaydo. Jack Kellog, you are in charge of this. You call the shots. Okay? I know you're just an intel agent around here. No rank, but…"

"Okay," Jack said.

"Nip, you're their drug connect. Manny, can you set up all this? What they need and want?"

"Yes sir," Manny said. "The airport is watchable from three angles. I have men that can tail comings and goings."

"I know you do. I know. Yeah, well, okay, do this. Y'all be careful, I do remember Dunker from the Sheriff's Office. A commander. He's a slippery smart operator. Dodged trouble his whole life. Detective Pathways?"

"Yes. My chief is very excited about your help, sir. I'm already working this murder full time and we… I…am full in," she said.

"I will officially declare this a team then, an operation, a task force. Give it six months for starters. We'll keep our own top-top secrets about it. I'll draw up the order. Open up a secure file. What will we call it for the file?"

He looked at Jack and Jack was not prepared for such nomenclature.

"What is your mission? Your goal?" Murth pushed.

"Well, sir, they are all killers and all of them on the take. We will…takedown the take," Jack said.

"Task Force Takedown, then," Murth said, noting it down on his desk blotter. "I see Weaver a lot and every Sunday at church. He'll keep me abreast of your progress. Ranger Wisdom has much confidence in you, Agent Kellog. I hope he's right. Any supervisor who wants you guys to work on something else, you say no. You can't. They bitch? You send them to me. This is important to get to the bottom of. Now, y'all geet goin on it."

Everyone stood up and made for the door.

"Weaver, you stay back for a minute," Murth said.

When Jack got to the door…

"Special Agent Jack Kellog!" Murth bellowed loudly.

Jack stopped and turned.

"Good digging, Mister Kellog."

"Thank you, sir."

They all left but for Weaver Wisdom.

"So, your man there…Kellog…he's okay now?" Murth asked.

"He's better than okay," Weaver said. "You turn him loose and he'll clear the field, Dan."

"Well, keep an eye on him," Murth said.

"I always do anyway," Weaver said. "He's my brother."

"I know you will. See ya in church Sunday," Murth said.

"Have a blessed day, Dan," Weaver said and left.

They all crowded into Weaver's office.

"No task force t-shirts or logos," Jack warned, only half-joking.

"Oh, that's too bad. I already pictured up one of a gator vomiting a narc," Nip said.

They all smiled.

"Yup, well," Jack started, "Path can you work on the locksmith list? Manny, the surveillance set-up. Once we capture some faces and plates, we can start running them down. I think identifying the players is good starting point. Especially that dude with the limp. Specially him. Nip, you drug guys stand by."

"Standing by," Nip said.

"And I'll sit here and clean my guns," Weaver said.

"I'm gonna dig into the Newlan thing," Kellog said.

"The vet that was found in the lake. I'll go to Huntsville and interview his cellmates. He no doubt bragged to them about his early release. And this woman Alice Powers, who owned the Ford pickup Skelton stole to escape. Manny, we might need a tail on her too.

Acorn offered up, "I'll do the initial bio work-up on Alice, too. But I will dig more into Skelton Rhoades activities of late. I knew him. Know how he thinks… er..thought."

Manny nodded at him.

"And this morning I'll try to keep a tighter lid on the Skelton Rhoades' DOA news at the hospital. Admin staff had to report the suspicious death to the West forge PD. It's the law. And you just know Dunker and Task Force will be calling all the PDs for a "lost suspect." And listen up! Y'all, remember they tailed and killed Paul Massaport, and when enough manure hits the fan over there, they will tail us and kill us too. Keep yer heads on a swivel for their tails."

"Yo! Swiveling, boss," Nip said.

Nip and Manny left. Jack sat and talked shop and life with Ranger Acorn, asking how he was, how things went after their Laredo shooting almost a year ago. Jack asked if he'd seen his kid up in the Panhandle lately. Acorn again committed to a complete, up-to-date background and current ground on Skelton Rhoades and Alice Powers. And yes, he'd seen and kept his kid over most of the summer.

Then Jack motioned for Pathways and Acorn to follow him. They did, across the back half of the investigations wing of DPS. Jack stopped at his desk in the open bay of the intel office.

"Acorn, I know you will probably be in the Ranger's office. Path, when you need a place to sit when here, call folks, whatever, sit here," Jack said, "I am hardly here. And you already know where the most important place is, where the coffee is., but..."

He pulled open a drawer and produced a Houston Oiler key chain with one key.

"This is an extra key to that back parking lot door to get in and out of here," he said pointing to a metal door.

"Just, you know, wear that badge on your belt, jacket open, like you have now, so's these cowboys don't shoot you. You'll get all the respect you need. You're a sister here."

"And smile a lot," she said.

"That'll hep."

He waved his hand for them to follow him again. They walked down the hall and into an office bay of secretaries – the "Coffee Klatch" girls.

"Here's the real brains of the operation," Jack announced going through the open door.

They all smiled, and Jack made a real quick introduction to the ladies.

"Here Jackie," Carol said and handed him a stack of photocopies.

"They're made from all the Harris County phone books," Carol said. "Copies of the Yellow pages about locksmiths. Some are doubles – they advertise in many cities. Some don't. I figure rather than chase a thick list of partial plate trucks, smarter to chase a smaller list of locksmiths and look for partial plates."
Jack took the list and handed it off to Pathways, then he turned to Carol again.

"Ranger Acorn here will need some help on two suspects. He'll be bugging you ASAP."

They nodded. Acorn smiled.

"Did you go see George Strait?" he asked Carol.

Carol spun around in the chair, smiled and gave quite a heartfelt review of the concert and her personal "admiration," of Strait. Jack and she giggled a bit and some of the other Klatch joined in with some teasing. Path watched Jack totally engage, laugh, talk and scratch his gray-streaked, black-haired head, combed back hair. Then they left. Acorn split for the Ranger's wing.

"They all seemed to like you," Path said.

"I like them," Jack said, "matter of fact. They are all really good gals."

Chapter 16: A Reason To Live

Texas State Penitentiary at Huntsville or Huntsville Unit (HV), nicknamed "Walls Unit", Admin Section...

Jack Kellog spoke with Corrections Lt. Gary Anderson in the prison admin office, and Anderson pulled all their files on Randy Newlan. The two stood in front a massive row of tall, old metal filing cabinets, with Jack resting an arm atop one. Anderson had drawer pulled out with a messy file open atop the open drawer.

"Ten months ago, we pulled Randy Newlan's file for a Task Force commander, a Sam Dunker. Says here of Gulf Coast Drug Task Force. Dunker brought a partner, says here a Greg Williams with him, with the Task Force. They visited Randy Newlan…let's see… two, no three times. Then, after that, aaaahhh….about two months later, says here Newlan was released early. Judge's orders. Don't know why. It doesn't say here. We just have the release papers."

"Okay. What judge?" Jack asked.

"Let's seeee here…Rose Wrights, Austin."

"Can I get a copy of that release?"

"Sure," Anderson said.

"Who can I talk with here that was tight with Newland?" Jack asked.

Anderson dug deeper into daily and weekly reports. He decided that a Foster Briggs, in the big house for attempted murder in his hometown of Archer City, was one of Newlan's main friends-known associates during Newlan's prison term.

"This Foster Briggs' file was pulled by someone here helping a Screed detective aaaaa…okay, says here, a Paul Massaport, three months ago," Lt. Anderson said. "See here? Look, here's his name and signature for the request." He looked up at Jack, "And he's the one that was murdered by that weird limping man in a church, isn't he? The dead detective. I saw that on the news. Man that was weird."

"He was. He is. Did Massaport get to talk with Biggs?"

Hmmm…okay, yeah, he did," Anderson said after scanning more of the papers. "He did and he left. Never got back with us on what was said. He just left."

"There's, I don't know, maybe a leak here? Or, maybe this Briggs contacted my suspect with the news that Massaport was here asking questions," Jack said. "You got records on all of Briggs' phone calls and such? Mail? After that Massaport meeting?"

"We do. We do. Somewhere else. We will have to dig that up. Different divisions," Anderson said.

"I might need that info too," Jack said. "And see if Briggs got a big commissary influx within a few months. Or something. Before or after Paul's Massaport's death."

"Sure. This is a big fucking deal, Kellog. Murder of a police officer. It'll take about a day or two to gather that up," he scratched his ear, "we're kind of a mess here. Computers are a coming they promise."

"Well, mail it to me, here's my card. And, I'm here now, so, I guess I'll talk with Briggs. See what he says."

"And ahhh…ain't you the detective that caught, that killed John Phillip Muzak last year? He escaped from here you know."

"I know. I am," Jack said.

"THAT was one weird son of a bitch. He needed killing. Thank you!"

"Yeah, well…I'm not a detective no more," Jack found himself saying yet again and again. "Just, just work Intel for the state."

"Foller me, We'll get cha to see Briggs."

In some 30 minutes, guards located and brought a hand-cuffed-around-the-front Foster Briggs into one of the interrogation rooms. Jack was already seated at the table. Briggs sat. Guards left.

"Now what?" Briggs said.

"Jack Kellog, State Police."

"Whoopy-de-fuckin do. Now what?"

"I am here about your old roommate, Randy Newlan."

"You got a cigarette?"

"Nope."

"Why are we talking. What's in it for me."

"Dodging an accomplice-to-murder charge," Jack said. "That's what in it for you."

"What!"

"You know that your old buddy, Randy Newlan is dead?"

"Yeah. Heard."

"How you hear?"

"A detective came in here while back and told me," Briggs said, shrugging his shoulders. "I heard he drowned in a lake. How's that murder?"

"Paul Massaport came here?"

"Yeah, something like that."

"Stocky guy, Black hair," Jack said.

"Yeah. He said was investigating the drowning. Routine. He wanted to know about any visitors Randy had and what they said to him."

"What did you say?

"What Randy said. Two police officers, probably plainclothes, came in to see Randy several times. Then

Randy got out early, early parole."

"And then Randy was murdered," Jack said, "and Massaport came in to see you about it. Then he was murdered." Jack said, "I think maybe you helped kill him?"

"Me? How? I'm in here. Murder who? Randy? Or the detective?"

"The detective," Jack said.

"I'm in jail, in case you ain't seen. So?"

"Somebody told the killer that the detective was here and talked with you about Randy's visitors."

"I got nothing to do with that. I ain't accompliced shit."

"How exactly did Randy get out early?" Jack asked.

"He said that some police, some task force wanted him to fly helicopters."

"Helicopters? To do what?"

"I don't know. Fly fucking helicopters. For the police. Police have helicopters."

"Why do you suppose that in a world out there of helicopter pilots, most NOT in prison, they would need to release an inmate to fly choppers?"

"Beats me," Briggs said.

"Beats you," Jack said. "He say?"

"No say. He was bragging that he was gonna be hero again, like in the Army. Get out and fly choppers."

"A hero," Jack said and stood up. "After that detective came and talked with you, two weeks later he was shot and killed."

"Bad timing. We all die at bad times, sometimes," Briggs said.

"I am checking your records. Your mail. Your calls. Your commissary. Your Christmas presents. Your momma's Christmas presents. If you told anyone that a detective was here asking about Randy's visitors? I'll charge you with accomplice to murder. That's how, in here. You're 38 years old. You have 25 to do. You could be out in 18 or 19. I'll put another lid on your jar for life."

"Who do I call to get you killed then?"

"That's an interesting question," Jack said. He put his boot up on the chair's seat. "A lot of people have tried to kill me. I'm still here. If you did call someone? Or you call in on me? In 18 or 19 years? If I'm still around? I'll kill you myself."

"What are you? Like 65?"

"Sixty-three."

"You'll be dead in 18 years."

"Ordinarily. But a person needs a reason to live."

Jack left the room. He said goodbye to Lt. Anderson. He had a gut feeling that Briggs didn't call the Task Force. Massaport was probably followed by the task force to the pen. A quick task force call to any prison admin office employee would garner Task Force help and they'd look up the visit for them. If Briggs did call the Task Force? Jack will try to charge him. And if the charge didn't stick? Well then, yeah, then Jack will kill him in 18 years. A person does need a reason to live.

He stepped out onto the vast parking lot and looked around the best he could to see if he too was being followed. Nothing he could see. Then he looked back at the admin gate and doors, the very place where John Phillip Muzak waltzed right out of last year, escaping dressed in his rigged-up, medical uniform. Then he looked up the roadway where Muzak hitchhiked off and later killed the stupid driver. Jack shot and killed an armed Muzak. The madman's ghost will always bang around in his brain.

Jack climbed in his Caddy for the ride back to Houston, all the while failing to see the distant Chevy pickup and Collier Jones watching him with a pair of binoculars.

Later that night, Jack drove through the plush streets of big houses and passed the giant trees on to his home in West Forge, to see a red Mercedes parked out front. It was Gail Canchas' car, and she knew all his alarm security passwords to get inside his house. Lights were on inside.

"Oh Gail," he whispered. He'd yet to warn her about all the possible danger.

He parked in the driveway, went inside with his thick, worn, leather notebook, and the married magazine reporter met him at the door and kissed him like she lived there, which she'd done off and on through the years.

"Mrs. Ballitross," Jack said, a quick reminder to her that she was married to Ernesto Ballitross, though she still used her popular maiden writer's name.

"Jack, sit," she said.

Jack tossed his hat on the dining room table. Gail already had a Coors out on the table and Jack snatched one from the fridge. They both sat at the kitchen table.

"Texas congressman Alexander Lamica is a big opponent to these Texas drug task forces," she said. "He considers them lawless operations, illegally seizing money and property and running roughshod over citizens."

"He's the hippy that wants all drugs legalized. Marijuana too."

"Yes," Gail said.

"Well then, he would think all that from the get-go," Jack said.

"But Lamica is demanding the state records from all the drug task forces and wants to hold hearings on them."

"What do they say about strange bedfellows? Any chance of that?"

"Maybe, I think so. Austin is becoming more and more hippy."

"Like they say babe, 'keep Austin weird.'"

"I talked with him this morning," she said.

"Well!"

"He is very interested in a Texican Monthly expose, crime article to force the issue. He needs, we need, some serious crimes to outrage the public and to get something done. Generic, I mean, no names yet. Like the ones you got."

"That might prematurely reveal my investigation, though."

"Yes, but there have been other task force problems in the state. More than rumors. They are unsupervised vigilante gangs. Or doing many illegal things. It'll take 3 or 4 months to get the article published. But if you can figure out what we can use, this might help kick off some big action and…"

"Gail, I have to tell you, this is getting deep. Kicking it off already and I could be followed, like Massaport was followed…" he threw a pointed thumb over his shoulder in the direction of her Mercedes outside, "and it's dangerous for you to come here. Probably dangerous to be seen with me anywhere. We have to…"

Jack continued to warn her inside the house, but it was already too late. Outside, Larry Drumwald had already driven by the house several times and scribbled down her license plate number.

Chapter 17: The Jenko Thing

Blast's Bowling Alley Parking Lot, Houston, Texas...

"I gots me a problem, Cin," Jerod Hoover told Cinnamon Dunker and Josh Elliot. The trio stood off on a far corner in the parking lot of Blast's Bowling Alley. Hoover looked bruised and beaten. "I paged you cuz we got robbed."

"What happened?" Dunker asked.

"Me and Harry and Merc and Stilts were delivering. Little Mexico Pizza, you know, that place. A pound of crack, some 'MJ' to Little Jesus. We wuz hit up by his new dealers."

"Outside? Inside?" Elliot asked.

"Inside! Lobby. Mother fuckers shot my man Merc. Little Jesus behind the counter? He be knowin this had to happen. He had to know what was gonna happen. He just ducked right away when we walked in. He traded us in for new dealers."

"He might have been scared. Jesus is about a half a wimp," Dunker said. "Your man… Merc… dead?"

"Not yet. He's at his aunty's."

"We'll send a doc. Who did it? You know?"

"Yeah, I know! Alexandrios brothers. Mexicans. They've been creeping around the outskirts of me and mine for about a month now. They picked up with come cartel rep who has big plans and they got new guns and got new balls. They even be trying to get me to hook up with their Mexicans or run me out of business."

"Name?" Dunker asked.

"The rep goes by Jenko. Cartel representative. All tattooed-up, mother fucker. Arms, neck, face. Walking advertisement of a dope man. He's got the Alexandrios gang all fired up and shit. Like they're minor league baseball movin to the majors."

"Were do they hang?" Dunker asked.

"They be somewheres near the Housing Authority, Houston. And they got a clubhouse like a warehouse, yeah, it's a warehouse in a warehouse row. Rented. That's all I know."

"Okay," Dunker said as he handed Hoover five $100 bills. "Spread this to your guys. Tell them they will be safe. Find out more if you can. I need to know exactly where they hang out."

Elliot handed Hoover a small notebook and pen and said,

"Write down Merc's aunt's address, we'll send the vet."

Hoover scribbled it down. The "vet" was a drug-addicted veterinarian Dunker used as a human medical doctor in such emergencies. When Hoover shuffled off, Dunker and Elliot leaned against their old Caprice on the lot, folding their arms.

"Reckon Little Jesus just wimped out, afraid of the brothers," Dunker said, "he's no planner. He knows better."

"Probably. I can see that. He shoulda called us though."

"Shoulda. Let's go see him," Dunker said.

"You know if they're dealing in the lobby, they'll be in there with guns," Elliot said.

"Yeah, and we're the fuckin Task Force. We'll have guns too."

Elliot smiled at that. He got behind the wheel and drove to Little Mexico Pizza. Dunker got on his phone and ordered up the Vet to go work on Merc at his Aunt's house.

Little Mexico Pizza was a crappy place in a crappy strip mall, in a crappy area on the crappy south side of Houston. Their crappy Caprice fit right in. They parked on far side of the lot, but even dressed down as they were, having two fit, tall, big white guys walk on such a lot and into this little dive storefront was odd. "Little Hay-zues!" Dunker shouted when he stepped inside.

Little Jesus was behind the counter, beside his wife who was folding up cardboard pizza boxes. No customers were there, but a skinny, Hispanic dude sat in the small lobby, minus any food on his table, just a cellphone on the table.

Little Jesus' eyes darted back and forth from Dunker to this guy at the table. Josh Elliot laid back a bit by the door. He flipped the open sign over to "closed."

"Who's homeboy?" Dunker asked, with a nod to the guy.

"He's…"

It didn't matter. The guy reached into his oversized jacket and Elliot drew his Magnum revolver and shot him three times. The sound and physical disruption of the guy and the table were surreal. He kicked the cheap table and other chairs off their legs, splattered and quaked down to the floor. The explosions rocked the shop.

Wife screamed. She ran in the back.

Little Jesus ducked yet again.

Dunker jogged around the corner of the counter, hauled Little Jesus up off the dirty tiled floor. Elliot grabbed the quivering, almost dead, skinny Hispanic dude and drug him back behind the counter.

When they all were all back there, Dunker stuck his .357 revolver under Little Jesus' chin. Elliot pushed the wife into a chair.

"That's now three bullets, count em, three rounds in your lobby. How's about one more in the kitchen?"

"Dey made me!" Dey made me. Dey say dey kill everyone here, me. Her. My kids."

Dunker put the pistol away.

"Who?"

"Terry Alexandrios," Little Jesus said. "Dey want to sell crack and dope right in my lobby and to people ordering my pizza. I don't want sales right here in my lobby. You know this. You know our deal. Deliveries only! Outside. But not inside here. I am stuck in de middle of…of death. De medio!"

"You are not in the middle. You are stuck with me and Hoover. And that's a good place to be stuck."
He patted Little Jesus on the cheek. Josh Elliot patted the wife on her shoulder.

"How about a couple of slices of that one?" Dunker said calmly to the wife, pointing to a combination pizza in the display case. She grabbed a paper plate and got busy.

Dunker called a number on his cellphone while he looked at an order form on the front counter. He called Calante's Merry Maids and asked for Mr. Calante. He read the address aloud from the form, but he followed up with-

"Got a clean-up, Pepino. I will send it to you again. Look at your pager for the address."

Pepino Calante of "Calente's Merry Maids" was a steady user of cocaine, but not a lost addict, but rather a functioning addict. To become a lost one, was to collect the rage from Dunker, something even worse than cocaine addiction itself. Calante had many related business problems that Dunker had solved, and he then started distributing marijuana to many of the houses he and his merry maids entered to clean. The maids would leave a bag of dope at a designated place in customer houses. Their monthly "cleaning" bill, re-flected this extra duty.

Dunker's Task Force had seized so much plant that they needed many dealers like Calante and Little Jesus. Plus, Calante, once a janitor in a chicken butchering factory in Arkansas, really knew how to clean up bloody messes like this one. Really good.

"If the Alexandrios people come here first, before I solve this problem," he took a big bite of the pepperoni pizza, "you tell them that their punk was shot by a drug task force police, and he did draw first. Tell them you had nothing to do with it. And you are being honest, amigo."

Josh Elliot searched the dead dealer's body. No ID. He pulled a big nickel-plated "show" gun, another .357 revolver, which was about half the size of the man's torso. Josh took his cellphone, and the gun.

Dunker finished the pizza and gave Little Jesus three $100 dollar bills and winked at him. The wife started mopping up the lobby floor. He stopped by her and gave her $100 bill.

"I got somebody coming for this mess, Carmen," he told her with a smile.

They walked out to the Caprice and looked at each other over the roof.

"Jenko. Jenko. I think this Jenko thing is a job for Bluto," Dunker said.

"Yup."

The next day at the hangar, Bluto spent a long time on the phone with their dealer Hoover. He collected more information Hoover learned from Little Jesus. Little Jesus told Jenko that the state police narcotics walked into the Little Mexican Pizza place and their guy in the lobby freaked out, pulled a gun and the narcs shot him, which wasn't too much of a lie, really. There was new intelligence. Hoover told Jenko that Jenko called him. Jenko wanted to meet with Hoover in a "join us," take-over talk no doubt.

The Jenko-Hoover meeting was set for Saturday noon, at a high school stadium parking lot. Bluto told him to say yes to the meet, but ordered him not to go to it. Bluto said not to worry about not going. Bluto said he would care of it all. After Hoover missed that meeting, Bluto told him not to answer the phone.

On Saturday, Dunker watched Bluto talk and prep with guns and cars. He knew Bluto was all over this and knew better than to ask or interfere with Bluto's plans. Once Bluto got going...

Saturday at noon, Bluto and Greg Williams were on the fourth floor of an office building, looking out through the glass wall with powerful binoculars at the stadium parking lot, a great distance away. Jenko was waiting there with three men on the lot, standing outside two black dually pickups. At noon, they started pacing.

"I checked with my amigos down south," Bluto said while scoping in who was obviously the main man.

"Jenko is with the Umbra Cartel in Columbia," not Mexico. Maybe they joined up with the Mexicans? I don't know."

At 12:20, knowing they were stood up by Hoover, and no doubt very angry, they left the parking lot by the looks of their faces and hand gestures. Greg Williams cell-phoned Collier Jones who was waiting somewhere below in a bland, Datsun Sentra. Collier

Jones then called Josh Elliot, also waiting in a Ford Thunderbird.

Their job? Tag team follow Jenko's truck till they parked somewhere.

"They are moving," was the message Greg Williams passed on.

Two hours later, Josh Elliot called Bluto…

"They're at a mini-warehouse in a line of connected mini-warehouses at 8817 Dolcimer. Number 12. Lots of cars on the lot. The warehouses are very small in length. The leasing sign outside the complex has a drawing of the interiors. They all look the same. Looks like regular glass front doors up a few steps. One side office just inside the front door. Big open area. Big garage door in the back."

"Okay. Watch the front and back," Bluto said, "Collier, you stay outside by the back until we let you in. Kill anyone that runs out the back door."

"Yes, sir."

Grenades. Bluto did not mess around. He shoved two in his vest pockets, while waiting in the car.

A thuggish looking guard stood out front of number 12. Greg Williams walked up nearby, looking up and down at a piece of paper in his hand, half-smiling and glancing at the front doors of each mini warehouse, as if searching for a location. He looked at the guard like he was going to ask a question. But instead when close, Greg drew and shot the guard dead with a silenced pistol. Then he pulled a black mask up from his neck and over his face. Bluto and 5 other masked Task Force members, all in common street clothes with jackets covering over their shoulder-strapped short machine guns, raced to the front door of the warehouse.

Bluto opened the glass door, pulled the pin and tossed a M67 grenade into the open-space warehouse. He stepped back. It rolled on in and blew with a mighty bang!

Bluto opened the door again the very second the blast ended and peeked in to see the post, shock, awe, destructive chaos of downed and stumbling men, splintered walls and furniture, and still flying, dusty debris. He tossed a second grenade in, this time even deeper and stepped back outside again, this time while lifting his shoulder strapped, short M960 Calico machine gun up from his armpit.

When the letter "t" of 'blast" ended, that very-split second, he entered and started shooting every living and dead thing in the warehouse. All the men out front piled in after him, SWAT-style in a line, ready to shoot, but Bluto, the efficient executioner that he was, had hit all ten of the ambushed guys at least twice with rounds.

Bluto saw the single office to the left and circled the damaged door. The big office window glass was blown away from the blasts. Bluto jutted his jaw toward the office and the men behind him circled it. Two "sliced the pie," peeking in the window from the right and left sides, to clear the interior.

"WAIT! Hold it," a voice from within shouted out.

"Come out!" Greg Williams ordered.

Terry Alexandrios kicked the busted door open and came out, hands up. He was chunked face down on the floor and searched. Other men poured into the office to search it.

Bluto said, "Get all the wallets and phones."

Task Force members ran to the metal back door and let Collier and his teammates inside. They started

searching the corpses. Bluto stepped to the office door
to see Greg Williams stuffing cash, cocaine and marijuana into a big canvass big he'd carried in on his belt.
Greg gave Bluto a thumbs up. The main idea of this
"raid" was obliteration, but also stealing some money
and drugs was always a plus.

"Who are you?" Bluto asked the man on the floor.

"Terry."

"Terry Alexandrios?" Bluto asked.

"Yeah."

"Your brother in here?"

"I…"

"Sit up and look around."

He sat up, hands up and surveyed the carnage in
the room. His jaw trembled and he gasped.

"That's...that's him. There."

Bluto looked over at the dead body.

"Jenko?" Pluto asked.

"That's him other there," he said half-pointed.

Then Bluto shot Terry in the face. Terry's head
jerked with a strange bone-breaking, crack-open
sound as he fell limp.

"Let's go!" Bluto ordered.

They gathered near the front door. Greg caught up
with them hauling the canvas bag bounty.

But just before they opened the door, a wide-eyed,
middle-aged white man dashed in, stopping short
when he saw the wreckage and the seven masked men
all dressed in common clothes. And…he saw some of
their guns.

"Who are you?" Bluto asked.

"I...I am the manager. I…I heard the explosion."

"Your name!"

"Robert Mulhouse."

"Robert, my name is Julio, and we are from the

Umbra Cartel in Columbia. This, what you see here, is a drug gang, revenge shooting. If you want to live, do not call the police for 30 minutes or we will come back and kill you slowly and painfully. In 30 minutes, call the police and then you can tell the police you met us and we are the Umbra Cartel taking revenge, but if you remember anything particular about us, we will put you inside five burning car tires.

"Ye…yes. Yes sir!"

"Who are we?"

"Umbrella Cartel."

"Umbra! The Unmbra Cartel. Who are we?"

"Umbra Cartel."

"Right. Sit down over there. On the floor, Robert Mulhouse, senior manager."

Bluto already had a Spanish accent, but he poured it on thick for Robert Mulhouse with this false Umbra lead, all to later, temporarily confuse the cartels and the police, plus put some extra heat on their local competitors, the actual Umbras.

They all walked out of the building, and off the complex to their cars on the streets outside. Still masked, they drove away in cars with fake license plates and split up, all to eventually, circuitously head for their Beachum Airport headquarters.

At the Task Force hangar, they all pulled their cars inside. All the cars had to be redone and plates destroyed. Dunker approached and counted heads. All present. All accounted for. A member collected all the guns to be cleaned, even though the only two guns fired were Greg's pistol and Bluto's Calico. They would disappear out in the middle of the Gulf, via their task force boat.

Josh Elliot dropped the heavy bag on a conference

table, smiled and emptied it. There were oooohs and aahhhs over its contents.

"The Jenko thing is dead," Bluto said walking up.

Dunker watched him approach. Bluto was shot in the hip in Puerto Rico by Cubans years ago. He could walk normally if he really thought about it, pulling his right foot in, and purposely pointing his right toes forward, but when not thinking about it, he had this strange, distinctive gait. Now relaxed and thoughtless, his odd walk was even more pronounced.

Dunker then turned his attention to the cash and drugs on the table. He'd split up the cash. Leaders like he and Bluto earned larger sums, but all the members got a happy amount, and then their own distribution system would sell the drugs through their various channels, like Hoover.

Chapter 18: An Ambush Was Ambushed

Galena, TX...

"I found him, Jack," Linda Pathways reported on her cellphone, after just two days of searching for the locksmith's truck.

"Great," Jack said.

"He has a shop in Galena. Harris County, on Place Ave. Has to be his truck. His name is Rick Sandavere. No criminal history, though."

"Hmmm, I wonder if he has a limp," Jack said.

"He does not. He parks out front. I watched him come and go a couple of times."

"Okay, we'll jump on him when the timing is right. Too soon now. Manny has set up surveillance at the airport, getting pictures, and will start tailing some of the guys to their homes. They are thinking about trying some quick fingerprinting on the outsides of their cars at night. Acorn is on Rhoades' background. My prison trip turned up nothing except what we knew already - that Dunker visited Newlan and got him out early. But I did get some information on the Austin Judge that ordered Newlan's early release. We can't go see her yet. It will tip them off."

"Sure."

"A lot is coming together. Fast. Be careful Path. Watch out."

"I will."

West Forge Police Athletic League Gym...

To stay off his beaten tracks, Jack had been working out at the newly renovated DPS gym, skipping his usual haunts. But the DPS gym could get very crowded with local troopers and the cadet classes in session working out there too. Plus, they didn't have some of the equipment Jack liked. So, he still returned to the Police Athletic League Gym in West Forge at least once a week. And he enjoyed helping out with the youth boxing classes.

Such was this Wednesday night. Tired, winded and sore, Jack packed up his gym bag in the locker room. Since his heart attack recovery, he'd worked out almost every day, mimicking his old boxing work outs of yesteryear as best his sixty-plus-year-old bones could. He did spend part of his PAL gym time helping some of the neighborhood teens with boxing drills and advice with the teenager boxing club. Though his short-lived pugil career was a total failure, he could still offer some wisdom and hold mitts for the kids. Otherwise, he hit the heavy bag and treadmills, and lifted some weights.

Given his latest threatening assignment, he did not want to run outside and become an eventual, possible, easy, lone, drive-by, task force target.

Guns in gyms were always a problem for cops. Leave them in your car in the parking lot and the car might be burglarized. Leave them in your locker and your locker might get burglarized. Leave them in your gym bag near you and bag might "walk away" when you turn away for a second, even in PAL Gym with a lot of police presence. The gym welcomed juvenile delinquents, especially for the boxing club which was risky and there were troubles from time to time. These last few days, Jack kept his .45 in a carry-around, Title Boxing, gym bag.

Gun back on his hip and covered by his Sears Member Only black windbreaker, in sneakers, jeans and a pullover shirt, Jack winked at some, waved at others, as he approached the front glass doors of the old building to head home.

"Night, Jack," Smiley-Pants Jansen said, a retired West Forge patrolman and amateur boxer, now the gym front desk employee.

"See ya, Smiley."

Jack cautiously stepped outside into the cooler night air and the parking lot. It had lightly rained and all around was shiny and wet. He knew the front doors were a "fatal funnel" for a trap. His left hand held the gym bag leaving his right hand free for a quick draw. No matter how quick though, an ambush was an ambush. A clever ambush was far worse. But he couldn't live life with his gun up, out and turning, scanning at every one of life's corners.

He approached his Caddy, head swiveling every which way. People in cars? People walking? Then he saw it and it struck him odd, like the stunning hot touch of electricity to his heart. A man seated in a car, across the four-lane, city main street and a bit north. The parked car was facing the wrong way. It faced south on the north side of the road. Someone had to cross two lanes of incoming traffic to park this way. Why? Well, Jack thought, better to see the PAL gym parking lot. All the other parked cars on that side of the street faced north.

The man behind the wheel could not see gym building itself, just most of the parking lot…and Jack's Caddy.

Nonchalantly, Jack opened the trunk and put the bag in. Then he returned to the gym.

"Forget something?" Smiley-Pants said, seeing Jack walk back in.

"Yup. My brains," Jack said, and he walked through the gym to a back, side door.

Jack slipped out on the side street, well out of the view of the man in the parked car. He walked west to a street corner, turned north and headed north for a short way on a street of older, small homes and an apartment complex. Then he turned right and east at the next corner. Finally, he hit the four-lane main street, well north of and well behind the man in the wrong-way car.

The street was a main one for West Forge and the newly renovated, downtown. It never really had heavy traffic. It was lined with old trees, wide sidewalks, old and new stores and apartments above the stores, here and there. Across the street where the car was, was a small park.

Jack walked briskly north again, then crossed the street over to the car's side. There he faced south too, looking at the row of cars all facing north, except…except…that…one.

He started south, and dressed in that black windbreaker, t-shirt, jeans and sneakers, he hoped he would look normal enough in the man's rear view side mirror, should the man even look backwards.

Closer. He got closer. The man's head and probably eyes were glued to the gym parking lot to his southwest, especially after he just saw Jack drop a bag off in his car and head back to the gym.

Then Jack got right up to the car window and the man's profile.

"Hey there!" Jack yelled, standing by the driver's open window.

The surprised man turned. It was Collier Jones, a Gulf Coast Task Force member Jack had met on his one visit to the hangar. And he was utterly shocked to see Jack Kellog, his pursuit, there right beside him.

Jack smiled.

"On a stakeout? Got something going? I thought

that was you Collier," Jack ad-libbed.

"Uhhh, ahhh…yeah," Collier said.

"I was working out over there, my gym is over there, and I always like to take a walk after a workout, Jack said, "beautiful night. Cool."

"Ahhh yeah, it is. Yeah, I am working on something. Yeah. Waiting on a car to drive by. Here on Main. Yeah."

"Need any help?" Jack asked.

"Ahhh naah. No. Just gonna report when the car drives by. A…a…you know, dope deal. You know."

"I know. You bet," Jack said. "Okay, well, you hang in there."

Jack backed away with a fake smile and turned north from whence he came. He knew he had screwed up this guy's mind, but real trouble was brewing for Jack. Like Paul Massaport, he was absolutely being followed and this early in the investigation! About five cars up, he crossed the street to the gym side, bound for the parking lot and his car.

Collier Jones sat, pissed. *REALLY* pissed. He'd been outsmarted and totally made by the old yokel-okel. How? Was this Kellog that freaking sharp? Or just very lucky like Dunker said about him. He cursed. Then he made a violent decision. If this Jack Kellog made him like this, this easy, then Jack Kellog was on to him and onto all of them. Collier steamed. What would Dunker do now in thus fix? What would Bluto do now? Right now? They'd kill him right now. That's what they'd do!

Convinced he made the right decision, Collier got out of his car, watching Jack walk across the street. He pulled his Browning pistol and held it "boot leg," pointing down beside his leg. He started after the investigator.

Meanwhile Jack was on edge. He knew the walk to his Caddy would be a dangerous one. Dangerous moments. With his head facing mostly forward, Jack peeked to his left until his eyes hurt, then he made some real quick glances to the street. Yup. Collier was coming.

Jack also pulled his .45 out and pointed it "boot leg" downward, counting the seconds. Judging distances. Counting. He guessed, he estimated, more from a positional gut decision on where Collier and what he would do. Jack decided to dart in the space ahead between two parked cars, a space just a few feet ahead. Dart and crouch.

Three steps. Two. One. Dart! Crouch! He made the cut. He did just as a bullet rang out behind him, which smacked into a storefront. Jack turned to see Collier now still in the street behind him one car back. Collier shot again, the round blasting down the avenue to who knows where? Jack circled out to the street, as Collier made for the sidewalk to get a car between them. Jack caught a glimpse of Collier and fired his .45. This big round slammed into Collier's left shoulder. It didn't knock him down though, and Jack could see his Collier up right and his torso twisted wide before him, his face scrunched in shock and pain. Jack fired again, center mass, interrupting Collier's attempt to shoot back. Instead, Collier sloppily shot the car between them. This time Collier did fall.

A few cars drove by, but a few cars stopped. Jack circled the parked cars and went in on Collier's back, his right shoulder up .

"No use!" Jack yelled. "Give it up. I'll call an ambulance."

"Fuck you!" Collier hoarsely, barely said.

"No. Looks like fuck you," Jack slowly whispered.

Jack closed in, pistol in one hand and aimed at the man. Collier had dropped the 9mm and it laid on the wet sidewalk. Collier gurgled. Jack's center mass round went a little high and was more of a lower throat shot. Not much blood, but a really bad place to be shot. Probably blew out the back of his neck, he guessed, torching the spinal cord.

"What's going on?" A man yelled from a second story apartment window.

"State police!" Jack yelled. "It's over. Call the city police. Call an ambulance."

Jack kicked the 9mm aside. He leaned in. A section of Collier's back by the nape of his neck was indeed perforated. More blood on the cement.

"You a dead man," Jack said, "a stupid, dipshit dead man."

"You a…" and he died.

West Forge city police started showing up, then the ambulance. Some of the older officers that arrived knew Jack, like one Jimmy Casulas.

"Jack!" Jimmy yelled.

"Jimmy, my first shot is still in him, second shot went through him. Probably in that wall. But he shot at me three times. Two are still here, there and in this car here. But one went way the hell down Main Street. I think somebody best drive down there and…I don't know…take a look around Make sure nobody's hit down there by the stray."

Patrol Sergeant Jimmy Malworth arrived and ordered an officer to drive south on Main and take a look around.

The EMTs got there and quickly declared the man dead.

Then none other than Jack's old police chief, West

Forge Chief "Shrewdy" Collins drove up, and stepped out of his sedan.

"Jumpin' Jack Kellog!" Shrewdy said, shaking Jack's hand.

"Chief."

"I thought you were through killing people in my West Forge?" Shrewdy said.

"Me too."

"Who he?"

"He…" Jack said with a sigh and resignation, "...he is a dirty cop, Shrewdy. And this whole thing is about to blow sky high."

"He part of that dead guy story at the hospital thing the other night, and why the admin said we were supposed to keep a lid on it? Best we could?" Shrewdy said.

"He is."

"Hmmm. You still have some pull around here, Jack. I came right away when I heard you were the shooter."

A young West Forge detective arrived and walked up to them. Jack recognized him as once a rookie patrolman.

"Hello there, Detective Acropo," Jack said, shaking his hand. "That guy tried to kill me, and I killed him back. His gun is right there."

Acropo was a little stunned at the synopsis.

"It's probably that simple, kid," the Chief said.

"I gotta make a few phone calls to the state," Jack told them.

"I'll bet you do," Shrewdy said. "I reckon some of this we have to keep secret squirrel too?"

"Ahhhh," Jack sighed, having to think about. "For just a day maybe. But this lid's gonna blow tomorrow anyway."

He pulled the cellphone from his pocket. The first man Jack called was Weaver Wisdom.

Chapter 19: On To Them. On To Us

"Last night a former West Forge police detective and now an intelligence special agent for the Texas Department of Public Safety, a Jack Daniel Kellog was ambushed on the streets of downtown West Forge. You might recall the name. This is the officer who waged a one-man war on the Texas and New York Mafia back in the 1980s and was fired last year from the West Forge Police Department for the brutal, public beating of a child killer. More recently he led a state police team to capture and kill escaped convict John Phillip Muzak that ending Muzak's murderous crime wave. Agent Kellog was ambushed by a man while walking on Main Street.

A gunfight ensued with Kellog killing his attacker. The shooting is under investigation by Texas Rangers, and they promised a press conference as soon as possible. Back to you Roger, Seth Sams, KPRX TV."

"That sounds like a man with a lot of potential enemies, Seth," added anchorman Roger Ingram.

Several copies of newspapers bearing much the same news laid on the big conference table in the meeting room inside DPS Houston headquarters the next afternoon. The whole State, Takedown Task Force were there, even Lt. Colonel Daniel Murth. Weaver Wisdom walked in with reports in his hand, and with the Ranger's arrival, Jack started the briefing.

"As with Paul Massaport, I was being followed by the Task Force. This time followed by a Collier Jones. I was to eventually be later killed at their chosen time and place. Followed by one of the Task Force members I met in their hangar, when I visited them last week," he further explained what happened and added, "everyone must be extra careful."

"This just in, Jack, "Weaver said, waving the papers in his hand. "This Collier Jones is not Collier Jones. Harris County medical examiners did their midnight shift autopsy as I asked them to rush it up. They ran the prints with the autopsy. His real name is Dane Achison, fired from Denver, once a detective three years ago. Corruption. Later arrested again for DWI and aggravated assault. There is an arrest warrant out for him. You killed a wanted fugitive, not a police officer."

"Perfect cover, huh?" Acorn said, "get a new set of impressive IDs as a task force cop. They must all be former corrupt cops and crooks. Dunker hires them like a recruiter."

Everyone nodded.

"The law states that a task force can hire anyone they want," Weaver added, "even bad guys as informants and undercover agents."

"And…give them false IDs, in case they work undercover. Okay, now hold on, get this," Nip said, "there was a helleva shoot-out, and dad-gum explosions too, two days ago. A warehouse district. Drug gang versus drug gang. Machine guns. Looks like a bomb or something went off. Witnesses looked outside their shops after the explosions to see what the booms were, and saw the gang leave and…and…one of them sons a bitches had a weird gimpy, limpy walk, witnesses said. The complex office manager told Houston narcotics and homicide that he ran into the warehouse after the explosions, thinking it was a fire. The gang caught him and told him that they were the Umbra Cartel taking revenge."

"Umbra…bullshit," Manny said. "Smart. But bullshit."

"This matched the times of the in-and-out log we turned in," Manny said. "A bunch of them left the hanger just before this and they all returned after this, but separately. This mysterious limper dude lives at the hangar. Sleeps there on a cot. Hangs out his laundry on a line out back. When he leaves and Jules follered him, he goes to fast foods places to eat and goes right back. Or he shops at HEB and comes back. He cooks his food on a grill he rolls in and out of the hangar. We've got blowed up face shots of him. Pictures of many of them, but good ones of him in particular."

"Manny, if they were following me, "Jack said, "they must figure that we are surveilling them. You got to get your guys outta there."

"We did what we could for a day or two, but yesterday we installed some cameras, like hunter's cameras, but very powerful and very small, filming the hanger's front and back. They're great cameras, like spy shit. CIA quality. Tiny little camo boxes up in some trees. They'll be hard to spot if they even try to find them."

"What's next?" the Lt. Colonel asked.

"Get me those pictures, Manny. I'll Ask the DEA to look at the photos. See if they can ID any of them," Nip said, "I can go do that in that morning."

"I'll get them to you," Manny said.

Murf nodded and said, "can we trust the DEA?"

"Oh, I think so," Nip said. "And I think Dunker and them are afraid of the DEA. Got to be, my guess. I think we can count on DEA to help. I know those guys. Bout time to tell them. I got a good friend over there, a real hound dog. Jessip."

Weaver winked, knowing Jessip Kline very well.

"Tell them that Dunker is working to buy a helicopter and transport drugs over great distances as in crossing state lines," Jack added. "Now, look, I saw Collier Jones in the lobby of the hangar. Dunker and them know I saw him. And this guy tried to kill me. The logical step would be I'd go there and ask Dunker about him."

"You can't do that," Weaver said. "They might kill you when you walk in the front door.

"Damn near did last time," Jack said.

"I'll go," Weaver said, "Acorn and I will go and just ask them about Collier. After all, a DPS shooting is investigated by the Rangers. Routine. Dunker knows his. And they will be expecting it. Worse, it's more suspicious if we don't go and talk to him. We have too."

"We can all play our parts, "Jack said, "but we both know about each other now, more and more. We're on to them. They're on to us. We're on to each other."

"This Alice girl," Ranger Wilderaydo Acorn spoke up. "I found where she lives, and she's got her truck back already. Driving it."

"I found the locksmith that made the key for the church," Pathways announced.

"And I found the judge in Austin that released Randy Newlan early," Jack said. "I want to know how Dunker pulled that off. Got a state judge to release a convicted felon. Soon, very soon, we have to hit them from all sides, all at once when the timing is right. Right now, we have no serious evidence to take any of them down."

They all agreed.

"Okay, listen, let's try this," Jack said, "Colonel, you go ahead and release the news now, that my attacker was just a wanted felon fugitive from Colorado, a..."

"Dane Achison," Weaver reminded.

"Dane Achison," Jack continued, "and Weave, tomorrow you two go to the Task Force headquarters and say…say that Jack Kellog …thinks… he saw Achison there. Say I thought, the look-a-like was a 'Jones something.' Use the word 'think.' And that, y'all have to go there to check it all out. Routine. No one knows what Achison and I said to each other last night, or how this shootout started, but me. Unless he called Dunker in the few seconds that we were apart. I sincerely doubt it. There was no time. And no way Dunker would not have told him to jump out on the damn street and kill me right there. He did that on his own. Impulsive."

"Makes sense," Weaver said, and Acorn nodded. Murf stood up and said, "I'll alert the media right now about the Denver fugitive. It'll make the noon, 6 and 10 o'clock news. They are already out in the lobby, banging down our doors this morning."

"And the morning news and papers," Weaver added. Then we'll pay the hangar a visit, mid-morning, tomorrow."

"And this is why God made the Texas Rangers," Jack said.

After some more discussion they all left the big room with plans. Jack and Weaver stopped in the hall. They leaned on the walls across from each other.

"How you doing?"

"Okay. Sore neck from looking over my shoulder," Jack said.

"How close this guy get?"

"I watched him come at me from across the street. We played tag around some cars, poppin shots. Could a gone either way. I got lucky. I'm okay. This ain't my first rodeo."

"Juuust asking. Just asking. Feeling desperate yet?" Weaver asked.

"Not yet."

"Cause, you get *real* frisky when you get desperate."

"You do too," Jack said, "don't get too frisky to-morrow. It's too early."

Weaver grunted. When the big man grunted, it sounded like a big angry bull, then he said, "Yeah. I'm cool."

"You know…DPS SWAT. Comegy…we need to get all of Manny's info on the hangar over to Comegy. Let him look it over early with his men. Make a plan. I got a feeling a big raid is in our near future. Might be World War three over there."

"Yeah. That's a good idea. I can set that up. I'll get with Manny on it too."

"I can tell them first-hand about the gear and set-up inside. After your visit tomorrow, you probably can too.   You know, I might just start up some description paragraphs for a search warrant."

"If we were in the army, we'd just drop a bomb on the place when they are all there," Weaver said.

"Yeah, well, this ain't Vietnam, Bubba," Jack said.

"It's getting closer every day," Weaver said.

Chapter 20: Lord's Work in Devil's Town

At 11 a.m. Rangers Weaver Wisdom and Wilderaydo Acorn walked in the front door of Ace's High and what was secretly the Texas Gulf Coast Drug Task Force headquarters. They were both dressed in "classic Ranger." White hat. White shirt. Tan pants, Boots. Tooled, tan leather gun belts with .45s. The iconic, cinco peso-based, coin badges. The only demographic difference was Weaver was a sixty-something-year old black man and Acorn was a thirty-something, year old Native American.

A small bell jangled with the door shove. They stood in the lobby. No one showed up. They stepped over to the lobby door to the hangar. Acorn shoved one of the two doors open.

"Hello!" Acorn shouted.

The Rangers were a bit amazed at what they saw. A military-styled SWAT van, a dozen cars, desks, meeting area, a weight-lifting gym, work-out area, a....

"Hello!" A call came back.

Several men approached the pair, recognizing immediately the two were Texas Rangers.

"Cinnamon," Weaver said with a smile to Dunker, recognizing him from past brushes in law enforcement meetings, not to mention the recent surveillance photos.

"Weaver!" Dunker said and shook his hand.

Weaver introduced Acorn.

Dunker failed to introduce the other three of his men that wandered toward them. He learned his lesson from Jack Kellog's prior visit.

"Whatcha doing these days?" Dunker asked.

"Oooh the usual," Weaver said melodically, "doing the Lord's work in the Devil's town. Now I got this shooting thing. How are you?"

"Okay. Okay. What brings you out here?" He knew not to ask how did they know where to find the head-quarters.

"Well…" Weaver started.

"Come on, come over here and have ya a seat," Dunker said, waving his hand toward their big confer-ence table.

One man quick, wiped clean the writing on the big erasable, white board next to the table. They sat.

"Coffee er something?" Dunker asked.

"No, no, we are coffee-ed out. Fact of business, we have cups of coffee out there now sitting in the car. And they are getting cold."

"Okay," Dunker said with a chuckle.

"As you might have heard," Weaver began, "some-body tried to kill one of our troops, Special Agent Jack Kellog out on the street in West Forge two nights ago. You know Jack. He's been here once."

"I do, just from meetings when I was with Harris County, and he visited us, came out here, offering his help weeks back. Shit, if you're an old-timer in our business, who ain't heard of Jumpin Jack Kellog?"

"Yeah, yeah, he's with us now. Intelligence. As you know that. Kellog killed this guy instead. Turns out, the guy was a felony fugitive from Colorado. Might a been a mafia hitman? Revenge from Jack's past? We don't know. Jack thinks he's seen him before though."

"Oh?"

"He said he looked very familiar, yeah, he says. He thinks. One of the places he thinks he's seen him be-fore? Might be right here, on his visit here."

"Huh?" Dunker said, with an accompanying sur-prised face.

"Have a look," Acorn said and he pulled from his

notebook a mugshot picture of Dean Achison-Collier Jones, and slid it across the table.

Dunker looked at it, bearing a protruded lower lip as he zeroed in.

"Hmmm. No," he signaled for the other men to step near and look over his shoulder.

They all shook their heads to the negative.

"We've had some officers come and go. A few. But not him. What name did Kellog say?"

"He doesn't remember," Weaver lied.

"Well, it wasn't here."

"To…be…thorough," Acorn said, "close this idea out, I know headquarters will ask us for this, do you have a list handy of all your task force members?"

Weaver smiled at Dunker , as though Acorn was probing too far to ask that. He pursed his lips for a whistle more like wind than sound, with almost down-right, disrespectful - a "these kids" expression at Acorn.

Dunker caught the supportive look, which probably tempered his response.

"Well Ranger Acorn," Dunker said, "you know with the Texas Task Force by-laws, we can't release any such information to anyone. Even to other fellow agencies. Even you Rangers."

"Ooookay, then," Weaver said, "We had to come by and check it out. Our money right now is still on an old mafia vendetta thing. Just the way it played out. Kellog killed a lot of influential players from the Cowboy Mafia and New York round here and those folks like the cold dish of revenge."

"The Cowbells Family," Dunker interjected.

"Yup," Weaver finished, standing up.

Acorn stood.

Dunker stood.

The others just gawked at them.

"We'll leave y'all alone," Weaver said as they headed for the lobby.

"Okay fellers, take care," Dunker said, remaining by the table and not seeing them out. No tour of the place was offered this time.

Inside, they all sat back down at the table.

"We knew that was coming," Dunker reminded them after he heard the doorbell clang.

"Man!" Greg Williams said, "but it sounded good. You think they are telling the truth?"

"Don't exactly know, but they got nothing to work with," Dunker said, leaning back in his chair. He ran his fingers up and down on a pencil, turning it over and over. "Collier's car was cool. No way to trace that back to us. Nor him."

"Those two Rangers on our watch list now?" Larry Drummond asked.

"Yeah but, well, no. I do know we can't be shooting Texas Rangers!" Dunker proclaimed. "You don't want that kind of heat. You think Bluto is bad-ass? Shoot a Ranger and whole Texas state police could turn into an army of troopers, raid and kill us all."

"You think?" Larry Drummond said.

"Hell, yeah, I think. And that Weaver Wisdom is some kind of a Ranger. Listen, everybody talks about Kellog's crazy past, but that big bastard was right there with him about every step of the way. Wisdom was just shot up by a fucking…Thompson…Machine…Gun in El Paso about nine months ago. He's back working! He's a manster! You don't want to tangle with him, or the Rangers, or that whole little army of redneck state troopers. They're mostly country boys, ex-military and hard core, patriots. That other motherfucker with Wisdom, that Acorn…you seen him. That look in his eye just now. He's a fucking Apache, or Comanche or something. Just…just leave them all be."

"I am not afraid of them," Bluto said, limping up to table. "They are all just flesh and blood."

"You hear all that?" Dunker asked.

"I did."

"Whatchu think? Truth? Dare? Or consequence?" Dunker asked.

"All of the above. But in the end, just flesh and blood. You all have to operate like the cartels. That's all," Bluto said and looked at everyone surrounding the table. "You kill everyone in your way. Soon, there is no one in your way anymore. Then you pay the rest off. And then you run everything. Texas and Arizona will fall first. Then like a wave, the other states going north."

Some of the other task force members wandered closer to hear Bluto. It was clear he was making a speech to all, but directed at Dunker.

"To conquer these states and the country," Bluto put a foot up on a chair with a grunt, and continued, "you kill all the problems. You kill four groups. Take notes amigos. You kill incorruptible politicians. You kill incorruptible police. You kill incorruptible re-porters. You kill the competition. You just kill and kill until someday they are all gone. You need to have the right people to do it. Like me, you know? And we have the perfect foundational operation for cover. The facilities and equipment. What we have here is the most perfect setup. We can never lose this. We must protect this. This man make it all happen."

And Bluto pointed at Dunker, then Bluto looked at everyone, made an eyebrow raising expression and grimace, then walked off. Others left the table also. They were all inside a brotherhood of a beautiful trap, greater than any mafia or cartel capture – once in? You can't get out.

"Greg," Dunker said, "Collier told me the other day that he collected a license plate. A car parked at Kellog's house."

"Yeah?" Greg Williams said.

"I ran it. came back to the famous Texican Monthly magazine crime reporter Gail Canchas."

"Yeah?"

"She has written big articles on Kellog," Greg said.

"I know," Dunker said. "She's a famous writer. Important. They are obviously friends. She is one of those incorruptible reporters Bluto talks about. We need to see what she is doing these days. Figure out a way to find out."

"Ten-four boss. Ahh…how?" Greg asked.

"Get creative. Have somebody follow her. Get me her phone number. Her home address. I am going to see my judge friend in Austin this week and get some wiretaps on some phones."

"She…that judge incorruptible?" Greg asked.

"No. Corruptible," Dunker answered with a smile.

"Ohhhh, she's the one…"

"She's the one," Dunker said.

Outside, Weaver and Acorn sat in their sedan and Weaver let out a painful grunt then a gasp.

"What?" Acorn said.

Weaver took a deep breath and said, "Two follow-up operations from that tommy gun in the last two months. Sometimes my left side seems disconnected from my right side."

Weaver lifted the top off of his 7-11 pecan-flavored coffee and sipped it.

Acorn nodded, not wanting to get deeper into

Weaver's personal recovery from being in that El Paso shooting. Acorn had visited Weaver in the hospital right after he was shot up.

"Dunker visit. We did that," Acorn said, "interest-ing."

"IN-triguing, Weaver said. "They know that we know. We know that they know," then he started to sing the old move theme song, "When we play our charades," as they drove off.

Chapter 21: The Last Stand of Chris Stands

Tanya Truman's head hung so low, chin on chest, melted into the office chair, that when she snorted awake, she felt like her neck had cracked in half.

"Ooo…oh…ohhh," she sighed as she lifted her head up inch by inch as if it was being cranked up by a crane. Deep sleep increases gravity! Her uniformed limbs were almost asleep atop the arms of the chair. She felt the numbness and worked her fingers to bring them back to life before lifting her arms.

It was 3:36 a.m. and she sat in the office chair she rolled up nightly to the third floor of the "Public Storage" warehouse hallway, a three-story building of indoor storage rooms. The outer walls of the whole structure was glass for the public to see the many doors of storage. Plus, visible was the life-size, cardboard cutout of a smiling waving, policeman lit up in the far corner of each floor. The corporation claimed that the one-dimensional, cardboard law enforcement figure psychologically dissuaded burglars. The remaining one story, larger warehouses spanned the fence-in area behind the building.

Every night at about 1 a.m. she rolled the lobby chair onto the elevator, up to the third floor, turned out the lights for the hallway. There she sat and tried to get some sleep. This nightshift job was her second job, third if you counted the Saturday morning gig at the counter of the Quick Stop. If someone arrived in the middle of the night as they rarely do, her pager would go off with the customer's press of the front door doorbell. Then she would claim when she got to the door,

"Sorry for the delay, I was making my rounds."

Her head finally upright, Tanya looked out over the nightlights of the city of Humble, Texas as her neck and arms came back to life.

"Whew! That was deep sleep," she said.

Then she spotted the odd commotion right down below her, way down below on the street, in the semi-lit driveway of the furniture manufacturing driveway across from her building.

"What the…?"

She stood up, stepped to the glass to see three police cars way down below, all parked haphazardly on the driveway. There was another car, a citizen's car, the driver's door wide open. Three uniformed officers, one white and two black were beating the holy hell out of a black man who was down and helpless on the asphalt. One stepped back to build momentum, ran up and kicked the man in the head like he was kicking a field goal in football.

She paced the hall not knowing what to do. She looked closely at the cars and could read the big police decals on the sides.

"Gulf TForce!" she said, "who in the hell is the Gulf TForce?"

She watched as the officers grew tired and winded from beating the man, who was now motionless. Was he dead? They stopped and conferred with each other, one so tired he rested against a car. Then they picked the limp man up and put him in the back seat of one of the police cars.

"You ain't even gonna call an ambulance? NO! Come on!" she yelled.

The police car with the man in the back drove off. One officer got into the citizen car, backed it up and parked it on the street. This area was somewhat of a business district and some people did park on the street, but most cars were parked in the parking lots. The officer locked the man's car up. He walked to his car, spoke with the remaining officer for a moment, and then they all drove away.

"I'll be damned," she said. "This is like Rodney King all over again. I sure hope they take that man to the hospital."

Tanya Truman pushed the office chair to the elevator knowing what she needed to do next. When down on the first floor she got behind her lobby desk and looked at the four TV screens. Public Storage filmed their premises as part of their security promise and contract. She rewound the entrance video tape and sure enough the entire beating was on film, even more violent and precise at ground level. She removed the tape and put in a new one.

"Ima gonna see about this," she muttered.

The next morning, once at home, she rounded up her three young kids for school. Her children slept alone in the apartment each night she worked. Once dropped off at school, Tanya went to bed.

The next afternoon, she woke up, made some coffee and put on the TV news. There was no report of any police beating, as well she'd guessed.

That night, reporting to work, she noticed the parked car was still there on the street. She was pretty sure that if the police were acting properly, the car would have been impounded.

She watched the 10 o'clock news on the little black and white camping, portable TV that the guards used to while away the boring lobby hours. She couldn't sleep upstairs that night after none of the TV news stations covered the incident. She used the firm's machines to make a copy of the tape of the beating.

At 3 a.m., she called the Humble Police and asked to speak with an officer.

"Is this an emergency?" the dispatcher asked.

"Maybe," she said, "If you think someone might be dying."

Two patrolmen arrived at the front doors.

"Last night I saw a police arrest. Over there. It wasn't any of y'all. Three cars that had 'Gulf TForce' on their sides. That a security guard company or something?" she said.

"No, ma'am, that is a drug task force that runs up and down our highways. Drug interdiction. We see them once in a while."

"Well, three of them beat the shit out of a black man right over there."

"Where?"

"I'll show ya."

The three left the building and they crossed the street.

"Right here," she said.

The officers shined their long baton-like flashlights over the driveway.

"This aaa…" one started to say and stooped over, "here's aaaa…this looks like a tooth."

"That's the man's car over there. They parked it over there and it's been there for 24 hours now. They left it." Tanya said.

"Did an ambulance come?" one asked as they walked over to the sedan.

"No. They hauled the man into the back seat of a police car, looking like he was dead, and they drove off."

They lit up the car with their lights. One asked for license plate registration on his handheld radio. Then he walked back to his squad car for more conversation with the dispatcher. The other officer returned to study the driveway. Tanya stood nearby with her arms folded, watching them.

The one on the radio back by the squad car returned to them.

"This car belongs to a Christopher Stands. He is reported missing. His mama reported him missing, yesterday afternoon," the officer said.

"Well…he dead. He was beaten to death," she said.

"That bad?"

"I know that bad."

"How would you describe it?"

"I'll show you and you describe it. I got it…on video," she said and pointed to a camera posted on the overhang above the lobby doors. She turned for the lobby.

The cops' eyebrows raised as they looked at each other. They followed her.

In the lobby, she ran the tape.

The cops were aghast.

"Yeah, yeah. He's dead," one said.

The other got on his handheld and asked for a detective, a patrol sergeant and crime scene person. In an hour, they arrived. All of them watched the tape.

"There's a dog going nuts in the back of the one car, look," the sergeant said.

"Drug dog. Yup," the detective said.

"They're all wearing gloves, look."

"Yeah," one officer said.

The crime scene man rested his arms on the tall office front counter and said aloud, mostly to himself, "Who are these guys?"

"We've seen their cars, Pablo. They run up and down the highways. Like the Highway Patrol, but they ain't."

"They ever arrest anybody here?" Pablo said.

"If around here, they take em over to Harris

County jail, not our city jail, I think. But they are all over the Gulf Coast. Up and down."

The shift patrol lieutenant pulled up outside.

"Lt. Brinkman's here," an officer said, "this is about to get serious."

Chapter 22: Pagers Explode

Beachum Airport...

"You did what?" Dunker demanded of three officers.

"We found Stands. Spotted his car. We knew, he knew that he owed us 9 grand and was hiding out from us," Reynolds Rebadoux said.

"We hunted for him like you told us and…" Officer Quinton Pressman said.

"I never said to beat him to death!" Dunker said.

"He got real pissy with us, boss. Disrespect. Mouthed off. Belligerent. We were not scaring him," Rebadoux said.

"Not at all, the son of a bitch. We roughed him up, just a bit," Officer Louis Etterman said, "then he fought us back. Fought back. Hard!"

"And we…," Rebadoux started.

"You beat him to death. You lost it, and you beat him to death," Dunker finished the sentence for him. He sat on a desk, groaned and rubbed his face.

"Pull the cars inside, in the back," he quietly told them.

"But nobody saw us," Etterman said.

"That you know of. You think. Where's the body?"

"Ah, in my back seat," Pressman said.

"Jeees-us. Okay. Okay, maybe that's best. We can get rid of bodies better than you guys can," Dunker said. "Get him in here. Is he stinking yet?"

"A little."

"A little. Zipper!" he yelled to another.

Zipper Miner jogged up.

"We got a body for a boat ride," Dunker said," when it gets dark, run it out damn near Florida and drop it."

"Ten four, boss," and zipper headed off for the body bag locker.

Dunker turned back to the three.

"And you left his car there?"

"We figured we needed to get out of there as fast as possible," Etterman said.

"Pull the cars in! Now!" Dunker repeated.

Bluto was nearby, listening in and chuckling. The three left the bay to pull the cars around back and inside.

"You should expect this," Bluto said as he walked up to Dunker, "everyone one of these guys you picked are confirmed fuck-ups. Fired losers. Some of them beat up people for no reason and got fired. Sooner or later their true nature comes out."

"I know. I… I thought…I think we can control them," Dunker said.

"HA!" Bluto said. "But you can't control stupid."

"Well, so far so good. No witnesses. But these guys have to learn you can't collect debts from dead people. Keep them alive and scared," Dunker said.

Three days later…

But, so far…not so good as Dunker thought. Actually, a worst nightmare. They were seen. And filmed! Three days later the film of the beating was on all the local Texas TV stations. The fourth day it was picked up nationwide. Worse, the enhanced TV studio film detailed the decals on the three police cars, "Gulf TForce."

Before the emergency meeting, four of the Dunker's men with penchants for technology made one more round searching the fields circling the airport for spies. Again, they failed to spot the latest super small cameras Nip had installed up in the trees. Once cleared, Dunker fired off all pagers for the 26 task force members. This called for another member meeting by lunchtime on the fourth day. Such a meeting would discreetly be held at the party house, but since that was burned down and not yet replaced, the hangar it was.

At noon, the three officers that beat Stands to death sat sheepishly in the front row, along with and beside the others, who had also already seen the video on television over and over again.

"What now boss?" Greg Williams asked.

"The interdiction guys have been seen in those cars up and down the highways for two years now. They've brought prisoners to the county jail in those cars. They have been seen all over east Texas, in and out of stores and restaurants from Brownsville to the Piney Woods. Bluto, can you change the decals on the cars?"

"Yes," Bluto said.

"We have four marked cars. Peters, you drove here in the fourth car?" Dunker asked.

Peter, glad he was off that work night of the beating said, "Yes."

"Good. It stays here for the change. We'll drive you home later. We'll change up the uniforms right now, from full black to white shirts and tan pants. We'll get them at K-Mart. Tan desert shoes. We have some old patches we didn't like back in the storeroom. We'll use them now."

"You, you…and you, you are now our new interdiction officers," he said pointing out a scattered three in the group. "Peter, you're still the fourth highway guy, you will be in these new uniforms and three of you (he pointed to beaters) will remain *in this hangar* in case the news or the law shows up. We can show them we don't use that black uniform anymore. And we need to be seen on the streets right away too, and with new decaled cars and uniforms.

"Charley, get their sizes and run to K-Mart."

Charley nodded.

"New look. Anybody asks? You don't know nothing about a beating, and if asked, say we changed our cars out weeks ago. It will be hard to prove otherwise. Right? Maybe some passing city police cars saw you all lately and waved, but how can they swear what day it was, really? We'll say…we all say we changed the car logos weeks ago and these beaters on TV? These ahh…these guys and those cars were police imposters, shaking down drug dealers in our name. Imposters."

"THREE police imposters? Three in full uniforms? Three cars? Who buys and outfits three imposter cars and officers?" one said.

"Ahhh well, rich drug gangs that's who!" Dunker said. "We have to say this. We have no choice. I will draft up something that says we heard rumors a while back that some cartel gang was going to copy us to raid and kill their competitors. And remember, this Christopher Stands guy has two drug dealing convictions on his record. The media has to find that out and report that soon, or later. Yeah, and when we heard that intel, we decided to change our look. A few weeks back. Got it?"

"Hmmm, that might work. It might," Greg Williams said.

"What else can we say? If the media finds out who we are, and they will, where we are, we will be flooded. And we can expect a visit any day, hell, any minute now really from…from Humble PD or Harris County, or the State even, yet again. The Rangers have already been here. Police brutality like this might… might even draw in the FBI. DAMN! Now that the state police knows where we are, our address will get around fast."

"Can we move? Should we?" one asked.

"Barbecue this place? We can move, yeah, but we shouldn't, couldn't burn the whole hangar down of this airport. Can't. The fire will be seen immediately. Fire trucks…no. It'll look like arson and a cover-up. But we could move, yes."

"Prints, boss. Our prints are everywhere in here," one said.

"Yeah, but if we move everything out," another said, "what's left? It's just walls, doors and windows. We can Mister Clean, power spray wash all that shit off."

"Let me think about it." Dunker said in a depressed sigh, "but, if we leave, there goes our chopper plans. We really need this hangar in an airport for the chopper. Damn. But…well…let me think about it. If anyone has any ideas? Like where we might move? Fast? Let me know, ASAP."

The group nodded.

"And YOU three geniuses," Dunkers said to the trouble-making trio, "you stay in here for several days. Like prisoners. Jeez! I have watched the news video a hundred times. It's a bit blurry and maybe you can't be identified, but we can't risk it. Your interdiction days are over. You'll be doing something else around here."

The three hung their heads in shame.

"Zip, the body gone?" Dunker asked.

"Out with the Gulf fishes, boss," Zip said.

"Good. Having no dead body delays their case. Fucks up their strategies and charges. It ain't murder yet. Just a beating without a body. Okay! You all are dismissed. Collectors kept collecting. The rest, go home. No work. Lay low. Watch your pagers. Somebody drive Peter home."

Most of them left. Bluto and Greg Williams approached Dunker.

"I will hide the cars with these decals in case the law shows up, until I change them out. I know where I can get new decals quietly made," Bluto said, "maybe, maybe it will say…it will look like, 'Highway Interdiction' with a state seal?"

"Yeah, that sounds good, Bluto. Good. I am thinking about moving. It will confound everyone, slow things down."

"Middle of the night move?" Greg asked.

"Maybe, yeah," Dunker said.

"What about Kellog?" Greg asked, "nobody's following him now since he shot Collier."

"Hmmm, yeah. Put Rebadoux on Kellog then. Get him up to speed with what Collier found out. We still have Jerome on the reporter, Gail Canchas?"

"We do," Greg said, "She's burning up the roads back and forth to Austin state capital."

"This will become a big article on the task forces I'll just bet. In Texican Monthly," Dunker said, "and on us. She'll wind up out here at some point asking questions. If no one knew where we were, we'd been better off. It all went downhill when Kellog found us."

"She has a webpage too, with articles on it, and she's already written something about the task forces and the Texas congressman that wants to cancel us all out."

"She's got a blog?" Dunker asked.

"What's a…blog?" Bluto asked.

"It's a new thing on the internet," Greg said, "People write on their webpages now like…like opinion columns in a newspaper. She's famous. I'll bet a lot of people read it."

"Just kill her," Bluto said, matter of fact. He shrugged his shoulders.

Dunker and Greg exchanged glances.

"Kill Kellog too," Bluto added, "Collier was right in trying to kill him the other night. An unsolved murder is an unsolved murder. The police get distracted and waste resources. It just makes problems…go away. One by one."

"Ahhh…" Dunker started to say…

"I'll do it. You two rearrange the deck chairs on the Titanic here. Change clothes and re-arrange people around. I'll get the decals right now. So, yeah, then I can take these two problems out. The Rangers too, if we need to."

"The…sinking…ship," Dunker mumbled. "Ooookay. Okay go ahead. But you and me need to buy that chopper first. This weekend."

Bluto made a facial expression, possibly one of impatience, that the two could not fully read as he walked off with that odd gait.

"Kill them? You think?" Greg said.

"I think. He's always been right so far," Dunker said.

"How in the world did you find Bluto anyway?" Greg asked.

"You do NOT want to know," Dunker said.

State police pagers exploded too when the morning news of the Chris Stands beating ran on Houston area television. Most of the message receivers were already at the DPS headquarters. They got together in the DPS narcotics office bay with Nip - the first to see the news and reach out.

"That's them," Manny said, "Those are their cars."

Kellog, Weaver, Acorn and Manny watched the film clip in a state of amazement, now a video tape Nip made of the TV broadcast.

"We have to tell Humble PD we know where they are," Weaver said.

They agreed.

"There's no body yet," Kellog said. "This poor bastard will wind up in a cement suit in the middle of the Gulf. Or the Atlantic."

"We'll watch all the films from the cameras at the airport we hid out there," Manny said. "It's McDugle's and Clipton's job to watch them and they are in the electronics room right now. The Task Force canine guys have been walking the fields all the way around the airport, hunting for surveillance teams or cameras. Like a dog will smell that out? They do not know to look up in the trees for our small camo cameras we hid."

"Good job, Manny," Weaver said.

"And, some of my guys followed some more of the task force members home this last week," Manny continued. "In the middle of the night, our guys crawl up and fingerprint the driver's car doors and trunks, you know where hands close the doors and trunks. We got lucky with some vehicles. We got some really good sets of fingerprints and even full palm prints. So far we were able to find matches for three of them."

"Yeah? What you find?" Acorn said.

"Three fired cops, brutality in Colorado Springs. Taking bribes in Chicago. One guy from Charleston, West Virginia was making traffic stops on women and trying to trade sex for traffic tickets."

"All out of state," Weaver said. "I am going to call the chief, Delarenzo at Humble PD They need to know the address of the task force right away."

"The proverbial feces is a hittin the manifesting fan," Nip said.

Chapter 23: The Killing Fair

Alexandria, Virginia…

The limo driver let Dunker, Bluto and their newest employee out in front of the Bellatron Convention Center. Dunker paid the driver, and the simple hand maneuvers involved caused him to adjust his expensive cufflinks yet again. All three men were decked out in expensive, yet classic suits. They had to present the roles of top dollar military and enforcement officials that were able to purchase anything from truckloads of 9mm bullets to small nukes at the annual Land-Sea-Air Weapons Fair.

The three melted into the arriving throngs of other well-dressed dignitaries of middle to late, aged men and women all in a muti-country, variety of uniforms and suits. All were bound to attend the demonstrations, lectures and interactions with salespeople and their array of militaria, dutifully posted in front of booths and roped off areas of vehicles, aircraft, guns and missiles.

All this would be entertaining to Cinnamon Dunker, but he was really only in the market for a big helicopter, big enough to carry cargo and people on long trips, ranging from Northern Mexico to South Carolina, with refueling pit stops. The manning and locations of these pit stops he'd worry about later.

Their new "friend" following them around was one Armond Pitchner, a former commercial airline pilot fired for his cocaine habit. Pitchner's coke jones got so bad he was scoring the powder in every city he flew to and from anyone he could find that sold dope. He eventually got reckless and on one hot Sunday night in Nashville, TN, he was foiled by an undercover DEA

agent. He was arrested and charged, and Delta quickly
fired him within one week. Shamed and divorced,
Pitchner was reduced to teaching fixed wing aircraft
flying lessons at a small Phoenix, AZ., Regional private airport.

One afternoon just a month earlier, Cinnamon
Dunker walked into that airport, winked and smiled at
him, and sat at the flight school's only desk.

"Are you interested in flying lessons?" Pitchner
asked while sitting down on the employee side of the
lobby furniture.

Dunker just smiled.

"For yourself or for a relative, perhaps?" Pitchner
continued.

"You fly helicopters," Dunker said.

"Ah, yes I do, sir," Pitchner said, "but I can't teach
that here. We don't have any choppers here. How do
you know…"

"We got, I will get choppers," Dunker said.

Dunker reached into his suede sports jacket
pocket, pulled out a brown engraved wallet, opened it
and tossed it on the desk blotter before Pitchner. The
gold badge was facing up.

"Texas Gulf Coast Drug Task Force. PO-lice,"
Dunker said, leaning in for the read. "There's way
more to the story than just that," Dunker said. "Right
now, I need a chopper pilot. The money? It's spectac-
ular."

"You don't know about me, Mr. Gold Badge."

"Oh, I know everything about you, Mr. Chopper."
Pitchner just stared at him.

"Your war record with various choppers. Your airline career. Your demise. Everything. It will all come
into play if you come to work for us. For me. This
ain't no ordinary operation I ramrod."

So, one month later, Pitchner was walking into arms dealer heaven, in a dark grey Armani suit with Dunker and the mysterious, Hispanic expert they just called Bluto.

Both outside and inside, the enormous convention center was teeming with heavily armed soldier-types in contractor outfits. There was even a jeep brandishing a mounted .50 caliber machine gun about every 50 yards on the parking lots. Snipers were on the rooftops studying the attendees with binoculars.

Inside the vast lobby, Bluto led the way to a series of security booths right in front of the many inner sanctum, closed doors. He spoke in Spanish with some men checking IDs. A man handed them papers and another door man scrutinized the trio, asked a few questions, and gave them IDs to hang around their necks. One requirement to get in was pre-proof from a bank that every guest entity had a $250,000 booty minimum on hand and available. This scrutinizing was underway at the nine other checkpoints to the right and left of them. Once approved they got to step inside the doors and onto the showroom floor.

There were numerous sections of collections to peruse. Missiles. Tanks. Arms. Humvees. Trucks, Satellites….and what they were looking for…choppers were in the far right sector. Dunker's eyebrows shot up and he smiled. They exchanged glances and Dunker and Pitchner started for the helicopter group. Bluto walked instead to a concession stand and purchased some black coffee. He'd seen, been around and used all this stuff before and wasn't so impressed. For him, it was all like a used car lot.

Dunker wanted one that didn't look too, too military. One that could-would pass somewhat as a civilian chopper if painted appropriately, as well as a police chopper. And there his eyes affixed upon the three Si-korsky SH-3 choppers. The Sea King. He read the sign beside them.

"The Sikorsky SH-3 Sea King is an American heli-copter built by Sikorsky. It was used by the U.S. Navy since 1961 for finding and destroying submarines, search and rescue, and utility."

Dunker liked the words "search, rescue, utility… and destroy."

"Can we help you sir?" A beautiful woman asked while approaching them.

"Yes, I think you can," Dunker said.

Chapter 24: The Peeling of the Shoes

Gail Canchas was a cheat. Married, she cheated with Jack. He's the only one, at least as far as he knew. They had an on-again, off-again, rather easy-going affair, sometimes years apart, and she and he loved it when their paths crossed on criminal cases. She had the excuse to work with him, or at times, was just in nearby Houston and away from her home in Austin.

Jack was drawn to her when she was nearby, but he knew there was no future with her. It seemed when he was younger, he was always a sucker, even a target of married women. He'd never married. Jack had a long affair with a rich woman named Linda many years ago who some of his friends say, especially the religious Weaver Wisdom, he wasted away all his "prime years."

Those are the years when men usually get married, have kids and raise them. Linda did all that with someone else. Time after time, her husband and kids had the priority, often leaving Jack as an outcast, second-stringer, feeling like a tenth-stringer. He eventually realized this empty fate when Linda had to ignore him. Such an affair was not a fully lesson learned, however, one not deeply enough because a few other married women came along "detaining him" even further. And one such detainer was the saucy, smiling, smart reporter, Gail Canchas.

He'd always enjoyed their banter, and at 60-something Gail still was attractive enough, a "looker," (he was no spring chicken either, she reminded him) and any little sign of age was overcome by her personality, charm and spirit. He thought her "effervescent." She could really burrow down on a subject. In short, Jack would rather have her around than not. And that's where all that stood, off and on, through the recent years.

She drove to Jack's West Forge home yet again to discuss the Skelton beating, this time in her husband's car. She'd left her Mercedes at their Austin home, as her car had a series of dashboard alert lights suddenly trigger that morning. She left her car in the driveway so their mechanic could come in by the next morning to check out the light show. Her husband told her to take his car because he planned on staying in for the whole night and watch war movies anyway. She told him her hot new case and article meant an overnight stay in Houston.

Gail had Jack's second garage door opener. She circled Jack's once, wide-eyed and searching for any tail or surveillance. She opened the three-car garage and parked inside. She had his house key and knew all his alarm, security codes. She carried her briefcase inside and paged him that she was there.

Jack arrived home and the kitchen table banter began, then came the…burrowing down.

"You know honey, in my stories, I always have a deep, personal angle," she said.

"Yeah."

"A personal story attached to the crime to make people feel what happened, and maybe this Skelton is one I could use as a skeleton."

"That, or the dead detective," Jack said. "That might be a better true crime angle?"

"Yeeees. You're right. The dead detective is terrible. So is this Rhoades/ story. And the folks like to read and get all upset and excited about someone being beaten by police."

"Yeah," Jack agreed.

"People don't riot when cops are killed. They riot

when cops beat up people."

"This is true," Jack said. "Probably by the time you write this and have a publishing deadline for your magazine, this whole case will have blow up like a bomb. You may as well start writing it. Otherwise, if it doesn't blow, these stories will interfere, and…and you know, tip off the case."

"I understand."

They wound up in the living room. Gail opened the top buttons on her blouse, sighed and plopped down on the couch, holding her glass of whiskey. She used her right foot to peel off her left shoe, then vice-versa, and Jack knew where this night was headed.

Chapter 25: The Bad News

Beachum Airport…

Once back from Virginia, the chopper on order, Bluto requisitioned Jerome, the team member assigned to watch Gail Conchas. Just after midnight, Bluto sat in the passenger seat of a Honda and smiled big at Jerome. Bluto was dressed in black head to toe. Black shoes, pants and shirt. His long hair was perennially, perfectly dyed black, along with his thick eyebrows. He grinned at Jerome because he seemed to be a bit excited. He had a small black bag with him, no doubt a pistol and ammo. He set it on the floorboard beside his feet.

"Vamanos," he said, and Jerome pulled out of the hangar. He touched the electric button and the one, open hangar door closed behind them.

They were off to Austin, about a three-hour drive northwest. Off to the Gail Conchas home. To kill her. Jerome was running back and forth a lot, ordered to keep tabs on the writer and he knew the way well.

As usual, Bluto was very chatty along the way, but usually about nothing in particular. But Jerome was dying to ask him a bunch of questions.

"How did you and Chief Dunker meet?" Jerome asked.

"Working," Bluto said and got quiet, then he continued as if to give in to explaining a bit about his past,

"I am from Puerto Rico. The Puerto Rico Police Bureau, like the state police. First patrol. Detective. Puerto Rico eventually formed a Narco-Terrorism Task Force after a huge grant from Washington. Puerto Rico is not a state…

"It's not? I didn't know that," Jerome said.

Bluto just looked at him funny and continued. "It's not a state, but the Federal Government has all kinds of narco money to spread around and we got some. They developed a "Strong Hand On Crime" program. The Feds picked me to be on it. Very military, they call it quasi-military. We got trained. We all went through special forces training. We kicked ass."

"Wow," Jerome said.

"We worked all over the Caribbean and the US coastlines. The Gulf of Mexico too. I met Cinnamon when he was a captain in Harris County. When I first laid eyes upon him, I knew he was deliciously corrupt."

"You did? How?"

"The way he looked at me and my uniform. Cinnamon is always reaching out. Big. Big ideas. He will not stay small. Cannot stay small. He knew I knew everything about the Caribbean and smuggling and grant money. We started to talk about the weaknesses of law enforcement and the success of the international drug trade. The law is stupid and complicated and cannot win. Crime is ruthless and lawless. He investigated my reputation and said he found out I was…ruthless." Jerome nodded.

"But we both have friends in Washington and these friends…hey… let's change that radio station to some country music, eh?" Bluto said, reaching over to the dial, and with that, it ended the history lesson.

By 3 a.m. they slowly drove past the Conchas house, an expansive place in a lofty neighborhood of large lots and lofty trees.

"Okay, now see, there's her car in the driveway," Jerome said. The Mercedes.

"Okay. Park over there," Bluto said.

They didn't care if a patrol car drove by and
stopped at this point, as they both had state-wide,
Texas police identification and could claim they were
on a task force, secret stakeout. That is, up until the
killing started.

Bluto pulled a pair of thin black gloves, and a black
pistol and magazines from the bag.

"You gonna use a silencer?"

"No. Because tonight I want to make this look like
a la familia suicide. Family murder-suicide. Who kills
their wife and themself with a silenced gun?"

"Yeah," Jerome said, "who?"

Bluto left the Honda and walked toward the
Conchas house. He crossed the street and stepped into
the driveway, searching for cameras and yard signs for
alarms. None. A few descending cement steps revealed
a basement back door. He pulled a small flashlight
from his pocket and studied the back door. He took out
a lock pick kit and within a minute opened the door,
listening for any alarms and looked for an alarm pad of
numbers on the wall nearby. None.

He crossed the basement room, appointed like a
man-cave. The electric gadgets, stereo and TV even
with the lights off, the equipment had enough red and
white lights to reveal the surroundings. With his gun in
his hand, he climbed the stairs. On the first floor he
stopped and looked around. More ambient light from
the streetlights outside illuminated the living room and
kitchen well enough to for him to see.

He moved for the second story stairs, a stairwell
that turned on a landing half-way up, the second half at
the turn was covered by a wall and he couldn't see
that upper second half. Fearing creaks, he stealthily
walked up until the stairs and made a sharp left turn...

But a figure of a man in his underwear stood on the

stairwell hallway a few steps up ahead, with a long wooden spear in his hands! He growled and lunged at Bluto and Bluto fell back down and hard against the wall. He landed at the turn of the stairwell. He lifted the pistol and shot the man twice in the chest. The half-naked man fell back, in a babbling shock. Bluto too was stunned by his crash. The man laid on stairs, gasping and almost still. Bluto raised the gun and from his lower angle, aimed at the man's protruding chin and the jawbone the prone figure above him. He fired again, driving a bullet into the bottom of the face and up through the head.

Bluto ignored him and the spear, and dashed up the stairs right past him and ran through the whole second story, searching every corner, every closet and under every bed, looking for her.

"Damn," he murmured. "No Gail Conchas."

He walked down the stairs, stepped over the dead man. The bullet had not exited the top of the skull. He lit up the weapon with his flashlight. It was indeed an ornate wooden spear from who knows where. A souvenir from a vacation? He chuckled at it, chuckled at the idea that from all the knives, bullets, hand grenades and bombs he'd survived, he was almost killed by a man in his underwear…with a spear.

He left the house by the basement back door, leaving it ajar to suggest a burglary gone bad, and walked to the car. He got in.

"Get her?" Jerome asked. "I heard three muffled gunshot way out here."

"No. Let's go. She wasn't home."

"Then who…," Jerome said, starting the Honda and slowly pulling off.

"I killed her husband I think," Bluto said, studying the neighboring houses to see if any lights were turned on or turning on, or if any people looked out their windows.

"He must have heard me come in, somehow."

"Man! But that is her car! I..." Jerome said.

"Well, she wasn't home, Jerome. I picked the wrong night. It will look like a burglar killed him. We'll have to get her another way. Another time. I'll just go for Kellog with Rebedoux in a couple of days."

Gail Conchas left Jack's house the next morning in her husband's truck. She tried to call Ernesto to find out about her car repairs. But no answer at their house, no answer on his cellphone. She called his office work phone at the Texas Department of Agriculture. Again. No answer. She still had something to investigate for another article in Galveston and decided she would try reaching him again later.

Later and at her destination address in Galveston, she tried all three phones again. Nothing. Then she called Janice, her husband's secretary.

"Gail, he has not showed up here, and he didn't call in," the secretary said.

"I have his truck. I'm in Galveston. And my car broke down at home. He said he would call a taxi to get to work," she said.

"Well, he's not here. He's an hour late."

"Probably something odd..."

"Do you have anyone that can go by the house?" Janice asked.

"I do. I do, Janice. I will call somebody."

She called one of the neighbors that had a key and asked her to check on the house and her husband...

Jack showed up at DPS headquarters, did some paperwork and then met with Manny, Weaver and Acorn in their CID bay.

"Yesterday, when the news hit the TV about the beating, that afternoon," Manny said, "a couple of their goons searched the fields for us again. They didn't find the cameras. Then ALL of them. Like the whole task force showed up at the hangar. Like 25 or so that McDugle could count. He saw them all drive up and go inside."

"Emergency meeting," Acorn said.

"I think so," Weaver said.

Jack's cellphone sounded in his pocket with a ring-tone of Garth Brooks' song, "The Dance." It was his attached melody to Gail's calls. A bad feeling came over him. He grimaced and struggled to pull the phone from his leather jacket pocket. He stepped back a bit and looked at it. It indeed was Gail. Something must be up, he thought. He stepped far away from the guys.

"Hello. Gail?" he said.

"JaaaaAAAAAAK! Jack! Jack...Jack..."

And then...he heard the really bad news.

Chapter 26: Gail

Jack closed his flip phone. He walked back to the group. Nip from Narcotics had joined in.

"Somebody killed Gail Conchas' husband last night," he said, "in their house. She wasn't home."

Weaver's head dropped and he stared at Jack over the top of his glasses.

"Like a burglar. A home invader, the police told her. They found him dead on the stairs, a big spear next to him they bought in New Zealand while on vacation. He must have heard something and…"

"A spear-spear?" Nip said, "Don't he have a pistola?"

"Apparently not," Jack said. "He's…he's kind of a liberal."

"Well, we know who did that," Acorn said.

"Probably. Could be. They have to be tailing all of us. I see Gail now and…and then…"

Weaver almost grunted at that, but held it.

"And they must have picked up a tail on her. She's a threat what with her reporting. I warned her," Jack said, knowing what all of Weaver's expressions meant. "I reckon I have to go see her. See the Austin detectives."

"Hold on Kemosabe, I'll go with you," Acorn said "you were first, and now you're next up again, you know. You need some back up."

"Yeah, you're right," Jack said.

Acorn met Gail last winter in Laredo when he and Jack were hunting the madman John Phillip Muzak. It made sense for him to go along. He also knew about his and Gail's on-and-off again "relationship."

"Yeah, be careful what you tell Austin PD," Weaver said, "they might march over here and blow up what we got working."

Jack nodded and said, "I think this thing gonna blow up real quick anyway. Well Chief, let's go."

He and Acorn snatched up some things and left for Austin.

"Where are you, honey?" Jack asked Gail on the phone, as they were entering the Austin city limits, with Acorn at the wheel. Jack mostly listened to her talk. Then finally he told Acorn,

"She's at her sister's house," Jack said. "I know where that is."

An hour later, her sister Helena answered the door.

"Hi Jack," she said solemnly.

He introduced Acorn.

Gail appeared in the living room in a robe wrapped over pajamas. She walked up. Jack hugged her. Long.

"Hi, Ray," she said to Acorn over Jack's shoulder.

"Hi Gail. I'm so sorry."

She took Jack by the hand and walked off to a formal dining room.

Acorn and Helena knew to stay back, and the sister guided the Ranger into the kitchen.

Gail started to cry. They pushed two chairs close together. She held his closest arm.

"They did it, huh?" She asked.

"I reckon," Jack said. "I'm sorry I got you in this."

"I would have been mad at you if you hadn't. This is big. Boy, I would have been mad at you if you held it from me. Don't you dare think that."

She turned a small kitchen hand towel over in her right hand, every few seconds dabbing her eyes with it.

"I...you know...I," she said, "I was not there. I was

with you. I…"

"If you were home, there too, honey, they would have killed you too. You are lucky you weren't home. Don't think twice about that. About us. You can't think that."

"Lucky. Yes, lucky. My car was in the driveway. You know. Broke down. They thought I…"

"Uh-huh."

"And they shot him in the chest and through the jaw, up in the head."

"He must have been above them on the stairs," Jack said.

"They wouldn't let me in my house. I saw the pictures. Oh, my poor Ernesto. He was in his underwear. Dead on the stairs in his boxer shorts. All these years, these crimes I've covered, and now it comes back onto me. Into me," she said, tapping her chest.

Jack leaned over and hugged her.

"I have to tell the Austin cops. Tell them what we know. Whose got the case here, do you know?" He said.

"Lee Trang. Homicide. Captain Gezealy knows I know Trang from other cases. Trang's a good man."

"Good. I don't know him, but we'll get in touch right away," Jack said and leaned away to shout," Chief! Lee Trang, Homicide."

"Got it, Kemo," Acorn said.

"We'll meet him right away. Are you staying here with Helena?"

"Yes. I will never go back. I will never go back in my house," she said.

"Well, okay, I guess. I get it."

"It's haunted now."

"I…okay, we'll see."

He hung his closest arm around her.

"This our fault, isn't it?" she asked. "What we do made this happen?"

Jack's eyes widened and he sucked in a real, big breath. He couldn't answer that one.

Chapter 27: Assault on Fort Kellog

DPS Headquarters, Houston…

"I can stay in your house," Acorn said, "sleep downstairs on the couch. They got me in a Motel 6 for now. You probably have better cable TV."

"Thanks, Chief, but no," Jack said.

Weaver knew why Jack wanted to be alone. Whatever happens in Jack's house, stays in Jack's house. He had plans. There can be no witnesses.

"Some guys tried to kill me in my house years ago and I have the best alarm system money can buy," Jack told Acorn. "The main frame of it all can be moved, rolled around and plugged into a box in the guest bedroom upstairs too. I'll sleep in there, and… and see what happens."

Weaver just shook his head. he knew what Jack had in mind.

Acorn started to understand the plot.

Jack's House, West Forge, TX…

Detective Paul Massaport was killed by one man with an odd, slight limp, probably the man Jack saw in the airport hangar. In a perfect world this damn hitman, killer would sneak in to kill Jack too. Oh, how Jack dreamed of this perfect situation. He'd made some other serious home invasion plans too, other than adding the moving the rolling alarm system.

That night, yes, he did tow the little rack of alarm controls and related small black and white TVs into the upstairs guest room.

In the big master bedroom, he piled up pillows and blankets to make it look like he was asleep in the bed. He would leave a dim night light on in there and the door wide open to fool any surprise "quests." He also sprayed the guest bedroom door hinges with WD-40 to hide any potential squeaks. He tested the wooden floor in the spare room, and the floor of the short distance in the hallway, walking and shifting his weight leg to leg, listening for creaks. None.

He propped a shotgun up against the guest room wall, though he favored a pistol for these close quarters. He placed a second .45 semi-auto handgun atop the guest dresser. He would sleep on the floor in the guest room, fully dressed but in socks, no shoes. He'd wear a gun belt, one much like his patrolman's rig. The trap was set for killers or a solo killer.

Would the killer creep straight to the master bedroom? Should the killer check the two guest rooms on his way down the hall to master bedroom, Jack would be ready for that too, his .45 in hand. He covered this guest bedroom window with a blanket, so as to create total darkness. Peeking into the room and seeing anything was nearly impossible without a flashlight, and by then, it would be too late for the killer.

With the potential bedroom trap set. He knew he still had to worry about an outdoor ambush, coming out of his house and going into his garage, and back. His travels. Otherwise, would a killer dare shoot him on the DPS parking lot? Not impossible. He would completely avoid the PAL gym for about a week, doing workouts at the DPS gym, which was more than adequate, but he had a personal commitment to the boxing classes, keeping him at the PAL gym.

Two busy days passed. Then the third night at three a.m. a back door silent alarm started softly buzzing on the alarm rack. Jack's eyes snapped open. He sat up and turned off the buzzer. That alarm had never gone off in years. This had to be the real deal. Then on the TV screen covering the kitchen, he saw a single man.

The man passed through the kitchen. Jack saw…he had a limp. No one else followed. He turned the sets off. Pitch darkness.

His two upstairs guest bedroom doors were purposely left open only a few inches. He could see the hall from the master bedroom. He stood, .45 in hand. He waited. He waited. He heard just a slight cloth-rubbing sound. Ever so slight. An arm on the wall of the stairs?

Jack waited. Then through the slim opening of the guest bedroom door, a dark figure limped by. Then by way of the dim master bedroom night light, Jack watched the invader walk to the main bedroom. Jack followed, gun up and stepped to the big room and saw the man in black by his bed, head down looking at it.

Jack's pistol was up in a single hand. He flicked on the light startling the intruder, while Jack slipped three-quarters back out in the hall. Most of Jack's body was now covered, and only his gun and face were exposed in the door frame.

"Drop it," Jack said solemnly.

The man turned. It was the mysterious man with the limp from the hanger. The man was a bit shocked, but then he smiled. He tossed his silenced pistol on the bed.

"Far enough? He asked.

"No, but it'll do."

Jack stepped into full view.

"Weeell, you caught me!" he said. "You caught me, but you know, all you got me on a burglary. That's all. By noon, tomorrow I'll be out on bail."

Jack just stared at him.

Still smiling, Bluto put his hands together in front

of him, suggesting he be handcuffed up front, which Jack knew "hands-out-front" was an invitation to eventually by choked by him, somehow, if the chance arose. Desperate cops in desperate situations took this "hands front" bait.

"Well, Johnny Lawman? Let's go then. Arrest me," Bluto said as he raised his hands up high and together, "do your handcuffing thing."

Jack said quietly, "No. This is my thing."

And Jack shot him in the clavicle, above any possible bullet proof vest height. The bullet - the cracking roar of it - the flash, encompassed the room like a small bomb. Then it was gone. Quiet. Just a slight smell.

Bluto fell back, making a wet gagging, gurgling sound. He fell back on Jack's nightstand, then slid off to the floor.

Jack holstered his gun, pulled the cuffs off his belt and rushed the man, flipping him almost over. Bluto was shaking just a bit of gasping, sounds from his mouth. Jack cuffed him. He patted him down while Bluto went limp and died. Pockets were empty. He was indeed wearing a bullet proof vest under his black shirt. Jack picked up the pistol on the bed and shoved it in his belt.

Next? Next the car, The killer got there somehow. He raced down the stairs and stepped out onto the front porch, slipping off to the side of it. Looking. Searching. Down the street, south, sat a strange car to the neighborhood, an Oldsmobile.

Jack dropped off the front porch and headed south across and through his and other neighbors' plush, landscaped yards, hugging their porches and house fronts.

When adjacent to the Olds, he saw a man in the

driver's seat. Jack made for the Olds, fast, as he pulled his pistol. Jack shot the back, side window into the empty back seat. Such a bang was like a stun grenade and man jolted in the front seat as though he was struck by lightning. His arms flew up and jaw dropped as Jack yanked open the door and hauled him out. "OUT!" he ordered.

With the driver, still shocked from the "stun gun-shot," Jack belted him across the face with the .45. Pistol-whipped, the man fell to the street.

"You pull out anything and you're dead right there!" Jack growled. "Hands behind your back!"

The man obliged. Jack pulled his second pair of cuffs from his old patrol gun belt and cuffed the driver. He shut the door, stood him up and shoved him toward his house.

"So, you two thought you were gonna kill me tonight, huh?"

"Well…aaa…I…ahhh."

A few nearby house lights turned on. Jack got the driver inside his house, into the living room and shoved him into a chair.

"Listen to me. You…you're now the face of everything. Everything. Every murder. Every crime. Everything Dunker's been doing. You are now the face of it all. Everything that happens from this point on is on you. Good or bad. It's all on you."

"You have nothing on me…I…"

"That's what that dead motherfucker said upstairs. If you are that worthless to me too? I'll kill you too. I'll just kill you right now."

"You…you can't…I am handcuffed. You can't shoot a handcuffed man!"

"Those come right off after I kill ya," Jack said within a growl.

"Ooohh I see, you think this is some kind of official police investigation." Jack said and grabbed him his jacket collar with his two hands and got inches from his face.

"You think I'm some pussy boy cop that plays by all the stupid rules that let's punks like you get away with murder? I'll shove you in my woodchipper out back, legs first, you piece of shit. Who sent you here?"

The man stared at him and Kellog's face looked like an angry devil's. The driver felt all the wind leave his chest. His head hung low.

"Yeah, well…Dunker did. Well, Dunker knows. Bluto planned it."

"Bluto. That's whose dead upstairs? Bluto?"

"Bluto! Yes! He's a narco-counter terrorist."

"He's now just a narco-terrorist. No counter nothing. He kill that detective in the church two months ago?

"Ahhh…"

"Did he?" Jack said and shook the man's torso with his left hand.

Yeah."

"He kill that man in Austin in his house the other night?"

"Yeah. The man with the spear? Yeah."

"You with him?"

"No. No. Jerome was with him. I was put on you."

"Put? On. Me? What? To follow me?"

"Yeah, yeah, that's all I did. I haven't killed anyone. Bluto does all the wet work. Most…most of it."

"What's your name?" Jack asked.

"Rubea…"

"Your real name," Jack said. "I know how you fuckers are."

"Charles Popperdale."

"Popperdale. What agency you get booted out of?"

"New Orleans."

"And Dunker recruited you."

"More or less," the man said.

"What you do in New Orleans?"

"I screwed up. Property room, I was stealing shit. Drugs. Stuff. Selling it off."

Jack let go of him and stood back.

"How bad is the task force?"

"Half the stuff we do is legit," The man said, "cover for us. The other half? Not. Like a cartel. Cartels and the Mafia are our models."

Charles, we are going to have a looong talk," Jack said.

Jack stepped farther back, and he pulled his flip phone from his pocket. He first called Weaver Wisdom.

"Got the shooter. He's dead. I got a live one. The driver," was all Jack said.

"In route." Those two words were all Weaver said.

Then Jack tapped out a very old number he'd memorized but hadn't called in almost three years.

"Hello?" said a groggy West Forge PD police chief "Shrewdy" Collins.

"Jack Kellog. Sorry to wake you, Chief."

"Ja…Kell…what…"

"Chief. Call out the troops. I got a dead man in my bedroom and his accomplice alive in my living room. These men tried to kill me in my house tonight."

"Two…kill…your house! Oh no, not again!"

Patrol officers and an ambulance showed up. The EMTs responding was just routine. Most of the responding midnight shift officers and even the EMTs knew Jack from the old days. Most of them knew to stand outside and not trample through a crime scene, but the crime scene man, jack's old friend, "Rightaway" Attaway was already upstairs probably taking pictures, even though a state team was in route to do so. Rightaway knew where not to trample. The shift sergeant, Al Crayon did enter the house. No doubt the command staff would soon show up and stomp all over the place.

"Guy upstairs is deader than hell. Let him be," Jack told the EMTs. "This guy's a little bruised. Me? I'm perfectly fine."

They approached the cuffed suspect, and started looking him over and asking questions.

"You alright Jumpin?" Patrol Sgt. Crayon asked.

"Yeah, fine. I was waiting for them to come in and get me. It was inevitable."

"I hate to say it, but, it…it seems like old times, huh? This all from the same group as the guy who shot at you on main street last week?"

"Seems like. Yeah."

"Rangers gonna work this one too?"

"Yeah, they have to. State shit. Weaver Wisdom is in route."

West Forge CID Captain Carterez, Jack's last CID boss before being fired, walked in through the open front door of the house. They did not get along.

"Kellog," Carterez said.

"Cappem," Jack said to his once captain. "You're still here. I thought you'd be a police chief by now. Maybe even here."

"What happened?" Carterez asked.

"Guy upstairs tried to kill me. Shoot me in bed, I was sleeping in another room," Jack pointed to the shooter's gun stuck in his beltline. "He had this. Silenced. I shot him first. This idiot over here is his

driver. He's under my arrest and I'll bring him in, book
him in the county jail, but first…a pit-stop at DPS for
an interrogation."

"He looks busted up," Caterez said, eyeing the man
seated in the chair.

"Yeah, we had us a little fight on the street by the
getaway car."

"Hmmm. A little fight. You look no worse for
wear," the captain said, scanning Jack's face.

"Only my pride's been hurt. We'll tow their car into
the state pound."

"We got a few calls that there was a gunshot out on
the street," Caterez said.

"Two gunshots. One upstairs and one out there during the arrest. I killed a car window."

"Jeeesus!" Chief Shewdy Collins shouted, bluster-
ing in through the front door. "You okay, Jack?"

"Yup," and Jack explained what happened. His version.

Everyone present knew there had to be a little more
to the story, but what happens in Jack's house stays in
Jack's house.

"Crime scene upstairs?" Shrewdy asked.

"Shooting scene, yes. Upstairs. He broke in
through the back door. Nobody's been around there…
yet, to look," Jack said.

Shrewdy looked around him at the home, recalling a
prior trip to this house, 12? 14 years ago, when three
ex-cons came there to kill Jack Kellog. Instead, Jack
killed all three in a bloody battle royal that concluded
in hand-to-hand combat. Shrewdy passed through the
two EMTs and up to the handcuffed man.

"You don't know much of history do ya, son?"

The man just stared at him, confused.

"You don't just come to Fort Kellog and try to kill

him. This ain't his first rodeo."

Texas Ranger Weaver Wisdom showed up with some state techs in uniform.

"Let's get the party started," was all the Ranger said.

Jack wandered off to the front porch. Some neighbors were on their porches in their pajamas and robes, gawking.

"Jaaack! Are you alright?" one woman yelled.

"Yes, Grace. It's over," he said walking down a few porch steps.

He waved to everyone he could see. "Sorry!" he shouted to all, "Y'all go back to bed. Sorry. It's all under control."

"Did they try to kill ya again?" a neighbor shouted.

"Yes Jason, but I won," Jack said.

He dug the phone out of his pocket, as the EMTs were leaving.

"Night, Jack," one said passing him by.

"Night guys," Jack said as he dialed.

The state medical examiner's van pulled up for their body work.

"Hello? Jack?" A groggy, Gail answered.

"Gail...I got him. I wanna let you know. He was like a hitman for the group."

"Was? Arrested? Or is he...dead?"

"Dead."

"Oh, Jack. Thank God. You...you, I have to get over there. But the funeral is coming up. This is such a big story. A book. It's a book."

"Okay. See you soon, probably at the funeral. I just wanted you to know. Bye."

He shook his head. Gail...Gail...Gail. Ever, ever with the story. Her husband is dead, and still...the story. The book.

Chapter 28: The Snitch

The next day, Charles Popperdale sat in the DPS conference room. He drank coffee from a Styrofoam cup.
Breakfast burrito food wrappers cluttered the table beside a tape recorder and a video tape camera set up by
Manny. The DPS holding tank section and interrogation rooms were too small for this fandango, so they
moved to one of the bigger conference rooms and stationed a trooper on the door.

Present were Jack Kellog, Rangers Weaver Wisdom
and Wilderaydo Acorn, DPS Narcotics Nip Budsten,
Manny from Surveillance, Screed Detective Linda
Pathways, Harris County Assistant District Attorney
Rygh Eadleston, Humble Homicide Detectives Sgt. An-
drew Archlando and Cornelius Wright. They'd waited
impatiently until 11 a.m. to officially begin so Austin
Detective Lee Trang could drive in. Trang arrived,
bringing with him an assistant district attorney from
Travis County.

Acorn advised Popperdale of his Miranda rights, but
he already knew to save his life he needed to cut the
biggest deal ever. So, he waived his rights and dis-
sected the entire Gulf Coast Drug Task Force operation, every legal and illegal case he could recall, from
local pot street busts to murder on the high seas.

Rygh took feverish notes for multiple arrests and
search warrants. Most of the arrest warrants were under
the officers' false names Popperdale knew them by, but
Rygh could use the old "otherwise known as" phrase
with detailed physical descriptions. Manny supplied a
file of real names investigated via the fingerprints on
parked cars his team collected at night. Manny had the
real names and photos of seven officers and why they
were fired or resigned from other agencies. Popperdale

identified them by a series of photos.

Rygh and his district attorney were shooting for a Texas organized crime prosecution and the targets were looking good for it. Texas had a very tough stance on organized crime, usually seeking the harshest possible penalties. Once convicted of organized criminal activity, one could end up in prison for life. The statute reads, "It is illegal for a person to commit or conspire to commit certain crimes with the intent to establish, maintain, or participate in a combination or in the profits of a combination or as a member of a criminal street gang."

There was a federal RICO crime charge available also, but that would mean the FBI, federal prosecution and courts and federal prison for the convicted, not the harsher Texas prisons. In the Screed, Humble and Austin murder cases, since the shooter Bluto was dead, Screed and Austin PD were looking to close out their murder cases, yet file cases on any accomplices.

Acorn also took serious notes along with asking questions, as he was rested and would sign all the subsequent warrants Rygh would draw up as the affiant, later in the day. Jack and Weaver were exhausted from lack of sleep, but they persevered on adrenaline.

Jack sat quietly in a chair off in the corner. "On the books" he was technically still on paid leave until the main street shooting investigation was completed by Weaver. Weaver had to at least pause the final clearance until the autopsy was complete and some ballistics were in. Weaver had collected Jack's second .45, but Jack quickly replaced it with a third. Leave or not, Jack was still irreplaceable, and though just sequestered to a corner, he was still very front and center.

Popperdale looked tired, but relaxed, like a man at a Catholic confessional just before the Saint Peter meeting at the Pearly gates. He claimed he'd never murdered anyone and wanted a witness protection deal, which was more than likely.

Manny's pager went off at 12 noon. They all looked to him. He turned the video camera off and stepped over to a big color TV set on a rolling platform in the corner.

"The news," Manny said, and turned the set on.

"That's right Ramon," the reporter said, standing on Jack Kellog's now sunny street, "there was a home invasion shooting here last night in West Forge, a quiet suburb of Houston. The DPS state police intelligence detective Jack Kellog, the officer who shot and killed an attacker just 6 days ago on Main Street here in West Forge, was apparently assaulted yet again, this time by an armed home invader. We do not have a lot of information at this time, authorities are quiet, but my investigation revealed the home invader was a Hispanic male. They confirmed that the medical examiner was called…"

"So, someone was shot, or I mean killed," Anchorman Ramon said.

"Correct. Who, we don't know yet. And Ramon, the police also have an accomplice under arrest…"

Beachum Airport…

"Shit," Cinnamon Dunker growled, watching the same TV news in the airport hangar common area. "Shit, shit, shit."

Others gathered around the TV set.

"They got Rebadoux?" Greg Williams said.

"Fucking Kellog. I told you he was real trouble," Dunker said ignoring the question.

"Bluto dead?" Jerome said.

"Shit. Probably."

They all thought Bluto was invincible.

"Will Rebadoux talk?" Greg Williams said.

"Probably," Dunker said, "his real name is Popperdale. When they caught him stealing in New Orleans, he talked. Burned all the guys with him in the property room thefts for a deal. Probably."

All the task force members present were gob smacked. They'd held down the "business as usual" persona for over a week since the street beating and fended off the first and only visit from the Humble police department, by playing dumb and fronting "the drug gang did it" story. The beaten body of Strands was still missing, so it wasn't listed as an official homicide yet.

"Bluto is dead," one murmured.

"I need a sniper," Dunker whispered, his head looking side to side as though he'd find a sniper at the big table.

Dunker's blurt was even more shocking. No one on the task force was a trained sniper. Dunker walked over to a phone and dialed what appeared to the members to be a long-distance phone number. He looked at the group and waved a "go away" hand gesture. They started to disperse, but as Greg Williams left the area, he overheard Dunker say,

"Yes. Department of Organizations and Association, please."

"Department of…what? Who or what was that?" Greg wondered as he was shooed away.

Chapter 29: Third Rate Romance

On the road to Austin…

Jack didn't know what to expect at the funeral of Ernesto Ballitross, Gail's long-time husband. Would she sit next to and stay by her sister up in the front row? Would she beckon Jack over to her. Did this change everything between them? Was she now free to be "with" him now? Did she really want that? Did he?

He pondered many things on the drive to the downtown Austin funeral home. He listened to a Frank Sinatra cassette tape, which he wondered was Frank's wounded tales of love lost, every tune like a three-minute movie, a good idea on this journey?

He parked his Caddy in the Trust's Funeral Home parking lot and left his hat in the car. He was dressed as normal, leather sport coat, white shirt and bolo tie, starched, pressed jeans and boots. He followed some of the attendees across the lot, up the stairs and into the lobby. There were many cars and a ton of people there because of Ernesto's high-falutin, state job, and of course, Gail's Texican Monthly people were there.

Inside, the big room was as large as a half-circle, designed church, and within the throng, he couldn't even spot her. But the funeral ceremony was about to begin, and she would already be well inside the auditorium and probably down front. There were no empty seats and He found some standing room and he stood up against the wall where he would rather be anyway.

The open coffin was front and center. Jack thought that the funeral home's morticians must have done an amazing job on Ernesto's head. Head shots usually meant closed coffins. The master of ceremony took the podium and introduced himself as Gregory Carone, the head of the Department of Texas Agriculture and Ernesto's boss. He began the eulogy and Jack quickly zoned out. He knew all about Ernesto's life, as he did the lives of all the husbands of women that had false-promised him a pending future. Plus, he had a lot on his mind what with the Dunker investigation and he was also busy looking up front to spot and spy on Gail.

And there she was, front and center. Sitting very close beside her, was a well-dressed man, black coif-fured hair, about 50. He put his arm around her. When Gail started to cry that arm turned into a hug. He gave her a handkerchief.

Carone spoke and then introduced several co-workers and they spoke of the wonders of Ernesto. Gail did not step up and speak. A prayer. Some hymns. The ceremony was over in 40 minutes.

People started to make the customary pass by the open coffin, which Jack never did any of these passes. He'd seen enough dead people. Strangers, relatives and friends. Gail was one of the first to stop, laid a gloved hand on the coffin rim, and was still under the tight arm of this man. Then the man guided her away and up the center aisle. She remained right under his armpit. She did not look around. She did not look for or see Jack.

"You must be Jack Kellog?" a man standing next to him asked.

"Ahh…yes."

"Gail has written about you in the magazine a few times, and I recognize you from the photos. I'm in the art department of the magazine."

"Oh, Okay. Yes."

"Ohhh, I tell ya, it's a good thing she's got Aaron, you know," the man said, nudging his head toward Gail and the man, "they've been…so close…so very close for years and now he's there fully to help her now. Trying times."

"Aaron, oh? Close, huh? Trying times. Very," Jack said.

"Yes. Very close if you get what I mean. I'll bet they get married now. Going to the cemetery?"

"No. This is enough, and I have to get back," Jack said.

"Houston?"

"Houston."

With stifling short steps, he slowly stutter-stepped with the attendees out of the hall and into the lobby. There, he could see out the giant lobby windows and onto the parking lot.

Outside, some people gathered around Gail and this Aaron guy. They were still standing very close. They spoke and shook some hands. Aaron guided her into the passenger seat of a new, black Mercedes Benz sports car, to the point of his guiding her in, running his lightly hand down her backside and leg to fit her in.

Rather than be seen outside by her, Jack felt the need to stop at the windows, surrounded by the morose recorded, organ lobby music, which sounded more like a horror movie soundtrack. He watched as this Aaron leaned over and kissed Gail, just a short "I'm here-for-you, how-you-doing peck." She leaned in for it, and their overall body language was apparent.

Jack stood there, kind of frozen. Many questions he'd pondered about Gail were just now answered. He'd never thought about this before, but maybe he was not a second stringer on "Team Gail." He was third, maybe fourth or further on down the bench?

Third rate romance. Low-rent rendezvous…as the old country song went. On the drive back to Houston, Jack removed the Sinatra tape. Why double down on lost love and those "quarter to three" saloon songs?

Chapter 29: The Exceedingly Thin Man

Cinnamon Dunker had lost his right-hand man. His hit man. Bluto was shot dead by Jack Kellog, the detective whom he thought of like a dangerous virus infecting his life. Kellog had to be stopped, if but for revenge alone. He had to prove to his guys he could kill the snitch and wipe out Kellog too. He thought of himself like a Godfather, a cartel leader, a lord, a baron, a king-pin. Pluto was a veteran of international drug wars and drug deals, but his approach to solutions always did border on the psychotic. But what Dunker was about to ask for…to commit to…wasn't that also doubling, even tripling down on Bluto's path?

It was a time to "take care of all the family business" like Michael Corleone would in the Godfather movie. Dunker was now desperate. He knew one man's testimony was about to topple their tower and send him and many of his people to jail and even lethal ejection, executions.

By now, the police veteran Dunker knew all the steps Jack Kellog would be ramrodding in a three-ring circus against him. He'd done it all himself in Harris County. He'd run such team circuses in the past.

He knew that Popperdale's confessions were either filmed, signed, sealed, and delivered, or about to be. But Dunker also knew nothing was better to slow down, befuddle or even blow up an upcoming police and courtroom action, grand jury or a trial, than a solo, dead witness. A key person that couldn't be cross-examined in a trial. So, he followed the instructions he'd been given by phone. He drove on down to the south side of Bush Intercontinental Airport, into a plethora of cheaper, airport hotels.

The Hotel Saint Faust was an old two-story motel

with indoor doors to hallways. Dunker respected the surreptitious choice of this interior door based, limited outside surveillance opportunity for the comings and goings of individual roomers.

Dunker was very careful not to be followed there. His contact demanded it. Just 5 hours after his mysterious phone call, he walked down one of the hotel's musty, stinky halls, carrying a folder of critical information. Dunker approached room 12 and knocked.

"Come in," a male voice said from inside.

Dunker didn't expect a friendly welcome, but this was still a surprise. In the dark far corner of the room, a man knelt on the floor on the far side of the bed, with only the top of his head and a hand holding a pistol, aimed right at him could be seen.

"It's me," Dunker said, stepping in.

"Whose me?"

"Karen's friend."

"Okay," the man said after hearing the proper phrase.

"I am very careful. Turn on the lights."

The man stood. He was in his early 30s, rail thin inside an untucked short sleeved shirt and baggy pants, with too long black hair.

Dunker flipped the switch. Why bother though, the lighting was terrible.

"You got here fast," Dunker said.

"They said it was an emergency. I do emergencies. What you got? Have a seat."

Dunker sat by the worn desk. The man sat on the bed. He laid the pistol beside him on the bed. Thus far, he had no discernable accent.

"There's a witness," Dunker said, "he needs killing. This is him."

He passed the man some papers that included several clear photos of Popperdale, and a written physical description.

"He's talking and gonna continue to talk, or at best, about to talk," Dunker said, "he's at the Houston DPS state headquarters in a holding tank right now. They will have to transfer him soon. At some point. County jail, maybe, but he's so important they may put him somewhere else, maybe even a safehouse."

"That big a deal, huh?"

"That big," Dunker said.

He passed the man several photos of the DPS building, which included the sally port area in the back from which criminals came and went in transport vehicles.

"So, he's still there now? Department of Public Safety?"

"Still there," Dunker said. "And here…here are all of the buildings, for blocks, with a view the sally port. From 50 yards to a mile. They told me you needed within that range."

"Uh-huh."

"Transfer could be anytime."

"Uh-huh."

"Here are the addresses of each possible building."

"I like one," he said, but didn't admit to which one.

He stood and walked over to a suitcase. He opened the lid. He put on medical rubber gloves. Dunker saw a rifle in there, in parts. The man reached in and grabbed a phone and a business card, handing them both to Dunker.

"I got a helicopter now if you…" Dunker started.

"No. No chopper needed. I need your number. Secured line?"

"Secured," Dunker said.

"That card's got my number," he said. "Can you make sure he's still in there, in DPS? You call me in two hours and tell me he's there?"

"I can. I've got two men watching the place right now. The target is still there right now.""Good. The state police. They have an inside sallyport?"

"No. Their building is old. It does not. The back of it looks like a loading dock," Dunker said, pulling a color photo from the file to show him. "The cars or vans drive up and the prisoners are walked out. They don't have or keep many suspects there. Usually all prisoners are taken, are held at Harris County jail.
Very few stayovers at the DPS headquarters," Dunker said.

"Does the Harris County Sheriff's Office have an inside sallyport?"

"They do," Dunker said.

"So, this shot has to be at the DPS headquarters. They have a van for this?"

"They do but not always. They often just run prisoners to the county in a state car," Dunker said, "couple of suspects? Then a white van. Special suspect or a long trip? The van."

"This one's special."

"Very special," Dunker said.

"Give your men my number too and tell them to call me if they see a transfer. That's it," the exceedingly thin man said.

"Ah, and now this one," Dunker said handing him an 8x10 photo.

The exceedingly thin man looked up at Dunker's face as he took the picture.

"This is a Detective Jack Kellog, state police," Dunker said. "He is the bane of my existence. The boil on my ass and I can't sit down. If he had a torturous death that would..." Dunker said.

"You say he's a cop?" the man interrupted.

"Yes."

"We don't kill good cops."

"Ahhh…oh?" Dunker said.

The two men stared at each other. The man handed the photo back.

"Ahhh. Okay. Good. Well, do I…how do I pay you?'

"You don't. They pay me," and the exceedingly thin man started packing a few things around him.

Dunker stood and made for the door, his departure totally ignored. No good-bye. The thin man had his orders.

Dunker left the room, then motel and walked out to his car. The very thin man was surely some sort of military vet, he could guess with a "hunter's watch-and-wait unique patience." The kind that snipers have.

A shot to catch Popperdale in a two-minute transfer would be tough. And a ballsy one taken at a state police headquarters. What did he mean they wouldn't kill cops? He made a mental note not to mention the murder of Detective Paul Massaport. That was done by the frisky Bluto, anyway.

He tried to guess the gear in that suitcase. Had to be a silencer-suppressor for a super, high-powered, long-distance hunting rifle. A precision rifle. He could only assume the man's experiences.

No cop shootings though? What kind of bad guy doesn't take out cops? Dunker also guessed that if anyone was going to kill Jack Kellog, it had to be him. And he would. That's what Michael Corleone would do.

Chapter 31: Snap of a Finger

"The guy you shot?" Weaver and Acorn were glad to catch Jack out in the DPS parking lot before they left. Screed Detective Linda Pathways was with him.

They all stopped by Jack's car with Pathways about to climb into the passenger side. Instead, she stood up by her side and listened in.

"Yeah? Which one?"

"This Bluto guy? The autopsy's complete," Weaver said. "One shot. Your gun. Lower throat. A front-to-front shot. All good. But Jackster…"

"What?" Jack said.

"Medical examiner says this Bluto guy has no identity. His fingerprints are a dead end. No records of him under any name exist. No history anywhere." Jack leaned against his state car, growled a short, classic, Kellog grunt and folded his arms. Pathways circled the car to their side.

"No shit?" Jack said.

"No shit."

"No tattoos or nothing?" Jack asked.

"None," Weaver said. "Shot before, stabbed before and even burned. Leg and hip jacked up, causing the limp, but no tattoos."

Weaver opened his polyester, western cut sports jacket and pulled Jack's .45 from his beltline.

"Here. Ballistic match. Shooting closed. You're back at full speed," Weaver said. "OOOficially." He also handed Jack a magazine from a pocket. They never took Jack's state badge during the paid investigation leave.

"Fuuuullll speed," Jack repeated, as if he ever

slowed down of late. He opened the back door, switched the .45 in his holster with his regular gun, traded magazines for a full load and dropped the back-up weapon on the back seat.

"So, my shooter," Pathways said, "is a John Doe."

"A very professional John Doe," Acorn added.

"Who are these people?" she said with exasperation.

"I may have a way to find out?" Jack said.

"Bats?" Weaver said.

"Bats. But it might take a while."

"Yeah, Bats. That'll work. Where y'all going?" Weaver asked.

"To snatch a locksmith. It's time," Jack said.

Weaver nodded and said, "yeah it's time to knit up the fish net."

"They moving Popperdale today?" Jack asked.

"Any minute now," Weaver said. "They're gonna transport him to the federal prison in Beaumont, away from Harris County. Nip cut a deal with the DEA to hold him there."

"Okay. Later gators," Jack said, getting into his car.

"Whose…what's…Bats?" Pathways asked as she slipped inside the sedan.

"You don't wanna know," Jack said. "He's a government guy I went to Mexico with to catch John Phillip Muzak years ago. I don't really know who he is or what he does."

Weaver and Acorn turned for the side doors of DPS headquarters.

"Who is Bats?" Acorn asked. "What is Bats? A bureau? Bureau of…?"

"Nope. No bureau. Just some guy. You ahhh, you really don't wanna know," Weaver said.

As Pathways and Jack drove beside DPS headquarters to a back street exit…

"What…is…going…on," Pathways declared looking at the back of the DPS building.

"Huh?" Jack mumbled, then looked to his left.

Several police vehicles were scattered about the back sally port area, which was normal, but the troopers around them were not. Some were running, ducking, some pulling their pistols, some shouting into their portable radios.

"Prisoner down! Shot!" Jack and Pathways heard over the state radio channel in his sedan.

"Wha….?" Jack said.

They saw troopers take positions beside cars, aiming their guns at…at what? High up? At buildings? At what and where exactly?

For the moment Jack did not know where to go or what to do. They both looked and guessed at the huge area that the troopers were aiming their guns at, just skyward and south

"Sniper!" came over the radio.

"Sniper to the south!" radio reports flooded the airways.

"Sniper!" Pathways repeated.

Jack, fearing such a sniper, drove wide off and further to the right, watching and listening to the radio.

"Coming from where?" the dispatcher asked.

"We don't know," one trooper yelled into his radio.

"South of here. High angle," another said.

Jack hit the gas pedal and left the parking lot.

"Best we can do is head south and look for a fleeing sniper," Jack said.

"What does a fleeing sniper look like?" Pathways asked.

"I don't know. Maybe someone with a suitcase? For a rifle that can be disassembled. Someone…looking around too much? Too nervous?" Jack said, cutting the steering wheel for the harsh cornering with the breakneck speeds he pushed the car. It jostled Pathways around. She quickly seat-belted in.

But, just two blocks away life proceeded as normal, Cars drove. People casually walked around. All oblivious to the crime just a minute ago and just north.

"State 101," Kellog reported in, "we are patrolling the general area south of DPS, looking for suspicious persons. None seen so far. Suggest others join this search."

"Ten-four, 101," the dispatcher replied.

Within a few minutes some other plainclothes units appeared, along with two Houston squad cars, to help in the search.

Within a few minutes more, additional Houston P.D. and the Sheriff's Office joined the search. With that net laid, ten minutes past and a frustrated Jack and Pathways returned to the sally port of the DPS headquarters. They saw an ambulance there. They spotted Weaver Wisdom and Wilderado Acorn.

Jack and Pathways both exited the vehicle and approached the back door lot.

"It's Popperdale," Weaver told them, "they got him."

"They got him, this fast? How…" Jack said.

Weaver motioned with his head for a transport officer to join them and explain what happened to Jack. The trooper walked up.

"Man! We walked the guy out, down the stairs over there, headed for our van. Just over there. Then, I swear, I ahhh, heard like a light zip in the air. A zip… a…swish. Then a…a…like a thunking sound. Like the sound you make, a sound like snapping your fingers? And our guy dropped like a rock."

Jack looked at the city landscape south of them. From that vantage, he could see numerous three-or-more story buildings jutting in and out of straight-line view up to a mile for or so.

"The guy was hit in the head," the officer continued, "he went lifeless. We each had an arm, he was between us, and we kneeled down with him like he was passing out. I…it took a few seconds for us to… you know…know what in the hell happened. This bullet must have missed my nose by about, like, like inches. He was shot in the side of his head. Round in and out before he fell because Roland remembers hearing the thunk and then something…the round…hit the wall over there. I didn't hear that."

Jack saw crime scene people already working on the hole in the brick.

"No shot heard?" Jack asked?

"None."

Jack grunted and added, "That far."

Pathways just stood there in shock. She studied the EMTs looking over Popperdale. Lost cause. Weaver had his hands on hips, shaking his head. Acorn wandered around the lot in disgust. Nip burst out the back doors, having just heard the news circulating inside.

"Oh damn, nooo!" Nip yelled out.

"Reckon we need a canvas of every one of those fucking buildings. Every floor. Every window," Jack said to Weaver.

"Probably get us nowhere," Weaver said.

"But we gotta," Jack said. He knew that if they ever caught someone for this, the defense would declare the police and prosecution remiss if such a search wasn't tried.

"We do. Gotta try. I'll get something started. The Colonel will…be…*pissed*. This happening in our backyard and all. He'll probably give me a lot of troopers to run a canvas.

"This shot is pro-beyond-pro," Jack said.

"Yup," Weaver said.

"Tells us even more who we are dealing with."

"Yup."

"Are we still going to pick up the locksmith?" Pathways asked while walking up to them.

"Yeah," Jack said, "give em somebody else to shoot next, I reckon."

Jack scrunched up his face, rubbed his nose and looked at Acorn.

"Chief?" he said to the Ranger.

"Yeah, Kemo?"

"Go pick up that girl Alice. She's a loose end over the pick-up truck, and they may kill her too. We need to talk to her, but we may need to save her life too."

"Ten-four." Acorn said.

Chapter 32: Locking Down the Locksmith

Galena, TX....

The duo drove to the locksmith shop that Pathways had tracked down two weeks prior. The time was ripe to confront him.

"There's the truck," she said.

"Looks like the one on the tape," Jack said.

He parked and the two walked inside. A bell peeled as the door opened. Inside, it had all the trappings of an established locksmith shop, an older one, with new and old products, some dusty, shoved and hung everywhere. A black cat crossed their path. A young boy sat on a stool on the customer side of the tall counter. They walked up to the counter and the boy was so engrossed in the Game Boy game in his hands, he didn't even see them.

They waited.

"Hey kid," Jack said, "You know where the owner is?"

"Huh?" the disturbed kid said.

"I'm right here, what can I do for you?" a squat man, about 50, with ruddy skin and messed-up thin, red hair, really faded forearm tattoos, in worn coveralls appeared from the back.

"Hello," Pathways said, "I'm Detective Pathways from the Screed Police Department. This is Special Agent Kellog, State Police."

He eyed both of them up and down.

"Y'all get locked out of your po-lice car or something?" he asked.

"And you are Rick Sandavere?" she asked.

"Yeah."

"Have you ever worked on a church door in Screed? Christ's Church?" she asked.

The man scratched his hairline.

"I'm not sure I know where Screed is?" he said.

"And you are thee Rick sandavere? That's your name?" Jack asked.

"What's yours?"

"Jack Kellog, like the lady said."

"Highway Patrol?" the man said.

"Wrong division. What's your name?" Jack said, now getting a little testy.

"Yeah, yeah. Rick, well, Richard Sandavere," the man said.

"Rick, we got you, on film making a key on the back door of that church in the middle of the night," Jack exaggerated a bit.

"Hmmm, weeeellll, ahhh, let me think about it. Okay, yeah there was a man that came in here couple a months ago, and said he needed a new key for a church, yeah, yeah, it was that church. Now that you mention it. Said it was emergency and I had to go out there. Now!" He chuckled, "I told him I had no free time and I would have to go in the middle of damn night to do it as fast as he wanted it."

They stared at him.

"Why not use a locksmith in Screed?" Pathways said.

"Yeah! I thought that too. Hell, if I know. Yeah. I want to tell you that people are weird about keys and security. I don't know, but yeah, yeah, now I re-member."

"Who was he?" Jack asked.

"Oh, I don't know. I don't remember."

"How'd he get the new key?" Pathways asked.

"He came back the next day."

"It's about 90 minutes away," Pathways said.

Sandavere just shrugged his shoulders.

"Paperwork?" Jack asked. "You got paperwork?"

"Ahh well you know, come to think about it. He paid me cash."

"No name?" Pathways asked cynically.

"Ahhh. I don't remember it, no."

"Cash or no cash, ain't you supposed to write something up for a job?" Jack asked.

"Mister, if I get cash, I don't write nothin up. That way I don't pay no taxes."

"Do you always make keys for strangers who want keys to doors of businesses and churches without any proof of a legal connection to them?" Jack asked.

"Sometimes, if I trust them."

"In case your innocent self is wondering," Jack said, "a police detective was murdered in that church a few days later. Entry was made through that very door."

Sandavere grimaced and produced another shoulder shrug.

"We need a statement from you about this," Pathways said.

"I, well, okay…well, now, I don't know. Maybe I need a lawyer?"

"I think it says in the Bible, Rick," Jack said, leaning on the tall counter, "that only guilty people need lawyers. If we leave here now, we'll be back with an arrest warrant, and ruin your little locksmith bond coverage and whatever else you got going on here. Might call the IRS."

"Noooo. You wouldn't stoop so low," he said.

"You need to come with us, and we need a statement about how and why you were making a key for a church door at 3 am in the middle of the damn night for a stranger. No voluntary statement? Then you will be an arrested suspect in a murder investigation."

"Well, so be it then. Bible or not, I will ask a lawyer what he thinks first," the locksmith said.

"You follow the news today?" Jack asked.

"No."

"Well, a witness against the drug task force was shot in the head in the back lot of DPS headquarters this afternoon. They didn't know if he talked, or if he didn't talk, or if he would talk. They just blew his brains out. They had a professional hitman blow his brains out from about half a mile away."

"So?"

"So…you're in the rat trap next, that's what's so," Jack said. "We are onto you. You! You're damned if you do and damned if you don't. With us you got a chance. If we arrest you? You are another risk to them."

"I think I will consult with my attorney," he said.

The three stared at each other.

"Who had his brains blown out?" the kid at the counter stopped playing his game and asked.

"My grandson. I watch him in the afternoons," Sandavere explained.

"Yeah?" Jack said. "Tell his momma she's gonna have to find a new babysitter pretty soon."

Pathways placed one of her business cards on the counter, then the two left.

They climbed back in Jack's state car.

"You got pictures of that truck?" Jack asked.

"I do."

"Can you write up a probable cause arrest warrant for that somabitch? We have enough to arrest him?"

"I can," she said, "after that fairy tale I can."

Jack nodded and said, "Seriously, they'll probably

kill him too if we arrest him, but we gotta do it."

"I know."

"Boss man, we got a problem," Sandavere said on the phone.

"Where are you?" Dunker asked.

"Don't worry, I'm in a phone booth," the locksmith said.

"Okay, what? Tell me the short version. I got no time, man."

And Sandavere ran down the events of the meeting with some guy named Kellog and a woman police.

"That's a…that's a terrible story you told them, Ricky. No cop is going to believe that. It's not an impossible story mind you, but unbelievable."

"What else could I say?"

"True. Well, but, ya coulda said nothing, but I understand. I see what you're saying, Ricky."

"Will they arrest me?"

"Probably."

"Do I need a lawyer?

"Yeah, probably. We have plenty. We have to meet about this. Sit down and talk. Make a plan. But they may start following you."

"Ohhh man! Really? Follow me?"

"Yeah, Kellog told you right out that we the enemy…a drug task force…had a man sniped. It's officially on. They know. It's now their task force versus our task force. But maybe we better meet fast before they can get you set up. You think you can lose a tail?"

"I think."

"Hmmm. On second thought, alright, listen, I am gonna have Greg pick you up. Back door of your shop. I know he can lose a tail. Then we'll meet somewhere, okay?"

"Okay."

"Ten o'clock tonight. By then traffic will thin out and a tail behind you is easier to spot."

"Okay."

They hung up.

"*JACK* Kellog," Dunker said with a growl.

Webster, TX...

Ranger Wilderaydo Acorn parked near but not right in front of April's small house. Her pickup truck, the Skelton Rhoades' escape vehicle, was not on the street, but maybe was in the garage? He knocked on the front door at first, then started pounding. No response.

He stepped off the porch and started looking into the front windows.

"She's gone, sir. Moved!" a man's voice came from the sidewalk behind him.

Acorn turned to see an elderly man walking his Chihuahua.

"Gone?" Acorn said.

"Yes, she moved."

"To where? Do you know?" Acorn said, walking up to the neighbor.

"We don't know, but we saw her, and a moving company carry her stuff out."

"I see. Do you remember if she still has that old pickup truck of hers? I'm sorry, I'm Ray Acorn, Texas Rangers."

Acorn shook the man's hand.

"I figured you were a Ranger, yes, sir. No, she must have sold the truck and has a nice new Mercedes."

"Thanks, I will ask around the street if anyone knows anything. She is not in trouble, she just knows something that we need to know. Do you know where she worked?"

"No sir, but she came and went at all strange hours, and she must have had a police officer boyfriend. We would see him from time to time."

"Thank you, sir," Acorn said.

Houston, TX...

The next day 30 troopers were assigned to Nip and tasked with canvassing the many buildings that the sniper might have shot from. Their mission was to check all rooftops and windows and ask questions. It was a needle in a haystack operation but had to be done.

That afternoon, with an arrest warrant for Rick Sandavere, Pathways and Jack drove back to the locksmith shop. The truck was parked outside, right where it was the day before. And to their surprise the grandson and a woman were standing outside the front door. The woman was pacing the sidewalk.

Pathways and Jack exchanged glances and exited his car. They walked up to the pair.

"You looking for Rick?" the woman asked.

"Mom, these are the police that talked yesterday about a man what got his head blowed off."

"Well, I'm about to blow the top of my head off. I've got to go to work and I'm trying to drop Bobby off with him and he ain't here. And he ain't answering his phone. That work truck is all he's got to drive around in."

Jack and Pathways just stood there sort of speechless for the moment, fearing for the health of there next main witness.

"Im-ma wondering if he ain't in there dead from a heart attack in there or somethin?" I called his friend Lawrence to come over. He's got a key. He'll be here any minute, but I got to get to work, ya know!"

Jack just grunted and nodded. He and Pathways retreated back to his car and leaned against it in contemplation, now also left to wait for this Lawrence guy with a door key to show up.

Lawrence did eventually cruise onto the lot in an old, blue El Camino that badly needed a new muffler. He got out and flipped many keys on a key chain until he found the one he wanted. He unlocked the front door and the woman barged in, followed by the boy, Lawrence and then Jack and Pathways. They swarmed through the whole shop like a SWAT team.

After a minute they all concluded that Sandavere was not there. He was…missing.

"Well, where in the hell could he be?" the woman asked.

Jack and Pathways had a few ideas, and hell was on their list.

Chapter 33: Mission Discombobulate

Beachum Airline Hangar…

"So, you say that every Thursday at dinner time, for the last four Thursdays, Kellog has eaten at Burning Heart Brisket?" Cinnamon Dunker asked his man, Conner.

"Yes, sir."

"Alone?"

"One time he had that big black Texas Ranger with him. There's a sign out front that says Thursday is a discount special. A blue plate special. Ribs."

"Hmmm," Dunker said, looking at Greg.

Greg nodded.

"This guy is driving us crazy," Dunker said, sitting on the edge of a table. "Greg, you, me and Conner are gonna get him this evening if he's alone, on that lot. We can't just shoot him the way things are now. We need to kidnap him and drop him right off in the gulf. He just needs to disappear."

"Why not just shoot him?" Greg asked.

"Weeelll, people I deal with, on a certain other level, don't hanker to shooting cops."

"They…people you deal…say what?"

"That's all I am going to say Greg. And right now is not a good time to be shooting cops. He just needs to disappear into a big question mark."

"Okay," Greg said, knowing not to pursue that topic any further. After all Dunker had procured a sniper so quickly, so efficiently, to shoot a man in the head from about half a mile away. Those are the people he deals with.

"Is that parking lot crowded at dinner?"

"No sir. The joint is in the slums. It's a shack. Some

people come and go with carry-out."

"What time he get there?"

"About six."

"Good then. Let's use a less-than-lethal riot gun. It's quiet. Rubber bullet. Knock him down. Knock him out and haul his ass away. We'll go out there, we'll take…MAN! I miss Bluto fixing up all these cars and trucks. We'll take that van over there, and a car. I'll run the gun. Cause, I want to be the one that shoots that son of a bitch. I am so sick of him."

Suppertime at the Burning Heart Brisket…

Jack was still careful about being followed and saw no tail. There were a few old cars in the parking lot, most he'd seen for years as employee cars. Levy Garret was the owner, and his 50s truck was there, and his nephew Bartholomew had the Datsun. The few other cars looked typical and okay to him. He got out, shifted his gun belt just a bit into the best walking position and made for the ancient, worn doors of the Burning Heart.

The meat was cooked in a pit out back and the air was rich with the smoke and smell of brisket.

Jack inhaled the rich aroma, and then…and then he barely felt a hammering impact feeling to the back of his head. He…

"Go!" Dunker yelled to Greg and Conner.

Jack was down and out cold. Greg pulled Jack's .45 from his holster and he and Conner grabbed Jack and towed him between cars and over to the old van. Jack was as limp as a dead man. Dunker studied the landscape and saw no witness to the quick event. No one exited the barbeque place either. He grinned.

The trio left in the van and their car drove off the

lot, with Dunker dreaming of a little revenge torture and kicking the one and only Jumpin' Jack Kellog out of their newly acquired chopper, well out over the Gulf of Mexico.

"He sure looks dead, don't he?" Greg, at the wheel of the van said.

"He do. Oh yeah. I hit him right where I wanted. Lower back, right skull and neck. Even a punch there could kill a man."

"Discombobulate him," Greg said with a chuckle.

Chapter 34: Ambushing the Ambusher

Over the Gulf...

Jack's face was numb but still felt his head bouncing up and down just a fraction of an inch. He winced and opened his eyes. He was lying on a dark green corrugated metal, vibrating floor of some kind. He was eye level with two western boots.

"Welcome back, Jack Kellog."

He heard this from above the boots. He tried to look up, but his neck and head were on fire from pain, and he couldn't think straight. Where was he? He still felt this vibration, but now over all his body. With a groan and a gasp, he rolled over on his back to see he was in a dark metal room of some kind. But the noise. There was an enormous roar from the ceiling! He was...he was in a helicopter!

"I wish you could have seen yourself, Jacko, when I hit you with the rubber dum-dum bullet in the head. I swear, I swear you flipped completely over. Head over heels. Wow-weee."

Jack looked toward the voice. It was Sam "Cinnamon" Dunker, seated on a metal bench inside the chopper. Was he dreaming? Unfortunately, not. Another guy sat on a bench on the other side, across from Dunker.

"You know it's ironic Jack. You stumbled upon us from an investigation about a dead chopper pilot. Yet here we are with a new pilot and a new helicopter! You didn't stop us. You can't stop us. We are unstoppable. And you know why? We are cartel personified. They, we, kill everything that gets in our path."

Jack coughed up some lumpy blood. He gagged. He thought of his gun, but he could tell when rolling over, his .45 was gone. He tried to sit up on elbows. His brain "spun," but he did manage the move.

"Wha…whe," Jack mumbled

"We are taking another joyride out in the Gulf of Mexico. Way out. So we can bury you at sea. You are not handcuffed because should you ever wash up? We don't want it to look like a Mafia "sleep with the fishes" deal. You will be just another drowned guy."

Jack rolled his right foot on its boot heel. He felt the weight! The weight of his snubnose, 5-shot .38 inside the boot, the boot top inside his jean pants leg. How to get it out fast enough! How could they forget to check for a backup gun? He rolled his left foot too to look like he was coming out of a coma and testing his body out.

"You will soon be living up to your nickname. Finally. You'll be a jumpin! Jumpin right outta this chopper. Your namesake personified. So, for your DPS funeral in abstentia, would you like any particular words said? I'll bet you and I have been to many police officer funerals. Any one of the words stick with you?"

Jack, gasping, jaw open and drooling, sat up and pulled his feet into a cross-legged, "Indian-style," position, his back-up gun closer to a hand. He slowly painfully inched his way over to lean against the bench next to Dunker's accomplice and he could look straight at Dunker. But his eyes were still going in and out of focus.

Dunker was dressed in a shirt and jeans. Jack cranked his damaged neck to his right to see the other man beside him, but his neck! Had they broken his neck? He could see that the man next to him had a magnum revolver, not in his hand but laying on his lap.

"The funeral words are so typical, aren't they? Officer Joe Blow was a husband, which you ain't one. He was a father, which you ain't either. He was a grandfather. No, not you. He was a member of the Blankety-Blank Church, which you ain't. He was a lifelong police officer, which you are, soon to be… 'were' one, and you have shot and killed so many bad guys, too many bad guys that Saint Peter has got to ponder the question, "is this Jack Kellog good or bad?' Heaven or Hell?"

"Where you gonna end up?" Jack asked.

"He speaks!" Dunker said, looking at his accomplice.

"Greg, he talks!"

"Where you gonna end up?" Jack asked again.

The chopper hit a sudden, surprise wave of air and shook the craft, almost lifting everyone about a quarter of an inch off their butts.

"I am a pretty smart fellow, and I am not worried about the Pearly Gates. I'll just cut another deal." Another serious air bounce hit them.

"Cut a deal. Your man Rubidoux cut a deal and you had him shot. You might cut a deal at the Pearly Gates and the Devil may cut you down like you did him. I understand the Devil is a helleva sniper."

"Ha! Popperdale!"

"Did you have that girl April killed?" Jack asked.

"Nahhh, we moved her away with a new ID. She was a sweetheart. I did her too many times to kill her."

"You had Massaport killed and that first chopper pilot."

"Oh yeah. That pilot guy was a war hero with PTSD problems. Got on drugs. He really thought we would help clean up the coast, knowing we would also wheel and deal with some with undercover dopers. Then he discovered we too were the dopers. We too want to dirty up the coast."

"So, you sold dope. Cocaine? Marijuana? Speed?"

"Oh yeah, and more. Tons."

"You kill that locksmith?"

"Oh yeah. We dropped him out here about the same place as your final splashdown. Oh, yeah."

Yet another huge air wave hit the chopper.

"Your highway guys beat up and kill that guy that's on the TV news?"

"They did. We did a helleva job covering that up too."

"You have your man sniped at the DPS parking lot?" Jack said.

"I did."

"Who do you know that could make such a shot?" Jack asked.

"I got professional connections. Nobody can touch me, Jack. I would tell you to remember that, but your memory will only last another ten minutes or so," Dunker said. "But even if they catch me? They can't do anything to me."

And you tried to drown Skelton Rhoades?"

"Yes. Drowning by way of a shackle. Devious idea. Look, I run a lot of bad cops and fuck-ups. I need to put the fear of God in them. Mafia fear. Cartel fear. We killed quite a few people with that underwater ankle, shackle trick. Bluto thought it up. He said we needed a gimmick, like the cartel's man-in-burning-tires thing. Strikes fear in all. In our world the ankle shackle was our thing, and if the body is found, the police just write it off as a drowning."

"You tell your new pilot (cough) about drowning your first pilot?"

Dunker put a pointy finger to his lips, smiled behind it and said, "Sssssshhh."

Jack was counting on another airwave. He was taking in deep breaths to garner up his strength.

"All this killing? You killed," Dunker said, "you killed my man on the street, and you killed my best man, Bluto."

"Justified, (cough) self-defense."

"Justified! You set up my set-up man. You ambushed my ambusher. What was the turning point for you. Figuring us out, Jumpin' Jack Kellog?"

"No one thing, "Jack said, "it all came together piece by piece. And I had a feeling."

"A feeling. You have had some good luck and good feelings your whole career. Up unnntil now."

This next air wave was a dramatic one. The bump, the bounce made all three almost lose their balance and position. Jack pretended that he really did. He rolled over in a ball and while the two others were recovering, he pulled up his jean pants leg and pulled out his revolver.

"GREG!" Dunker cried out.

Too late. From the floor, Jack fired three times into Greg, into his gun arm and chest. Greg's magnum pistol fell onto the metal floor.

Dunker dove for the loose pistol just as Kellog did too. Dunker did grab the gun, but the barrel was aimed at the bench at that second. Jack's gun wasn't. Jack landed half on top of him and put his snub nose right up against Dunker's right temple.

"You let go of that gun," Jack growled, "or I'll punch a .38 right through yer skull."

"Hmmm," Dunker growled, thinking about his chances, then he let go of the magnum and Jack grabbed it with his left hand. They separated but both remained on the floor.

"What are you gonna do now, cowboy? Tell my pilot to turn back?"

"Something like that."

"He won't," Dunker said.

Jack slowly stood up. He switched gun hands and approached Dunker. Now, with that big magnum in his good hand, Jack struck Dunker in the head with the magnum barrel. It was a wallop and the crime boss fell against the metal bench. Headfirst and hard. But not before Jack hit him again with the gun. Then again. Then…one more time. It felt really good.

"Now you sleep that shit off, mother fucker," Jack said.

Jack looked at the accomplice, Greg. He was dead. One of Jack's rounds hit him in the face.

"Yeah, fuck you too," Jack said to him.

He noticed that this Greg, although in plain clothes, had a police belt on. He pushed him over on the bench to find the classic, handcuff case in the small of his back belt position. Jack stuffed his two guns in his beltline and took out the handcuffs. Jack cuffed the unconscious Dunker's hands behind his back.

Then, Jack looked Greg over again, especially the black police belt. They were about the same size, so Jack unhooked the whole police belt from Greg's body and put it on. He shoved the magnum revolver into the holster.

With the snub nose in hand, he walked to door and stairs to the cockpit. The pilot did not turn around until he felt something touch the right side of his neck. It was Jack's snub nose.

"Hi," Jack said.

"Wha…"

"You hear that gunfire back there? In the back?"

"Yeah."

"Well, I've killed Greg and just about bashed your boss's brains in. So, it's just you and me and we are gonna turn around now."

"What are you gonna do? Shoot the pilot? We'll crash. You'll die."

"Oh, I won't shoot cha up real bad. Shoot your ear off. Graze your face. Shoot off your nose. Something like that. Hell bubba, you have to eventually go back anyway. How's about right now?"

The pilot took a deep breath and banked for a turn.

"I tell ya what," Jack said. "You fly to downtown Houston. Can you get there?"

"Yeah."

"You land on the DPS parking lot, let me and Dunker and that corpse called Greg off on the lot, and I promise I'll let you go fly away free. But if you go back to the airport, you'll be caught in the middle of the biggest police raid you've ever dreamed of. Deal?"

"Deal."

"Good. Will cellphones work out here?" Jack asked.

"Not well. When we get closer to Galveston they will."

Jack looked out the front windshield. The world was dark but for a few distant speckled lights.

"Galveston?" Jack asked.

"Yeah."

"Good. Let's have your phone. Hand it over. It seems I have somehow misplaced mine."

The pilot handed off his phone and Jack left to check on Dunker.

When Jack returned to the cockpit about ten minutes later, he saw the brighter lights of Galveston. He jumped back and called Weaver Wisdom.

"Ranger Wisdom."

"Weave, it's me on another phone. I've been kid-napped by Dunker and was about to…"

"WHAT?"

"They were about to drop me in the Gulf. I shot one guy and beat Dunker into a coma. I cut a deal with the pilot to fly in and land on the DPS parking lot. It's a big bird so have some troopers clear an opening. Bigger than the small pad we got for smaller choppers. Can you record this? We need a warrant to raid the airport NOW!"

"I got your number, I will get on a recorded line. Wait a minute. I'll call you back."

They hung up. Jack heard Dunker moan.

The phone rang five minutes later, and it was Weaver.

"Okay, go ahead I got the Colonel, Acorn and some of the guys here too. Speaker phone."
Jack recited all the things that happened and what Dunker confessed to.

"You got to get the fastest warrant together with Rygh that you can. Prep SWAT and support while its being written. Hit the place, Weave! Hit it and take it all down!"

"On it now," Weaver said.

They hung up. Jack returned to the cockpit.

"Troopers are clearing a big space for us to land. And, the Rangers and SWAT are about to raid the han-gar. I'm telling ya, Ace, don't go there. Here's your phone back. I don't know your name and our deal still sticks. You drop us off and fly away."

"I will fly back to the coast, land on an empty beach," the man said taking the phone in his hand, "I'll call my wife and she'll come get me."

"You have a wife and you signed on for all this

shit?"

"I did. I need the money. I use to be somebody. A veteran Delta pilot. But I…"

"Let me guess. Drugs."

"Yes sir. Drugs. I dried out and started teaching flying lessons. Met a nice Mexican girl. But this Dunker showed up with big dreams. I thought I could sock away some loot."

"You pilots!" Jack said.

Jack noticed he still had his wallet in his back pocket! He pulled it and extracted a business card.

"Here. My name is Jack Kellog. Call me if you get in a jam. Or you need some help. I don't want to know your name right now, so I don't have to lie later under oath. Just call me and tell me you are the chopper pilot that took me home from my murder. I'll know. Maybe I can help you sometime."

The pilot took the card. He reached back and shook Jack's hand. Jack then patted his shoulder and returned to watch Dunker. Once back there, he stared at the crazed commander. He wondered where his favorite .45 was. He wondered why they didn't search him for back-up guns. He wondered why Dunker didn't have a gun. Why didn't they cuff him. These are all rookie mistakes. Or lazy. Or way overconfident. Jack selected the way overconfident assumption.

Adrenaline now dumping, his neck and head started to ache and stiffen up. He touched the lower, right back of his head, the general places where he learned from his failed boxing career that boxers cannot legally strike…the "rabbit punch" area. Very dangerous place to hit. Now, it was incredibly painful to the touch, and he yanked his hand away. Dunker said they shot him in the head with a rubber shotgun bullet. Dunker said that he'd flipped head over heels. From the sickening pain, he believed it.

Troopers were on the big back DPS lot with flashlights guiding the chopper in for a landing. After all, on the sides of the chopper read, "Police," and they did not know the whole sordid tale. The big prop winds blew every loose speck on the lot elsewhere.

The chopper landed, but the pilot kept the blades slowly spinning. Jack threw the side door open, and he rolled the dead Greg out. Then he struggled to lift Dunker up, to the door and dropped him out like a sack of potatoes.

Jack slowly, gingerly slipped out onto the ground. Crouched over just from reflex - the spinning blades were some 20 feet above, Nip and some of his narcs ran up to them. The chopper started its lift off. Jack was so weak, the chopper winds blew him over flat.

As the guys grabbed Dunker, Nip, who heard the whole recorded phone call an hour earlier from Jack, got to Jack first on the parking lot.

"My God man, are you okay?" Nip asked, sitting him up, then standing him up.

"No," was all that Jack could say.

With Nip's arm around Jack, they made for rear bay of the headquarters building.

"I am…" and Jack seemed to lose his strength in his left leg. He almost went into a kneel. Then Jack's right leg gave out, and then he passed out, pulling Nip down on the asphalt with him.

An ambulance was already standing by.

"Get that ambulance over here!" Nip yelled.

Chapter 35: Taking Down the Take

Beachum Airport, the next morning...

Betty and Emile Hutash sat quietly in the quaint Beachum Airport coffee shop, awaiting their flight to Tulsa, Oklahoma to see their kids. Emile was preoccupied with the financial pages of Houston Chronicle, to the point that his cigarette ash finger-flicking was missing the metal ashtray by about a half an inch. This dismayed poor Betty, but before she could cluck about it...

"Emile, is the President in Texas? Flying out of here too?"

"Huh? No. Clinton is in Europe. Why?"

"Look at all those black cars," she said. "It's like a motorcade."

Emile turned to look through the big front glass windows to see at least 6 black SUVs and several black vans. Betty could see farther down the airport road.

"There's a whole lot of cop cars too," she said, "maybe ten? I see even more turning in."

They watched the official looking parade zip by the terminal, heading for the hangers on the far side of the airport.

"I hope there's not a problem. I hope all that doesn't delay our flight," she said.

Rangers Wisdom and Acorn were mid-way in the procession. They watched as their state SWAT vans up front zipped onto the task force hanger lot, one for the front and one for the back, followed by two Harris County SWAT vans, front and back. The men in black jumped out and swarmed the hanger. State cars pulled up next to SWAT and troopers in regular uniforms dashed into the one neighboring business on the innocent, left side wing of the horseshoe-shaped hanger, to warn and protect all the employees inside. Weaver stopped his sedan, up on the airport road. He and Acorn got out.

Nip, with four of his drug agents and Manny in a van pulled up by the Rangers. They exited the van and wandered near them.

"We're all here except for Jumpin Jack Kellog," Nip said. "The main man. And where's Pathways?"

"She's here," Weaver said poking a thumb up the road, "she's back there in a Screed PD car. In the line."

"How's Jack doing?" Manny asked.

"We went by the hospital this morning," Acorn said. "He's almost in a coma. Serious concussion."

"Won't be the first time," Nip said. "That guy's got a hard head."

"Could be the drugs, but he tried to talk with us, he couldn't. He just mumbled and went back to sleep," Acorn said.

Weaver rested his arms atop the sedan roof and observed the hanger attack with frustration.

"Wish that was you?" Acorn asked.

"Once upon a time, I was," Weaver said.

He remembered the times of yesteryear, before SWAT when he and other investigators were - "the SWAT team" - and they got to raid and invade. Since SWAT, their routine orders are to remain safely outside until SWAT cleared the buildings, which bothered the action-deprived Ranger.

The state crime scene van stopped on the airport main road, as did at least 15 to maybe 20 state, county cars, along with two Screed PD squad cars. Each vehicle had three to four LEOs inside. The troopers, deputies and cops bailed out with shotguns and proceeded to encircle the entire hanger, standing at the ready.

This formation was a political-revenge statement. A detective was killed in Screed. A state intel agent Kellog was almost murdered – three times! And the Harris County Sheriff's Office was disgraced by a former employee. These overwhelming numbers were an angry show of force.

Weaver spotted Gail Canchos and several photographers getting photos of the troops and the outside action.

"There's Gail," Acorn said.

"Yeah, I see her. I don't know how she found out this was going to happen." Weaver said. "Jack surely didn't tell her."

"Oh, she is addicted to our police radio channels," Acorn said, familiar with her methods from the Muzak manhunt."

Pathways, now in a Screed uniform complete with a tactical look that included a bullet proof vest, walked up to them.

"Path," Weaver said. The rest of the crew nodded.

"Rangers," she replied and winked once at the others.

"No gunshots so far." Acorn said.

"Yup," Weaver said.

Then a face-masked SWAT member appeared in the front door and waved his hand. Things were safe now. Weaver shook his head at this safe-wave, as he did every time since God invented SWAT. He sighed.

"Let's go," he said.

He, Acorn, Pathways and the crime scene team started in first for the secure hanger. As they got closer, they heard the angry shouts and orders from the SWAT men inside, corralling and controlling the inhabitants.

Three officers had three members face down in the lobby. They were cuffing and searching them. Once inside the hanger, they could see SWAT covering the facility and barking commands to the captured. Some were busting open lockers with crow bars, some searching the Task Force cars.

Weaver, Acorn and Pathways split up to look around. The scene inside was the exact same layout as the Rangers' last visit.

State SWAT commander Captain Comegy peeled off his mask and approached Weaver.

"Eighteen arrested, Weave," the Captain said, "they had three badly beaten men in their holding cells over there. The crooks treated us like rescuers when we showed up. One guy cried and 'thank God.'"

"Yeah. There's probably a crazy story with each one. But, no trouble from any of these guys, huh?" Weaver asked.

"No. We blew in and they all folded like cheap suits."

But Comegy spoke too soon…

Gunshots.

A task force member, once prone and unseen on the roof of their big tank-like, personal carrier, apparently could no longer hide up there as hanger search expanded.

All the police ducked as this idiot slowly, methodically sprayed the interior with 9 mm pistol rounds. He slipped off the safest, far side of military vehicle. The SWAT teams started to peek above their quick cover positions to see where he was.

Weaver caught sight of the man dashing out through the big open, back doors in a last-resort, last-ditch effort to escape.

"Riiiight…" Weaver said.

He and others half-stood as the man dashed away into the sunlight, whereupon he died.

Three shotgun blasts in about two seconds. The first hit the criminal full frontal, pushing him back, but before he could tumble, a second caught him in his lower right side, standing him, spinning him back up for the third to hit and drop him like rag doll.

Some of the pellets that spread and missed the man scattered through the right insides of the hanger and somehow during the "shots-fired" the encircling officers outside managed to get clear of any crossfire.

"Suicide by cop," Weaver commented.

"Anybody hurt?" Captain Comegy yelled. "Check each other out!"

After inspecting each, inside and outside the hanger, all were unscathed.

"Where's their new chopper?" Pathways asked.

"You're gonna have to ask Jack about that when he wakes up. Seems he pulled some kind of a 'Kellog' with their new pilot to get him back on dry land."

"A…'Kellog,'" she said.

"A 'Kellog,'" Weaver said.

Chapter 35: This Ain't Over, Bubba

Two days later…

Jack woke up in a hospital room. Alone. In the dark.
He was in a hospital gown, without even his watch. He
did not know exactly where he was, what time it was,
nor could he remember what happened to put him
there. He was attached to numerous machines and
plastic tubes. He had a medical collar around his neck,
one that people usually wear from whiplash, car acci-
dents. Any movement of his head to look around really
hurt. Did someone fuse his neck? What? It was dark
outside the one window of the private room. What happened…

"Jack?" came a male voice as the room door
opened, "Jack there's a woman here to see you. Are
you alright? You want to see her?"

Jack's head lifted a few inches off the pillow – serious wave of pain - and saw that the request came
from a unformed Texas state trooper at his door.

"Ah, ah yeah," Jack said, not really knowing what
he who or what he was allowing.

And Gail Canchas walked in.

"Oh, my Jacky," she said.

She went to some wall shelves and turned on a
lamp which cast the room in a soft-light, yellow-white
hue. She slid up a chair by the bed, sat and grabbed his
right hand. Jack could see she'd been crying.

"Jacky, the trooper out there said you were stable
and going to be alright."

"I guess. I am, I don't know."

"What happened?" she asked.

"How's about you first," he said.

"They, the State and Houston police raided the task

force headquarters at the airport the early morning after you landed. They hit it like a hurricane. No police were hurt. They arrested 18 members of the task force. One task force member was killed. Gunfight.

They're still picking the place apart now."

"You were there?"

"Yes, I left after a while, Our photographers are still there. They found three beaten men in their jail cells."

"They…so…I…this…"

"It's pretty much over, Jack. You won."

"I…won," he whispered.

"Acorn said you were shot in the neck!"

Jack thought for a few seconds, then said, "Yeah, the… with a rubber bullet. From a shotgun. A less than lethal shotgun. It must have hit my head too. I…they didn't like…operate on my neck or something? Fuse my neck?"

"Oh Jack, no. No operation. It'll get better. Your neck is fine. Weaver said they tried to throw you out over the Gulf!"

"Yeah, they were gonna…they were gonna, but they got lazy. Overconfident or something. They didn't search me, Gail. I still had my boot gun."

"The gun you killed Muzak with."

"That one. That same one. Yeah."

They stared at each other. Jack's memory was jelling. So to was his memory of the funeral.

"So, Gail. Are you gonna marry that guy? That co-worker of yours at the magazine?" he asked.

"Oh, I don't know."

"You don't know. You might?"

"I might. I am not good alone, Jack. You know that. I need somebody. Around every day."

"Uh-huh," Jack said.

"I know what you are thinking. I have told you all

this before and you know it. I told you that I could never marry you, Jack. About once every year or so somebody almost kills you! You almost die. And here we are again, Jack. Look at you. I can't live like that. Like…like this. I have told you that over and over."

"You did. You have," Jack said.

"Many times. Well, this is what all that would look like. What it has looked like for years. Us, Jack. And this is what it will continue to look like. I can't do it."

"And yet, Ernesto died, not me."

"He did," she said harshly and teared up, "and it's not fair to say that. And you know it's not."

"Yeah. I know."

"I…I hugged and kissed him goodbye that evening, in my arms…and …he was right here in my arms," she raised her arms up in circle. "Then… then just 5 days later he's in a cremation, they…they disintegrated him into dust, to ashes. My baby!" Then she really broke down, crying, babbling and wheezing.

Jack squeezed her hand. It was the best he could do. After a moment, with a paper towel she pulled from her jacket pocket, she patted her eyes and calmed down.

"Sorry," he said.

"Don't be. I saw you at the funeral," she slowly admitted. "I didn't know what to do, what to say to you," she said.

"Yeah, you would be slumming it by saying hi to me in public." He was only half joking. "You could have waved. Winked. Smiled?"

"No! You deserve more than that. You deserve so much more, so much that I couldn't do there in the funeral for my dead husband. Couldn't stand to do. Couldn't say. So, rather than break down to the floor, on my knees, Jack, into pieces right in front of you and everyone at the funeral, I did nothing. I had to leave. Leave you alone. I have been to funerals. You have. But when it's like this one…mine, I mean his. Ours."

Jack just stared at her, trying to believe her, yet not. Yet a little.

"Gail," he started to shake his head and it hurt. Big time.

He groaned.

"Don't move your head, stupid," she said in a whimper.

"What are we gonna do now, Gail," Jack asked.

"You gonna marry that guy and still come around to my house?"

"I don't know."

"You know I have been in this mess before…triangle mess," he said.

"I know. With that Linda bitch."

"She wasn't a bitch. It's a lot of my fault. I…am I just like some kind of addict? And she was the drug. You're the drug. Or the drug dealer?"

She took a deep, deep breath and let it all out in almost a whistle. She wiped her eyes again.

"Okay. Are you going to tell me exactly what happened on that helicopter?" she asked, regaining her composure. Her work was the only road to composure.

"Yeees," he said begrudgingly. "You know I will."

"Tomorrow? I can come by tomorrow. The magazine has stopped the press for this story. I don't have much time. But I know you need more sleep too. Is tomorrow okay?"

"Yeees," he said.

"This is a book, Jack. A bestseller. First a magazine article, then the book. Dunker is the evil genius with… with tentacles everywhere. He…"

And Jack fell fast asleep.

Next morning…

Weaver Wisdom and Acorn walked into the hospital room. Jack was trying to eat breakfast off of the rolling food tray, and the tray was too low for his head and neck brace. Plus, food kept slipping off the too-small plastic fork.

"Gentlemen," Jack said.

"Howdy stranger, how you doing?"

"I am in and out of sleep for two days. My neck and back feel like I was interrogated by the Spanish Inquisition. Drugged. How are you?"

"Boy howdy, did you miss it," Weaver said. "Surprise! Surprise. Lord almighty, they sure were surprised when SWAT busted in."

"I bet they were surprised," Jack said.

And Weaver began telling the insider's tale of the multi-SWAT raid on the Gulf Coast Drug Task Force hangar. Jack was all ears. The TV news was only beginning to put the details together. They probably would never know the whole truth and nothing but.

"But, brace yourself though, there's some very strange news," Weaver said. "Bad news."

"What? Bad?"

"It's 10 a.m. now. At 8 a.m. this morning, Cinnamon Dunker…"

"Yeah?"

"He bailed out of jail," Weaver said.

"Impossible."

"No sir. Rygh appeared at the arraignment, repping the State for organized crime charges. There were Feds already there. Feds from out of state, had D.C. all over them. Ones that I've never seen before. The Judge…"

"What judge?" Jack asked.

"Freddy Marks!"

"Freddy Marks let him go?"

"Rygh said, Freddy met with these Feds before-hand, and Patricia, you know his court stenographer, told me out in the hall later, that the Feds called a special meeting with the judge at 7 a.m. before the arraignment."

"The Feds!" Jack said.

"Then at 8 am, Freddy set the bail at one million dollars and his attorney…"

"Who's his attorney?"

"Don't Know. Never heard of him. We don't know him. He's in from out of state. Talks like a Yankee."

"A high-dollar lawyer?"

"Yup. His attorney posted the bail with a promissory note. The boy is out! Everyone else is still in jail. All 18 of them. No bond. They had no lawyers, just public defenders. And we have troopers hunting down the rest of the task force at large, at the addresses Manny gave us. Six more we know of."

"These other guys will probably sneak back home and assume their old real identities."

"Yup. Could be. Some think this is over but there is a lot of work to do. Rygh needs a case filed on each one of them. Nip and his drug guys are on it and Acorn has been assigned to us too. You are too. As the commander. It's gonna be a full time job for a while."

"I guess you're here for a while, Chief," Jack told Acorn. "And since I am in charge, I may just keep ya here."

"I am," Acorn said, "I like it better here. Near the Gulf."

"Don't mention the Gulf for a while, okay?"

"Me, the colonel wants me as a consult for you all," Weaver said. "I still have my own caseload the Ranger cappen wants me to work on. But yeah, Dunker posted

bond. They unhandcuffed him and he walked right out
the courthouse with his Yankee lawyer. But! He
stopped right by me, a foot from my face, to say something to me."

"He did?"

"He stopped, looked me dead in the eye and said, 'I
am untouchable. You'll never take me down for anything. I know people.' Then he walked out."

Jack was dumbfounded, but added, "you know,
now that I think about it, he told me the same thing on
the chopper. And he knows who people? What people?
You know that sniper he hired was a real-deal killer.
Those kind of people? Why didn't they just snipe me
too?" Jack asked.

"Come on. They hated you, bubba. Dunker wanted
a closeup kill. Listen up, I don't know, but with all the
Feds there? Have you called Bats yet?"

"No, not yet. I still have too," Jack said. "Maybe he
knows something or can find something out. I got his
card in my desk at HQ."

"How's that neck?" Acorn asked.

"Bad. I feel like a sledgehammer hit me right here,"
Jack said barely touching his neck brace. I reckon
though, that's my only medical problem. That and a
concussion, I guess. From that damn dum-dum bullet."

"Now you know what it feels like to be a protester.
Yeah, the nurse told me you have a very bad concussion," Weaver said. "But, you are still the head honcho
of the Takedown Task Force, but the Colonel said you
are off for a few weeks."

"The hell you say," Jack said, "I've got stuff to do."
Weaver just nodded, almost chuckled, then said, "you
have time off and mandatory therapy on your neck. A
doctor will have to release you back to work."
Jack grimaced and grunted. They both know Jack will

still work.

"And hey, we found your .45 in Dunker's car on the airport parking lot. We got it in evidence," Acorn said.

"The crime scene guys have to process it as part of the kidnapping charge."

"We've got your snubby too," Weaver added, "part of your shooting."

"Okay. I got plenty more at home," Jack said.

"And we towed your car back to the DPS lot from the barbeque joint," Acorn said.

"Levi was pretty pissed when he heard they nabbed you in front of his place," Weaver said. "He has that Tech-9 behind the counter under the register. Dunker is lucky Levi didn't see you shot. He told me he will comp you a few free rib dinners."

"Ha. Huh. Just a few," Jack said, "oohhh boy."

"Some back-patting, ooo-ficials from DPS will be coming to see you today. This afternoon. Play nice. They are just now starting to like you. We gotta run, bubba. Saying our prays for ya," Weaver said.

"I need em," Jack said.

Then Weaver stopped at the door, turned and pointed at Kellog.

"Bats!" the Ranger said emphatically.

"I know," Jack said.

He picked up the plate to eye level and half-shoveled the rest of the breakfast into his mouth.

A nurse walked in with a big smile and said, "Time to pee, Mr. Kellog."

Chapter 37: Bats

Three days later, DPS Headquarters...

Clad in his neck brace protruding above his usual
leather sports coat, white shirt, bolo tie, jeans and
boots, Jack was a bit of an abstract celebrity at HQ, for
his first morning back for a visit. He was still on medical leave.

Lots of folks came by to see him, including the Colonel, who said he did "a great and dangerous" job. The
intel office Coffee Klatch girls gave him a get-well
card and a homemade carrot cake. Jack left the impres-
sion with the Colonel and all others that he was just
stopping by to get his car and some personal things
from his desk and locker, but actually neck or no neck
pain, he was in full work mode.

He walked to his desk and opened a side drawer.
His neck brace interfered with his ability to look down,
but he glimpsed the old ammo box of loose business
cards and removed the lid on a box, of which he stored
cards from various people. After a thumb-through, he
found what he was looking for. A simple white card
that read, "Bats" with just a phone number and the
words, "Leave a message." Not even his last name on
the card. Bats MacNamara. Was that even his real
name?

He recalled the moment when Bats handed the card
to him down on the US and Mexico border, back when
he and Bats went into Mexico to hunt down John Phillip Muzak. It was a number of years back. He always
assumed "Bats" was a nickname, but he didn't know.
Jack never knew exactly what position Bats held in the
US Government. Department of Justice (his claim and
badge), or the CIA? Or both? Or something else?

He dialed the number on the card. It rang. Bats' recorded voice answered with, "Leave your name and number. Say no more here. I will call you back."

Jack left his name and cell phone number. He wondered what would become of that left message. Judging from the wild past, was Bats still even alive?
But right then his phone rang, which startled him.

"Jumpin Jack Kellog! How in Hades are you? I hear you got over that bad heart attack and had a face-to-face again with our old buddy Muzak."

"I'm fine. Better. And yeah, I did."

"And you killed him."

"I did," Jack said.

"Good. As well you know he was a son of a bitch. I still keep a few tabs on you dude, now and then. I am glad to see you put an end to John
Muzak down in Laredo. And now you are working with the State. Good. Good choice."

"Governor Bush so ordered," Jack added. "I was not on anybody's first choice list for the job."

"You're too good a man to put out to pasture."

"The pasture seems pretty tempting now and then."

"What can the DOD do for you?" Bats asked.

"Me and a Ranger Weaver Wisdom…"

"Wisdom. Know him. Met him. A police meeting. Good man," Bats interrupted.

"We have cracked open a very corrupt State of Texas police drug task force."

"Name?"

"Gulf Coast Drug Task Force."

"Okay. Go on."

"They've killed a Texas city detective and tried to kill me. They have murdered numerous people around us. One professional sniper killed a witness."

"Ohhhh yeah, yeah, I read about that. Super shot.

Killed a state's witness.

"Then the commander tried to kill me. Personally. Tried to throw me out of a helicopter."

"No shit."

"I killed his accomplice and pistol whipped him. Brought him in."

"Nice work."

"Yup. But now once caught, the commander claims…"

"Name?"

"Sam. Samuel. The nickname 'Cinnamon,' Dunker."

"Okay. Go on," Bats said.

"Dunker told me and told Weaver that he was untouchable. And in court he was surrounded by the Feds. He says he also works for important people. All kinds of Feds were at the court hearing and got him bailed out last week, and…"

"Okay!" Bat's interrupted, "that's all for this phone call. Listen. I have to be in San Antonio in a few days. I got a private jet for this trip. Ain't Uncle Sam grand? I can stop and see you in Houston and we will talk. Alone. Open space. No phone shit."

"Well, we can meet here at my DPS office and…"

"Nope. Nope. Nope. Name another place. Open place. Just us home boys."

"How about the San Jacinto Monument?" Jack asked.

"Okay, I have no fucking idea what that is, but I will be there."

"It looks a little like the Washington Monument, only taller."

"Everything's bigger in Texas. I'll take your word for it. I'll be there Thursday, 2 pm. That good for you?" Watch your back, Jack. I'll see you Thursday."

Chapter 38: Double Dog Rogue

San Jacinto Monument, La Porte, TX...

The history textbooks say, "The San Jacinto Monument is a 567.31-foot-high column located on the Houston Ship Channel in unincorporated Harris County, Texas, about 16 miles due east of downtown Houston. The monument is topped with a 220-ton star that commemorates the site of the Battle of San Jacinto, the decisive battle of the Texas Revolution.

At the appointed time and place, Jack parked his Caddy and walked on the open grounds of the San Jacinto Monument tower and museum. Within a few minutes a black SUV pulled up on the lot and the one and only Bats McNamara exited the rear, right passenger door. As before he was dressed in a black suit, tie and shoes, dark sunglasses. As he walked toward Jack he smiled and popped a thumbs-up.

"Your neck?" Bats asked, pointing to the neck brace, "from the helicopter fight you told me about?"

"Kinda. To capture me Dunker shot me with a dum-dum round from a shotgun. In the…in the head and neck area. Knocked me head over heels out cold. They coulda just shot me, but they wanted me to disappear."

"Damn! Hey, this is a great place, Jack. You know I read up on this place. The builders consumed 3,800 sandwiches and 5,700 cups of coffee while whipping it up. Something huh?"

Jack chuckled. He pointed to some isolated park benches. They sat. Bats crossed his legs and spread his arms out on the back of the bench.

"Other than your neck collar, you look good Jack, about what you looked like when we were in Mexico. You recovered from that heart attack very well," Bats said.

"As they say – 'been working out.' But I had that nervous breakdown too married to the heart attack."

"Nervous in the service." Bats added.

"You look the same."

"It's the suit. And the dyed hair. I'm a legend in black."

"I see," Jack said with a smile. "Johnny Cash said 'I'd love to wear a rainbow every day'…"

"But I'm the man in black," Bats finished.

Alone in the park, Jack told Bats the whole sordid story. Bats mostly stared straight ahead at the park and at the towering monument.

"Listen Jack. I looked into this some," Bats said and turned toward him on the bench. Sweeping off his sunglasses, he propped a bent leg up on the seat between them.

"Here's the thumbnail sketch. Our wonderful government is worried about the drug cartels, and you know, hell I am too. We all are. I'd like to drop MOABs on all their factories south of the border, but we can't. Now, they have spread production out into…maybe hundreds of homes with families. We just can't bomb them anymore. It's too late. There are segments, sections of our government, a little rogue, but with a lot of money and power. They are so secret, they can do what they want. Try what they want."

Jack leaned in to and listened intently.

"It's just like these state drug task forces," Jack said.

"Yeah, times a hundred, though. A thousand maybe. It's the Feds! An entity. Lets call it that for now, a government entity dreamed up this plan. Above the law. Enforcing drug laws, yeah, but beating and torturing people for intel. Knocking off key drug people. Who else could fight for these three things in complete secrecy? Have a war with the cartels and kill a lot of them and get away with it? Consistently? These drug task forces working in secret isolation. Some of them. Not all.

Some other states now have these drug task force programs. Uncle Sam sends money to the states to support the war on drugs. Some of that money is earmarked for these independent task forces. Well, this entity decided that some of the task forces could declare a real war on drugs. Like a shooting war. An elimination war. Kill dealers, mules, screw the arrests and court. Just eliminate."

"They have killed a cop and tried to…"

"I know! It sounds like your local group went more wild, even more rogue than rogue. A rogue task force within a rogue entity."

"Double dog rogue," Jack said.

"Yes! They are deep cover, with all the legal mechanisms to become their own mini-drug cartel. In the wrong hands"

"In the wrong hands. So they…the Feds hired Dunker? Recruited him?" Jack asked.

"They didn't hire him. The state hired him. The Feds recruited him later, yeah. It looks like it. They saw in him, enough of a criminal to do the dirty work. Best I can tell he is also paid directly from the feds too. No Austin middleman for this 'extra' money. And some of these outfits, who knows how many, get paid on the side by this rogue entity within the federal government. Like the CIA recruits spies and informants, they recruited Sam Dunker."

Jack nodded. It made sense.

"The…entity. Who is it," Jack asked.

"What will you do if I tell you?"

"I would confront any politician that…" Jack started.

"Whoa, Jack. Slow down, hoss-man. This isn't any politician. I don't think politicians know anything about this. Maybe…maybe one really high up one suggested this once and walked away from it? But these are government employees doing this. I remember years ago when they made you testify before Congress about the Mafia."

"Yeah."

"You won't be testifying about this to anyone."

"Then, who exactly is doing all this?" Jack asked again.

"I am looking into this. It's top-top-secret shit, but I am a top-secret mother-fucker. Tell ya what, give me your business card and in a few days, a week or so, I will mail you an envelope, with a piece of paper in it with a name and an address. But look, you cannot just ride up to Washington D.C. and shoot him like Matt Dillon. But you'll know who it is. And I can tell you this much already, they are not in this to shoot and kill cops. Exactly the opposite. They love cops. They love soldiers. They love the country. And then maybe… maybe you. Or somebody will do something about Dunker. Figure out something that will shut him and this down."

"What will become of Dunker, you think?" Jack asked.

"He's already out on bond, which is off-the-charts bewildering to me. Texas or no Texas. The Feds could up and charge him with a big federal crime, walk in and take him right out of a Texas jail and put him in a federal pen for a while. A short while to look good. Then the Feds could change his name and hide him away."

"I think he's close to his wife and kids," Jack said.

"Jack, Jack…they'll pack them up to, like in the witness protection program. Or, give him a whole new drug team in San Diego, or Boston, or someplace. New name. New game."

Jack's eyes widened.

"Or he might just…disappear," Bats said.

"Disappear like, as in dead?"

"Yeah. Maybe. Dead. Maybe."

"Or a Witness Protection Program? A cover up?" Jack said.

"Don't know. Maybe."

Jack tried to hand him his new state business card.

"Don't need it. You're already in my radar," Bats said, waving off the card. "I gotta run Jack."

Bats stood.

Jack stood.

"Well, sir, gotta be in San Antoine. Don't shake my hand. You'll leave fingerprints!"

Jack chuckled.

"If you need me for anything, any time, call me."

With a stiff neck, he watched Bats McNamara walk back to his SUV in waiting.

This was all a bigger takedown of a bigger take.

Chapter 39: Organized Associations of Organizations

Six days later…

Jack was still attending physical therapy, and still sneaking in and out of the DPS office, pretending to be on medical leave while working on case files at home and in the field. He stayed off the police radio. Everyone knew Jack though that was still unofficially "on the case."

On one quick sneak visit back to his office desk, he saw a small pile of mail. One letter had an odd return address. It had to be from Bats MacNamara. He opened the envelope to find a single piece of folded paper. A business card was inside the folds. The card read-

JANETTE REDERICK
Department Of The Federal Association
of Organizations
12335 Bankston Blvd, Room 2789.
Washington D.C. 20005

"The Federal Association of Organizations?" Jack whispered. "What in hell is that? What does that mean exactly?"

He knew, it was obviously government gobbledygook. It could easily be the reverse of nouns, the "Organization of Associations." It smelled of a government shell game.

He left headquarters with the envelope, paper and card. He would be calling Weaver up when he got home about this. It was time for a visit to the Capital, and not shoot someone like Matt Dillon would, but he needed a Matt Dillon type to go with him. It would take the prestige of a Texas Ranger to pull off exactly what he had in mind.

"D.C.?" Weaver said into the phone mouthpiece.

"I will pay my way and I will pay your way too. It would be hard to explain all this Bats mumbo-jumbo to your Ranger captain, my sergeant and the Colonel for them to authorize the flights and hotel. But Weave, we've got to go!"

Two days later. 12335 Bankston Blvd. Room 2789, Washington D.C. ...

"Ms. Rederick will see you now," the secretary advised Jack and Weaver.

They stood from the lobby couch and entered the freshly opened office door.

"Have a seat, gentlemen," Janette Rederick said, pointing to two chairs in front of her uncluttered desk.

They did.

"And what brings you two to my office? I can't say I have ever met a Texas Ranger or for that matter, a Texas detective before."

"To be blunt, ma'am, "Weaver started, "We have received information that this office is financially supporting a rogue, Texas drug task force."

She stared at them with an intrigued expression.

"You..." she started.

"What exactly do you do here?" Jack asked.

"We act as a middleman, a banking, bill paying service you might say for some, not all, of the U.S. Congress. Or, if not the Congress, for various departments in the US Government that control their own budgets and send monies to other organizations for missions, growth or goals."

"Like to drug task forces," Jack added.

"It's possible yes. There are usually 'attachments' with the money, lists of requirements as to what some of the money must be used for. They tell us where to send the money and we send it. We don't know anything, more or less, about the why of it."

"They. Who are they? Can you look up exactly who sent this money and who exactly is getting the money for the Texas Gulf Coast Drug Task Force?" Jack asked.

"If it is true and we are sending them money, I am afraid not sir. I cannot. That is not open to the public or police."

"What if we got a search warrant for that information?" Weaver asked.

"We would contest it. Sorry. We always do. About the only thing we can respond to is a Congressional subpoena."

"Federal or state?" Jack asked.

"Federal."

"These people have tortured, murdered numerous people and a police detective and have tried to kill me three times," Jack said.

This seemed to set her back. Her head actually moved back an inch or two with that news. She said, "You have a drug task force that has allegedly killed and has also tried to kill a law enforcement officer?"

"Alleged? Yes. Tried? That would be me. Three times," Jack said, raising his hands up, three fingers up.

"The dead detective was a military war vet, a city detective. Married, and father of two."

"In Texas?"

"In Texas," Weaver said.

"That's…that's terrible," she said.

"Yeah," Jack said.

"We are here about the task force commander, Samuel Dunker," Weaver said. "Agents of the U.S. government were at his arraignment. They had a pre-bond meeting with the judge. Dunker is now out on bond."

"On bond? After murder and attempted murder?"

"He told me he knew people and he was untouch-able," Weaver said.

"He told me the same, just before he tried to throw me out of a helicopter," Jack added.

"Un…touch…able," she repeated.

"And how did you know to contact us?" she asked.

"Like the lesson from Watergate," Weaver said. "Follow the money."

Jack pulled from a folder he was carrying, newspaper clippings from the Houston Chronicle. He placed them on her desk. Then he placed a thick copy of the organized crime indictment next to them.

"What's all this?" she asked.

"It's the criminal indictment of their whole operation and everything we've documented they've done," Jack said. "That we know of. They did more. Way more as we are uncovering more information as we arrested members try to cut deals."

She swung the papers her way and much closer to her. She spent a moment looking them over. Then she leaned back in her chair and laid her arms on the arm rests.

"I cannot guarantee any one thing," she said. "I can try to ask some government sources about this. I would be surprised if the fund allocators would stand for the murder of law enforcement." Can you leave me your business cards? Can you give me a little time about this?

"Yes."

"Yes."

They pulled out cards from their wallets and laid them on the desk.

"We need some help on this, and this Dunker must be punished for what he has done," Weaver said. "We are worried he won't be."

She collected the cards and the men stood and left.

They departed the offices and walked to their rental car out on the parking lot.

"What do you think?" Jack asked.

"I don't know, bubba. We just have to wait and see. Not much else we can do."

Chapter 40: The Devil's Got Him Now

One month later, West Forge, Texas…

Jack, sans his neck brace, had case files all over his kitchen table. The still unmarried as yet, Gail Canchos sat across from him, her laptop open, typing a hundred miles an hour, asking Jack questions and reviewing papers. Though it was the early afternoon, she was still in her pajamas from her overnight stay.

This open sharing of insider legal documents was questionable, but they knew to trust each other on what news could or could not be publicized.

Jack was still on medical leave, recovering from the concussion and in physical therapy for his neck for another few weeks. But everyone at DPS knew Jack was actually toiling away on Task Force Takedown, pulling strings, pushing moves, coordinating options, and prepping the court cases on the members. Speedy trial time limits were in place on all the gang members but not Sam Dunker. His lawyers, now a full team from Washington D.C., with only one token, Houston lawyer on the team, were confounding and postponing the legal process.

Jack's cell phone rang with Weaver's individual sound byte, a segment of the Walker, Texas Ranger TV theme song.

"Weave," Jack said.

"Jack, been listening to the police radio?"

"No, sir."

"Jack…Acorn and I have been in a car, monitoring all the Harris County area PD radio traffic running in the background."

"Yeah?"

"League City PD dispatched an ambulance and city

squad car to Sam Dunker's house about lunch time." Jack put the call on the speaker phone option so Gail could listen in.

"We heard this address on the air and went along too. I am outside Dunker's house right now. Jack…Sam Dunker is dead."

"Suicide?" Jack said immediately.

"Ohhh no. Drowning, He drown in his pool. In his backyard pool."

"Dro…"

"Acorn and I got here and walked in the yard just when the EMTs drug him out of his pool. They started working on him, but he was swollen dead."

"Yeah?"

"He was wearing swim trunks and… and Jack, he had that bruise…that big bruise on his ankle, with fresh cuts. That same sized, shackle bruise…"

"Whoa," Jack said.

Gail's jaw dropped.

"I guess…" Jack started to say.

"I guess," Weaver continued for him, "I can only guess that someone in Washington D.C. did look into the matter, huh? Like we asked."

"I guess! All the right people," Jack said. "Dunker broke the rules of their game. Killing cops was one step too far. But he's a cop?"

"Not a good one. By all rules, he was a criminal."

"Who found him floating the pool?"

"His father lives in the back of the house. Wife at work. Kids at school. The LCPD officer said the old man is about half-blind, half deaf. But he looked out the window and saw Dunker face down in the pool."

"Huh! I wonder, will the medical examiner know to check the water in his lungs to see what kind of water is in there? Sea water? Lake water? Or chlorinated pool water?"

"I don't know, but I ain't asking," Weaver said. "I ain't pushing it. My guess is it'll just go down as an accidental pool drowning, and all the scandalous stories will disappear."

"I think so too. I'll call Rygh right away and tell him," Jack said.

"The Devil's got him now," Weaver said. "Cut him down."

They hung up. He and Gail were speechless for a moment, then Jack said,

"Some kind of justice has been served. I don't know exactly what, from who. But some kind."

Epilogue: Conjugality Speaking

Four weeks later…

Things returned to normal, or whatever normal was for Jack Kellog. The state task force was finished. The DAs office took over and was running interviews, plea bargains and setting trial dates for the drug gang. Jack was back in rotation for normal intelligence duty, which for him could be pretty boring.

Word at DPS headquarters in Houston and Austin was that if he'd take the next sergeant's exam, he'd be promoted. But routine DPS promotions usually mean divisional changes. New sergeants go where new sergeants are needed. And he could not move into the highway patrol division or the Rangers since he was never really a trooper to begin with. He would have to remain a sergeant in criminal intelligence.

He heard whispers that they might use him as a sergeant in a "special projects" category and ship him around the state for certain problems, which he thought interesting.

Otherwise, he was not so sure he would take the test, anyway. It would be too boring being office bound and bossing people around in the division. But the idea of working special projects all over Texas did intrigue him.

As he expected, Gail sort of "retreated" away from him and back into her busy Austin lifestyle, not needing Jack so up close and "personal" for her next thrilling article and book. Jack would soon be the subject of another Texican Monthly article and in a second big book like he was in the first *Be Bad Now* book years ago by a Hollywood crime writer. Gail said this book would tentatively be called, *Takedown the Take*.

Another book. He both liked and disliked the idea.

Unlike the first book from years ago *Be Bad Now*, he would not get any royalties from *Takedown the Take*, but Gail swore she would "take care" of him somehow.

He took this day off. This afternoon, Jack was in his Caddy, on his way back to the women's prison, to see Inmate Number 474898, Shelly Mongrieves for another conjugal visit. Why not? The sex was memorable. And he hoped this visit would not include some new, otherwise, ground-breaking, gangland, criminal intelligence coup from her like last time.

Well. Only half hoping...

Jumpin Jack Kellog returns in **Clutch Hitter.**
Houston Astro baseball superstar Ali "Presto" Mustafa had a season ending injury in August 2001. In September, he was flying into New York City but suddenly, emotionally, he declined the flight at the gate, at the last minute, even abandoning his luggage already on the plane. That flight crashed in the World Trade Center. In December, the FBI started to routinely investigate these few, last minute bailouts before the deadly 911 flights. The Feds, very busy, asked Texas State Intelligence Special Agent Jack Kellog for a routine small favor. "Hey, Jack, will you stop in and ask Presto, why did he not fly that morning?" Routine? Up until the time mysterious people suddenly started trying to kill Presto...

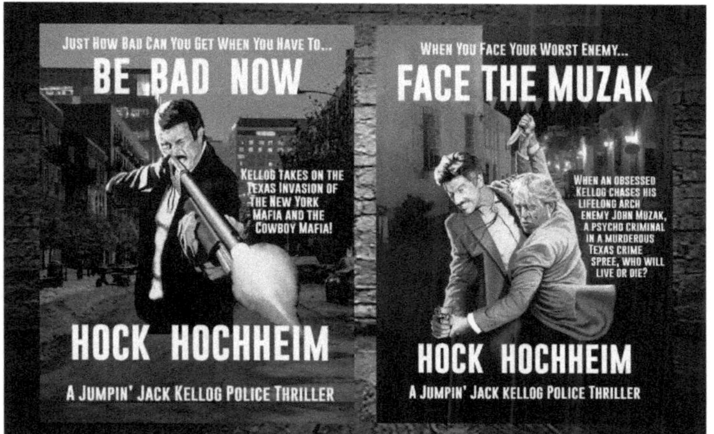

The two prior Jack Kellog adventures. Type the titles into your web and find them. Ebook, paperback and audio book.

The Gunther westerns. Type them into your web a nd find them. Ebook, paperback and audio.